"Don't g
Our bargain still stands."

"I know." Determinedly, Rosamond lifted her chin. "I fully intend to hold up my end of our deal, too." She swallowed hard, then gave him a deliberately steely look. "I can't wait to leave here and help you kit out your new lodgings at the stable!"

For a long moment, Miles could only gaze at her with admiration. "I'm impressed. That almost sounded convincing."

"So did your dedication to fixing that window," Rosamond pointed out. "Yet here we are, chatting away instead."

Miles laughed, knowing he should skedaddle inside but wanting this easy closeness to last between them...the way it once had every day. "You're a hard taskmaster."

"I like to get things done, that's all. Now that I've decided what to do, there's no benefit to wasting time."

Miles disagreed. He crossed his arms, still studying her. "I think you'll find that some things are best done slowly."

Her brow arched. "Like window fixing?"

"Like kissing."

Author Note

Thank you for reading *Morrow Creek Runaway*. I'm happy to share Rosamond and Miles's story with you, and I'm delighted to introduce you to the Morrow Creek Mutual Society, too. I hope you enjoy reading about all the intrigues and escapades going on there. If you do, please tell your friends! Join me for another book in my Morrow Creek miniseries, too—it includes *The Honor-Bound Gambler*, *The Bride Raffle*, *Mail-Order Groom* and several others (including some short stories and an ebook exclusive), all set in and around my favorite corner of the Old West.

If you'd like to try a sample, you can find complete first-chapter excerpts from all my bestselling books at my website, lisaplumley.com. While you're there, you can also sign up for personal new-book alerts, download an up-to-date book list, get the scoop on upcoming books, request reader freebies and more. I hope you'll stop by today!

As always, I'd love to hear from you! You can follow me on Twitter, @LisaPlumley, "like" me on Facebook at facebook.com/lisaplumleybooks, send email to lisa@lisaplumley.com or visit me online at community.harlequin.com.

LISA PLUMLEY

MORROW CREEK RUNAWAY

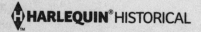

Recycling programs
for this product may
not exist in your area.

ISBN-13: 978-0-373-29823-5

Morrow Creek Runaway

Copyright © 2015 by Lisa Plumley

All rights reserved. Except for use in any review, the reproduction or utilization of this work in whole or in part in any form by any electronic, mechanical or other means, now known or hereinafter invented, including xerography, photocopying and recording, or in any information storage or retrieval system, is forbidden without the written permission of the publisher, Harlequin Enterprises Limited, 225 Duncan Mill Road, Don Mills, Ontario M3B 3K9, Canada.

This is a work of fiction. Names, characters, places and incidents are either the product of the author's imagination or are used fictitiously, and any resemblance to actual persons, living or dead, business establishments, events or locales is entirely coincidental.

This edition published by arrangement with Harlequin Books S.A.

For questions and comments about the quality of this book, please contact us at CustomerService@Harlequin.com.

® and TM are trademarks of Harlequin Enterprises Limited or its corporate affiliates. Trademarks indicated with ® are registered in the United States Patent and Trademark Office, the Canadian Intellectual Property Office and in other countries.

Printed in U.S.A.

USA TODAY bestselling author **Lisa Plumley** has delighted readers worldwide with more than three dozen popular novels. Her work has been translated into multiple languages and editions, and includes Western historical romances, contemporary romances, paranormal romances and a variety of stories in romance anthologies. She loves to hear from readers! Visit Lisa on the web, like her on Facebook, or follow @LisaPlumley on Twitter today.

Visit the Author Profile page at Harlequin.com.

To John, with all my love.
Happy 25th anniversary!

Chapter One

*March 1885, Morrow Creek,
northern Arizona Territory*

Miles Callaway was a man who didn't believe in second chances. He'd never needed to before. But on the day he arrived in the tiny territorial town of Morrow Creek, perched at the edge of a pine-dotted mountainside and bordered by its namesake sparkling creek, he decided to try for a second chance anyway.

After all, he'd traveled two thousand miles to find this one—to find the woman who'd slipped away from him back in Boston. Any woman who could inspire that kind of devotion was special.

On the other hand, so were the five hundred dollars he'd accepted for finding her.

That was more money than Miles had ever seen in one place in his whole lifetime. Even now, with most of those greenbacks stashed safely away in his battered valise, he felt conspicuous—like a miner who'd just pickaxed himself a gold nugget or twelve and was carrying around all that plunder stuffed in his britches pockets.

Around him on the town's main street, horse traffic

kicked up dust. Passersby lingered on the raised-plank boardwalk to talk. Several calico-clad women meandered in and out of the businesses surrounding him, carrying parcels of goods. Miles spied a mercantile and a millinery as he walked past—also, a newspaper office, a book depot and a telegraph station. Like most other small towns he'd passed through while headed west, Morrow Creek seemed both bustling and peaceable. Its church was as prominent as its saloon. Both appeared equally revered.

Stiff and vaguely achy from his long train journey, Miles shouldered his valise and then stretched his legs with brisker walking. Moving felt good. So did the cool springtime air on his face. Inhaling a lungful, he almost grinned. In Boston, the air felt as thick as scorched pea soup. It looked black with soot, and it burned all the way going down. Compared with that, the territorial air he drew in felt like a kiss from Mother Nature herself.

He could learn to like it here.

Especially if he found Rosamond McGrath.

Squinting ahead, Miles focused his attention on Jack Murphy's saloon. Even though it was scarcely past noontime, the place looked busy. That suited Miles just fine. He was secure in the information that had brought him to Morrow Creek, but some of the facts he'd garnered were months old now.

Before making his move, he needed to know more.

There was no better place for a man to get his bearings than the local saloon. He could clear away the railway dust with a pint of Levin's ale, swap yarns with the locals and wrangle the remaining details he needed. If he followed that with trips to the telegraph and post offices, passed by the jailhouse and made sure he tamped down his impatience long enough to approach Rosamond McGrath in a sensible fashion, Miles knew he could prevail.

He had to prevail. He'd already spent a year trying.

He'd sacrificed his job and his principles for this search. Because of it, Miles was a different man from the jovial stableman who'd left Arvid and Genevieve Bouchard's employ and journeyed westward from Beacon Hill, determined to find a woman who sometimes felt more like a ghost than the flesh-and-blood runaway housemaid she was.

Not that that description adequately described Rosamond McGrath. Or Miles's feelings for her. But for now, those feelings of his were beside the point. What mattered now was making a smart approach. He didn't want to spook Rose. He didn't want to send her scurrying away again, the way she'd done so mysteriously before. Miles was a man who persevered, no matter what. But that didn't mean he had to struggle uphill both ways.

He could make damn sure, this time, that he played his hand shrewdly. So, with his gaze fixed and his mind clear, Miles sent his boots clomping across the boardwalk and up into the lively two-story saloon, where piano music played and men like him congregated…and sometimes shared more than they should.

Thank Providence for whiskey, Miles told himself as he shouldered his way inside the dim saloon, inhaling the earthy scents of spilled liquor and stale tobacco as he went. Thank heaven for all its useful, tongue-loosening qualities, too.

Setting his valise safely at his feet, Miles tugged his flat-brimmed hat over his face. He gave his bearded jawline a rueful rub. If he wanted to appear presentable, he needed to shave. But as it was, his dark facial hair and overgrown shoulder-length locks made him look less like a respectable, citified carriage driver and more like…well, more like a man who didn't intend to take no for an answer on the questions he had.

So, bearded and determined and equipped with more money than any man ought to wisely bring into a place where drinking and gambling held the upper hand, Miles ordered an ale from the barman and got down to the business of locating Rose McGrath.

Rosamond McGrath Dancy was in the small fenced yard behind her house, playing with the children in her care, trying for the umpteenth time to learn the rules of baseball, when a surprising summons came from Bonita Yates, her friend and assistant.

"I'm sorry to interrupt all the frivolity, Mrs. Dancy." Bonita stood in the meager shade of a scrub-oak tree, speaking loudly to be heard over the boisterous children shouting their advice to Rosamond. "But you have a gentleman caller."

A gentleman caller. Those unexpected words made Rosamond's grip on her baseball bat go slack. At home plate, she missed the next pitch, thrown by little Seamus O'Malley, Maureen's son.

Rosamond frowned. "You know I don't see gentleman callers. Fetch Seth. He'll know what to do to get rid of him."

At her mention of one of the two burly "protectors" Rosamond employed, Bonita shook her head. "Seth let him in."

"He did?" Rosamond darted a glance to the second of her protectors, Judah Foster, who'd been stationed here in the yard. His quizzical shrug only increased her sense of unease.

Everyone in her household knew better than to allow

strangers inside the house. Especially if those strangers were men. Especially if those men wanted to see her. Most of her rules were designed to avoid exactly this situation.

Entirely alarmed now, Rosamond lowered the tip of her bat to the ground, her baseball lessons all but forgotten.

The children cried out in exasperated impatience.

"Don't quit, Mrs. Dancy!" yelled wiry, bespectacled, blonde Agatha Jorgensen. "You almost hit the ball that time!"

Nearby, Grace Murphy nodded. "Agatha is correct, Rosamond. You have your batting stance mastered. Now all you need to do is work on your timing." As a notorious suffragette and advocate of equality, Grace had been the first to suggest entertaining the children—girls and boys alike—with athletics. She'd also spent quite a while tutoring Rosamond in the finer points of the sport she so enjoyed herself. "If you keep practicing, you'll be joining my Morrow Creek ladies' baseball league in no time."

"I'd like that, Grace." Rosamond tossed her friend a shaky smile, grateful—not for the first time—for her encouragement. It was partly due to Grace's determined intervention that Rosamond's unconventional household had been allowed into Morrow Creek in the first place. Reminded of that unconventionality—and all the misunderstandings it sometimes engendered—Rosamond swerved her attention back to Bonita. "Why did Seth let him in? He knows better than that." Both of her security employees did. "I'll have a talk with Seth. After he sends away whoever—"

"It's Gus Winston." Seth Durant strode in through the side yard, temporarily abandoning his post at her household's front door. With his broad shoulders, gunslinger's

attitude and fierce demeanor, the elder of her two protectors was the approximate size of her front door—and
usually barred intrusions just as capably. Until today. "I
knew you'd want to see him before he heads off to San
Francisco with Miss Abigail."

"Oh. Well, of course I want to see him!" All smiles
now, Rosamond handed her bat to Tommy Scott, who was
awaiting his turn. "Here, Tommy. You try batting next.
The rest of you…make lots of scores!"

"They're called runs, Mrs. Dancy!" shouted little Tobe
Larkin, full of sass and exaggerated forbearance. He'd
recently come to the territory from California with his
widowed mother, Lucinda. Both were temporarily taking
refuge with Rosamond. "When you're playing baseball,
scores are called *runs*."

"Yes. Thank you, Tobe." Growing up in faraway Boston, Rosamond had never spent much time with other
children. She'd worked in a factory, like her parents, until
she'd been orphaned. After that, she'd been apprenticed
as a housemaid in a fine Beacon Hill household. Her days
had not been filled with games and childish pastimes.
"I'll master this eventually."

"We know," the children chimed in cheerfully, having heard the same axiom from Rosamond endless times
already. I'll master this eventually was something of a
catchphrase for Rosamond. She hadn't realized she used
it as often as she did until her friend Libby Jorgensen
pointed it out to her with surprising admiration.

"You're so determined, Rosamond," Libby had told
her that day, shortly after they'd moved into the house.
"That's what makes you different from the rest of us.
That's what made you able to get us here, all the way
across the country, after Mr. Dancy—"

Rosamond had cut off her friend curtly, unwilling to

hear any more about the man she'd briefly and disastrously been wed to. Elijah Dancy might have unwittingly enabled Rosamond's new life by obligingly getting shot at a gambling table, but that didn't mean Rosamond felt a speck of gratitude for the man.

In fact, she had yet to meet the man she felt grateful for. No one who truly knew her would have blamed her for that fact.

But if any man were to come close, it would have been Gus Winston. The lanky, bandanna-wearing stableman had approached Rosamond's household with an open mind and endearing enthusiasm.

You have a gentleman caller, she remembered Bonita saying. She had to get busy. She couldn't keep Gus waiting all day.

Breathless with the aftereffects of her athletic endeavors, Rosamond patted her bedraggled, mostly upswept auburn hair. Vigorously, she brushed off her bodice and her bustled, lace-trimmed skirts. Playing baseball wasn't strictly among her duties as the lady of the household, but whenever one of the children asked her to join in, Rosamond simply couldn't resist. She loved hearing their raucous laughter and seeing their little faces smudged with dirt…but wreathed with smiles, all the same.

You have a gentleman caller.

When would those words not stop her heart?

She'd escaped from Boston, Rosamond reminded herself firmly. She had nothing more to fear from the Bouchards or anyone else. She'd made a new life for herself in Morrow Creek.

A life that left her—a supposed lady—hopelessly untidy.

Nonetheless, she faced Grace brightly. "How do I look?"

Her friend assessed her. "You look perfectly invigo-rated!"

Hmm. That wasn't terribly helpful. "Bonita?"

"It's Gus," her assistant reminded her. "He won't mind if you're slightly less stringently ladylike than usual."

Bonita's teasing grin reminded Rosamond that to ev-eryone here, she truly was ladylike. Despite the gossip and whispers that had initially greeted the arrival of her Morrow Creek Mutual Society—and the ladies therein—no one in town suspected Rosamond of anything untow-ard. Her neighbors approved of her.

Almost a year after her ignoble departure from Bos-ton, Rosamond had created the haven she'd always longed for. In the unlikely refuge of Morrow Creek, she was fi-nally secure.

Unless a particular and unwanted "gentleman caller" arrived, that is. If that happened, all her security would be shattered.

Rosamond couldn't bear to consider it. "I'll be back for the next round," she assured everyone. "Good luck!"

"It's the next *inning*!" Tobe called. "Inning!"

But Rosamond gaily waved off his assertion and headed for her private parlor, hauling in a deep breath as she went.

If nothing else, she was in charge here. She had friends, security, a family of rescued women and their children, and a useful occupation to occupy her mind. She'd done good work here.

As proof, Rosamond reminded herself, she was about to meet the first and most satisfied client of her mutual society.

The just-married Mr. Gus Winston, waiting in her parlor.

Chapter Two

Within half an hour of his arrival at the saloon, Miles had the dispiriting realization that he'd become an expert at subterfuge. Wholly without meaning to, he'd become a man who knew how to pick a lock, when to trade cash for information and where to find answers that didn't send him off cockeyed on a wild, time-wasting goose chase. He'd learned how to suss out the truth and how to protect himself. He'd had to. The kind of people he'd dealt with were neither reputable nor trustworthy.

At this point, maybe he wasn't, either.

But the urgency of his search had demanded more from him. More, maybe, than he'd been willing to give at the outset. But he'd had no choice then. Now that Miles was so close—now that he knew Rosamond McGrath was within reach—he couldn't quit.

He'd always been able to handle himself, of course, Miles recalled as he studied his ale. He had the usual masculine willingness to fight, if the outcome of that fight mattered. In his time, he'd settled a few disputes with his fists. He had the musculature that came from hoisting horse-and-carriage equipment from dawn to dusk, the wits that came from growing up in the hardscrabble city tenements and a hardheadedness that owed itself, quite naturally, to his Callaway forebearers.

Each of them was as stubborn as a stuck mule and more than eager to boast about it. But they also had the charm of several fallen angels to sweeten their obstinacy. Miles's own father had possessed unholy amounts of charisma…coupled with an unfortunate unwillingness to quit playing faro until his pockets were empty.

Too bad he could always finagle the faro dealer into letting him play a mite longer on credit, Miles remembered. Without that damnable charm of his, Silas Callaway might have been able to save and move out from the grimy tenements. That certainly would have pleased Miles's mother. But none of the Callaways had ever really expected to leave the rougher side of Boston—at least not unless it was in service to someone like the Bouchards.

In the end, Miles had been the only one who'd left.

He'd brought some of that infamous family charm with him, though, he reckoned as he signaled the barman for some food. He'd twisted the Callaway charisma into use not for gambling but for a greater cause.

For Rose. For finding her, just as he'd promised, and for—

"You must be Callaway." A huge, friendly-faced man wearing homespun trousers and a loose buttoned shirt stepped up to the bar beside Miles. He ordered, then nodded at Miles. "The man with all the questions about Mrs. Dancy and her establishment."

Mrs. Dancy. Miles still couldn't get used to that.

He knew Rosamond had married. But how? Why?

Had she really, as Genevieve Bouchard had insisted, become smitten with Elijah Dancy and run away with him in the night?

He couldn't believe the woman he'd known would do that.

Even if she had, she would have written to someone. To him.

Knowing there had to be more to this situation, Miles nodded calmly at his interrogator. "I am. You know Mrs. Dancy?"

Another, more curt nod. "Yep. But I don't know you."

With new respect, Miles eyed the man. He had the burly build of a stevedore, the jovial demeanor of a gambler who always won big and the jaded gaze of someone who knew better than to trust an outsider.

"Miles Callaway." Miles offered his hand to the man. "I'm new in town. I couldn't help hearing about Mrs. Dancy's place. I don't mind saying, it's got me mighty intrigued."

The man laughed, then accepted Miles's handshake. "Daniel McCabe. I wouldn't get yourself all het up about Mrs. Dancy's society, if I were you. It sounds scandalous, but it's not."

With a genial nod for the barman, McCabe accepted what appeared to be a midday meal of beans, bacon and bread. All around them both, the business of the saloon continued apace, full of low conversations, clinking gambling chips and quickly dealt cards. More whiskey flowed. Clouds of cigarillo smoke drifted toward the ceiling, almost obscuring Jack Murphy's painted image of a cavorting water nymph behind the bar.

"The Morrow Creek Marriage Bureau?" Miles repeated the name he'd heard used. "Sounds scandalous to me—and to every other man who doesn't want to get hitched in the next week."

Another laugh. "Officially, it's called the Morrow Creek Mutual Society," McCabe informed him. "But around these parts, we took to calling it the marriage bureau pretty quickly." He aimed a speculative glance at Miles. "If you don't want to step into a wedding noose, what's your interest in Mrs. Dancy?"

"I'm an old friend of hers."

"You don't say?" McCabe sized him up. "Such an old friend that you don't know where she lives or what she's been up to?"

McCabe's genially voiced question belied his sharp demeanor. Despite his easy ways, this was no country bumpkin. This was a man who would fiercely protect the people he cared about. Reevaluating his initial opinion of him, Miles regrouped. Usually, folks overlooked whatever logical inconsistencies arose during his questioning of them. Especially when they were knocking back ales. Daniel McCabe was different.

"We didn't part willingly." With real mournfulness, Miles stared into his ale. "I aim to make up for that when I see her."

"Aha. You poor lovelorn fool. You need another drink!"

Generously, McCabe ordered him one. Somehow, Miles had stumbled onto the best tactic for use with the big man—love.

After glimpsing the wedding band on McCabe's hand, Miles understood where the man's good-natured resignation toward romance came from. Possibly his guardedness, too.

After all, true love didn't always run smoothly. Miles knew that for himself. He'd waited too long with Rosamond. Now she—

"We become damn fools when some woman turns our heads, don't we?" McCabe proposed, offering a toast. "Here's to you."

Miles raised his glass, then quaffed. The moment he and Daniel McCabe sealed their newfound camaraderie, other saloon patrons began drifting nearer. If Miles had been fortunate in sniffing out information before, he was doubly lucky now.

Everyone, it seemed, wanted to help McCabe's buddy.

In very short order, Miles learned where Rosamond Dancy lived—and with whom. He learned what her mutual society did and how popular and sought-after an admission to it was among the local menfolk. He also learned, discouragingly, that gaining a personal interview with Mrs. Dancy was next to impossible.

"She's practically a ghost," Hofer, the mercantile owner, confided in a dour tone. "She hardly comes out. Not ever."

"She just keeps things running, quite efficiently, behind the scenes," added Thomas Walsh, editor of the *Pioneer Press* newspaper. "I find her ingenuity very admirable, myself."

"You ain't getting no place near her," opined Mr. Nickerson, who ran the Book Depot and News Emporium. "'Specially as a stranger to town. If Mrs. Dancy doesn't want to see you, her two bruisers make darn sure you stay away."

That put Miles on alert. "She has guards?"

"Two of 'em. Seth Durant and Judah Foster. Head-knockers, they are." The barman, Harry, raised his arms high over his head. "Big as apes, both of 'em, and twice as mean, too."

That was a complication Miles hadn't counted on.

"I would advise you to stay away," old Doc Finney put in, sipping his sarsaparilla. "A woman who is both secretive and uppity is dangerous to a man's well-being. A man only gets so many heartbeats per ticker, you know.

A woman like that'll use them all up, faster than you can say 'Bob's your uncle.'"

The men surrounding him appeared intrigued by that.

"Exactly how," McCabe wondered with a twinkle in his eye, "would all those heartbeats get used up extra quickly, Doc? Because some of us are hog-tied to uppity women ourselves." Here, he aimed a meaningful glance at Jack Murphy. "We might need to consider protecting ourselves from overexertion."

All the saloongoers guffawed at that, but Miles was too busy contemplating Doc Finney's description of Rose to wonder about the salacious possibilities inherent in his warning.

Most likely, secretive would describe Rosamond these days. So would uppity, if an opinionated old coot like Finney was doing the describing. Back home, Rosamond had certainly known her own mind. Miles had definitely found her this time.

"Just don't try getting into that society by fibbin' that you know Mrs. Dancy 'from back east,'" a lumberman warned him. "I tried that, and her hired men dumped me in a ditch."

Miles had expected Rosamond to be wary. Given everything he knew about her entanglements with Arvid Bouchard, she had reason to be. Still, he'd been counting on her being eager to see him.

So, if the truth were known, had the Bouchards.

After all, Miles was the stableman who'd helped Rosamond feed apples to the Bouchard household's horses. He was the stableman who'd carried heavy loads of coal for his favorite housemaid. He was the stableman who'd pined for his Rosamond from afar…and now found his best chance at being near her again thwarted by two hired thugs and a whole town's worth of gossipy, intrusive menfolk.

Well, Miles hadn't gotten this far by quitting easily.

He'd traveled for weeks by rail, horseback, ferry and foot to tell Rosamond McGrath his true feelings for her. He now stood less than a mile from Rose—his Rose. He was not a man who would be daunted by a few complications.

"I can get into the marriage bureau." Miles swallowed the rest of his ale in a single gulp. He eyed the assembled men. "By this time tomorrow, I'll be Mrs. Dancy's favorite client."

Or I'll die trying, Miles swore to himself.

Not long after that, he said goodbye to his newfound friends. He picked up his flat-brimmed hat, shouldered his valise and set out to make his vow as real as the ill-gotten money that still burned a hole in his bag…and in his heart.

What I won't do, he promised himself further, is tell Rose where that damn money came from. That would not endear him to her—nor would it encourage her to trust him. To get what he wanted from Rosamond, Miles needed her good regard and her trust alike.

He needed a second chance. He was damn sure about to finagle himself one, no matter what he had to do to secure it.

Rosamond was saying her farewells to Gus when she first heard the kerfuffle at her front door. She tried to concentrate on what her very first client was telling her about his new bride and their plans, but the sounds of raised voices and scuffling feet stole her attention. What could be happening now?

Sensing the same disturbance, Gus broke off. He cast

a worried glance down the hallway, beyond the parlor's entryway where they both stood. "Sounds like trouble. You want me to go an' help your bruiser put down all the hubbub?"

"No, thank you, Mr. Winston. That won't be necessary." Thinking of scrappy Gus Winston getting into a scuffle, Rosamond hid a smile. "I'm sure Mr. Durant has matters well in hand."

A firm, raised male voice contradicted her statement.

A familiar firm, raised male voice. It couldn't be.

But if it was…

Wholly unexpectedly, a host of memories flooded Rosamond. She could smell hay and horses and fresh green apples. She could feel the heavy burden of the coal bin being chivalrously removed from her grasp. She could reexperience the heart-pounding excitement and surge of pure joy that had come every day from venturing to those Beacon Hill stables and seeing—

"Don't sound too much like he's got things in hand," Gus observed dourly. He turned toward the hallway, ready to help deal with the disturbance. "I should be goin' anyhow. Abigail—I mean, the new Mrs. Winston—will be waitin' on me."

Gus's reddened cheeks and shy smile at his mention of his new bride reminded Rosamond of all the positive effects she was having here in Morrow Creek—and pulled her sensibly away from the fanciful memories that had swamped her, too. There was no reason at all, she chided herself, to be thinking fondly of—

"Miles Callaway!" The stranger's words carried easily from her house's guarded doorway to the parlor. "All I want to know is if Miles Callaway has been here to see Mrs. Dancy."

Rosamond swayed. She felt her insides somersault.

It couldn't be him. It simply couldn't be. Not here.

But it definitely sounded like him.

For a heartbeat too long, Rosamond wanted it to be him. She wanted it to be Miles, her Miles, come to her door in Morrow Creek—no matter how unlikely that would be. Even if it was Miles, she assured herself dizzily, that didn't mean she could trust him. It didn't mean—

"Mrs. Dancy?" Gus's worried tone cut through her haze of disbelief. "Are you all right? You look about to tumble over. You've plumb gone white as a sheet, too." Protectively, Gus shooed her toward the upholstered settee. "Go on. You better have yourself a little sit-down. You want me to get Bonita?"

"I— No." In midretreat toward her settee, Rosamond stopped. She squared her shoulders. "I'm fine, Mr. Winston. Truly, I am."

Gus peered disbelievingly at her. "I ain't swallowin' it. It ain't like you to fib, anyhow. I know that for certain."

Rosamond almost laughed. Gus had no idea.

"Let's just get you off on your wedding trip with Mrs. Winston." Deliberately, Rosamond steered herself and Gus back to the parlor doorway. Her heart threatened to burst through the bodice of her practical, ladylike dress. Her hands trembled. But that didn't mean she intended to dither uselessly in her parlor. "In the meantime, I'll sort out the trouble with Mr. Durant."

"You? Pshaw." Gus waved. "That there's men's work."

"Being a good husband is a man's work," Rosamond demurred. "And that is your job now, so don't delay!"

"Well, if you're sure you don't need my help…"

"I am. Positively." Another rumble of voices came from the entryway. Rosamond was dying to know how there could be another man on earth who sounded so like Miles. Her Miles. "Bon voyage!"

Almost ushered out, Gus stopped. "Huh?"

"Have a nice trip with Mrs. Winston," Rosamond amended.

"Oh. I will." Another blush. "Why didn't you just say so?"

Because I'm conspicuously trying not to sound like a runaway housemaid. She'd once heard Mrs. Bouchard say bon voyage to an acquaintance. It had struck Rosamond as sophisticated.

"Because here at the Morrow Creek Mutual Society, we like to create a sense of occasion for our clients." Deftly, Rosamond maneuvered them both a few more feet down the hall. Now she could almost glimpse the man who stood facing down Seth. Given her protector's size, that was saying something. Any man who wasn't immediately dwarfed by Seth had to be considerably sized himself. Six feet at least, and very strongly built.

Just like Miles. His considerate ways had seemed twice as incongruous when paired with his massive size and his rough-and-tumble job as head stableman and driver. His smiles had seemed twice as rare, too, coming from a man who'd been reputed to enjoy a brawl or two.

"There. Well, thank you for becoming one of our clients." Formally, Rosamond nodded at Gus. "I wish you all the best."

He eyed her prim stance, then lifted his gaze to her face. "Aw, shucks, Mrs. Dancy. Ain't no call for formality 'tween us!"

Gus lurched forward, then startled her with a tremendous hug. He wasn't a large man, but he had the wiry strength of a man who worked hard for a living. Besides, even the smallest man was stronger than a woman—a woman who didn't want him to touch her, didn't want him to envelop her, didn't want him to take—

Feeling smothered in panic, Rosamond shoved Gus. Hard. He stumbled backward, momentarily looking like another man—a man who'd laughed at Rosamond's paltry efforts to protect herself.

Arvid Bouchard had viewed his former housemaid's resistance to his unwanted advances as proof of her Irishborn, redheaded, working-class "liveliness," not her wish to escape him. He'd pursued her relentlessly. Eventually, stuck with no place to go and no one to turn to, Rosamond had simply gone numb to what was happening with her employer. She'd seen no other choice.

She'd paid dearly for her inaction, too.

"Don't touch me." Rosamond raised her head, her gloved hands balled into fists. "Don't ever touch me! Even my friends and the children here don't—" She broke off, realizing too late how inappropriate this was. How shocked Gus looked. It was true that Rosamond could not bear to be touched. But Gus's gesture had been an openhearted farewell, not an attempt to hurt her. He was still gawking at her, in fact, still trying to figure out what had caused her outburst. Rosamond couldn't explain. "Oh! I'm so sorry, Gus. Please forgive me. I didn't mean it."

"I reckon ye did." His knowing tone didn't blame her for it. He gave her a measuring look. "I'm sorry for it, too. Most folks won't mean you no harm, but sometimes— well, you only have to ask Mrs. Cooper about that one. Sometimes folks do want to hurt a woman. Daisy had herself an awful time with—"

Rosamond was confused by Gus's mention of the livery stable owner's new wife, a renowned cookery book author and now stepmother to little Élodie Cooper, but she didn't have time to ponder the matter further. Because just as Gus was winding up his commiserating speech, the duo at her doorway parted.

"She said not to touch her," the stranger growled.

Rosamond had a brief impression of dark clothes, fast movements and pure masculine authority before all tarnation broke loose. The stranger stepped protectively between her and Gus, his arms outstretched to shield her. Seth shouted and pursued him, having evidently been given the slip at the door. Gus straightened like a cornered rooster, not giving a single inch.

Astonished, Rosamond stared at the back of the stranger's head, at his brown hair falling in collar-length waves beneath his hat and at his broad shoulders stretching the black fabric of his coat, and wondered why a bearded outsider who smelled like whiskey and cigar smoke had decided to come to her rescue.

She couldn't shake the impression that this man could have dodged her protector at any time. He simply hadn't had sufficient motivation to do so—until Gus had touched her.

"Nobody asked you to git in on this." Gus's eyes narrowed. His weathered hands curled into fists. "This here's a lady's house. You ought to learn to mind your manners."

"So should you. Start by saying goodbye."

"Why should I?" Gus demanded. "You gonna make me?"

Oh, dear. If Rosamond didn't do something, they'd come to blows. More than once, she'd seen Seth or Judah dispatch an unwanted or rowdy male visitor to her Morrow Creek Mutual Society. Typically, those men worked with their fists. She didn't want to see Gus mixed up in a melee. For whatever reason, she didn't want this stranger to be on the receiving end of one of Seth's mighty sockdolagers, either. As a onetime railway worker, Seth was as strong as an ox and twice as ornery.

Gus shifted a sideways glance toward Seth. The two of them appeared to be formulating a plan, but they were about as covert as a pair of cantankerous mules resisting being saddled. "Who kicked up his heels an' made you boss, anyhow?" Gus goaded.

The stranger didn't budge. "When I see a woman in need, I step in. Any decent man would do the same."

Again, his voice sounded so familiar. Raspy, faintly accented with a secondhand brogue, roughened by the coarse environments of tenements and stables. He sounded just like Miles. Or maybe Rosamond only wanted him to sound like Miles...

"It's my job to step in." Seth took a swing. He missed.

How had he missed? He was always so effective. So tough.

Seth looked shaken by his failure to topple the stranger. So did Gus, whose eyes widened—then narrowed again in renewed readiness. All three men froze in wary postures, leaving the air fairly vibrating with tension and combativeness.

Seth had missed. He'd failed to protect her.

Rosamond quailed, distracted from her musings about Miles. For the first time, the fortress she'd fashioned for herself here in the Arizona Territory felt in real danger of crumbling. Maybe Seth and Judah weren't so very tough, after all. Maybe if genuine danger came calling, Rosamond would find herself all on her own. Just the way she'd always been.

The notion terrified her. If her own house wasn't secure...

Well. She'd just have to make it secure.

"All of you, stop this at once!" Rosamond stepped from

behind the shielding arms of the stranger to sweep a chastising glance at them all. "Gus, please give my best wishes to Abigail. Seth, please return to your post, lest some other miscreant try to invade this house today. And you, sir—" she swallowed hard, hoping to dredge up a bonus quantity of courage "—should leave immediately, before I take it into my mind to stomp your foot, wring your ear and drag you out of this house myself."

A heavy silence descended. More than likely, all the other ordinary sounds were drowned out by the furor of Rosamond's heartbeat pounding in her ears. Then, gradually, the laughter of the children playing outside returned. It was followed by the steady ticking of the grandfather clock to Rosamond's left.

She drew in another fortifying breath, not quite daring to look the stranger in the face. She both did and did not want to confirm that he wasn't the stableman she remembered, wasn't the man she'd thought of so often since leaving Boston, could not be Miles Callaway, come thousands of miles to arrive at her door.

"Please don't make me repeat myself," she warned.

Gus tipped his hat. "Thanks kindly, Mrs. Dancy." He had the audacity to wink. "You sure know how to throw a lively bit o' entertainment here at the marriage bureau, that's for sure."

Gus saluted, then left with a grin. Seth, for his part, retreated the merest quantity of steps, then mulishly stopped.

"Since when have I not meant what I said?" Rosamond asked.

Improbably, the stranger laughed at that remark.

Seth, looking more embarrassed than she wanted, stomped all the way back to his usual post in the entryway. From there, he surveyed their latest visitor through distrustful eyes.

So did Rosamond, albeit from beside him. Clearly, in the end, shielding her household of women and children was up to her. Her protectors, Seth and Judah, could only do so much—especially if she were the one causing all the trouble.

Reminded of her earlier overreaction to Gus's bear hug, Rosamond winced. The poor man hadn't deserved that. She'd physically retaliated against him! She'd berated him. She was so sorry for that. It wasn't at all normal to dislike being hugged.

It also wasn't normal for anyone to get the better of Seth. Yet her latest visitor had easily gotten past Seth and avoided his blow, too. Who in the world was he? And why was he there?

Miles Callaway, she remembered the stranger saying. *All I want to know is if Miles Callaway has been here to see Mrs. Dancy.*

This man was looking for Miles. He'd unwittingly roused Rosamond's bottled-up memories at the same time, but that wasn't his fault. If Miles was in any trouble, Rosamond wanted to know.

She'd liked Miles. She'd more than liked Miles.

He'd been her staunchest ally in the Bouchard household. He'd been a friend, and, yes, the subject of her girlish daydreams about love and romance, too. She hadn't ever admitted as much to him. In fact, she hadn't ever done anything much more audacious than smile at Miles. But Rosamond had entertained youthful fantasies about holding his hand, about dancing with him, about learning why he seemed so strong and yet so trapped in Boston, why he seemed so charming and yet often so alone.

Those girlhood fantasies felt very far away to her now. They were part of another life—a life when she hadn't had a hole in her heart and a soul-deep need to bar the door at all times.

"Sorry to bother you, ma'am." With the scarcest turn to acknowledge her, the stranger tipped his hat. "I'll be going."

He took several strides toward the door.

In a moment, he'd be gone. Just the way she'd demanded.

But his voice still rang in the air, so reminiscent of...

Well, so reminiscent of the one man Rosamond had never been able to forget. The one man she'd never truly wanted to forget.

"Wait! Please." In a trice, she'd caught up to him. She touched his sleeve, caught his questioning glance at her overly intrusive gloved hand, then regrouped. Hastily, Rosamond took away her hand—but not before she felt... something...pass between them. "I heard you talking earlier. I'd like to know everything you know about this... Mr. Callaway, was it?"

He hesitated, his bearded face mostly cast in shadow by his hat and his collar-length hair. Then he unwisely accepted her sham uncertainty at face value, just as Rosamond had intended.

This...Mr. Callaway, was it?

As if she hadn't dreamed of him.

"Are you asking me to stay?" he asked. "All I wanted was to question your hired man. I heard you never entertain visitors."

"Today, for you, I'll make an exception. Please." Valiantly, Rosamond cast about for a proper inducement. Now that she almost had this man right where she wanted him—in a position to reveal whatever he knew about

Miles—she didn't intend to quit. "I have tea! You must be thirsty after your travels."

His posture sharpened. "My travels?"

His wariness confounded her. "You're carrying a valise."

"Ah. Yes, I am." He lifted it in a rueful gesture, his tense shoulders easing with the motion. "It holds everything I own, some of what I've borrowed and none of what I need." His gaze shifted to her household, then arrowed in on her parlor doorway with no effort at all. "Right now, I need tea."

That meant she'd won, Rosamond knew, and felt curiously buoyant. If she could not see Miles Callaway again, at least she could find out what had become of him. After all, she would likely not be the only one who'd left the Bouchards' employ.

Miles, as she remembered him, had loved an adventure. He'd also possessed a lightheartedness she'd envied on occasion.

This man did not seem quite so sanguine.

But then, he wasn't her Miles, was he? He couldn't be. She and Miles were thousands of miles apart. Neither of them had the means to cross that distance. Rosamond herself had only done it through extraordinary and trying circumstances. It was preposterous to think that an ordinary stableman could have followed her this far—or that he would have wanted to.

All the same, he very much seemed to be Miles! Rosamond needed a closer and clearer look at him to know for sure. She intended to get herself that closer, clearer look at him, too.

Just to be on the safe side. Just to indulge her silly, woebegone sentimentality at this mysterious stranger's expense.

"Excellent. Right this way." Rosamond indicated the way forward, watching alertly as he preceded her.

She had not come this far by trusting lightly, though. Nor by skipping any of the necessary precautions. So she signaled for Seth to fetch Bonita, added an extra bit of cautionary instruction to her request for tea service and then joined her new guest in the parlor.

Chapter Three

Miles had never felt more jubilant in his life.

He'd found Rosamond. He'd found her. At long last, his Rose was seated directly across from him on her fancy upholstered armchair in her fancy Morrow Creek parlor, looking beautiful and pert and just a little bit thinner than he remembered her.

Worriedly, Miles examined her more closely. The experience jarred him. He'd never seen Rosamond in anything but a tidily pressed housemaid's uniform and her requisite cap. While she'd lent a definite sparkle to those stiff and unbecoming duds, it was still odd to see her wearing a high-necked dress with a tight bodice and a full bustled skirt. Her gingery hair was a little more tumbledown than she probably intended it to be.

She seemed older. Wiser. Infinitely more cautious.

Also, she seemed, just then, to be distinctly blurry.

Confused, Miles blinked. He gestured at his teacup. Sitting on the polished tabletop before him, it was now empty of the sweetened hot liquid Rosamond had so adroitly served him earlier. He'd swilled it all in record time and then polished off a refill, too, unexpectedly dry-mouthed and in need of something to do to settle his big, restless hands.

"Is there any more tea?" he asked.

"There is. But I'm not sure you should have more. It seems to be affecting you quite strongly. More strongly than usual."

Her words made sense, given how peculiar he felt. It was as if his head were floating a few inches above the rest of him. He hadn't had enough ale at the saloon to be drunk. What was this?

The truth was, though, Miles felt too good to care.

Because he'd found Rosamond. She was all right. She was safe. Everything he'd done till now—everything— had been worth it.

"Looking at you, I feel like dancing a damn jig," he told her. All three of her. "You're well. I'm thankful."

Thankful scarcely described the depth of relief he felt. He wanted to bawl at the depth of relief he felt. But a man did not weep. So Miles only uttered another grateful swearword, shaking his head in wonderment as he went on studying Rosamond.

If only she weren't pretending not to know him...

"Hmm. Yes, I am well," she said. "Given our situation, I'll forgive you your coarse language just now, too. I can see the jubilation on your face." She peered wistfully at him. "For a variety of reasons, I believe what you're saying is true. I believe you are glad about something."

Serenely, Rosamond folded her hands atop her skirts. Even while scrutinizing him as if he was her long-lost love, she seemed the very picture of ladylike decorum.

Miles told her so.

She smiled. "Thank you. You seem the very picture of someone I once knew. He was a stableman and driver in Boston."

There was that disingenuousness in her again. It had begun when Miles had taken off his hat and coat, and hadn't abated since. He didn't like it. But two could play that game.

"Boston? Pfft." He waved again. "The only good things in Beantown are rivers and bridges and a mother's love."

She seemed to find that amusing. "Then you've been there?"

"I've come from there. To find someone."

"To find Miles Callaway, you said. The thing is, I am very struck by your resemblance to the Miles Callaway I once knew."

Her tense posture suggested she didn't trust that Miles Callaway. That's why Miles didn't own up to being himself straightaway. That and the tales he'd been told of Rosamond having visitors from her past hurled forcibly from her house.

Launching a scuffle with her security men would not endear him to her. Nor would being made to explain— too soon and in too much detail—exactly how he'd come to be there in Morrow Creek.

This was not the sort of reunion he'd been hoping for.

"Mmm. I reckon I have that kind of face." He had the kind of face, it occurred belatedly to him, that felt weirdly numb. He stroked his bearded jaw, then cast a suspicious glance at his teacup. Rosamond's tea had tasted strange, but he'd been too polite to say so. On top of his long travels and the ale he'd already consumed at Jack Murphy's saloon, that tea had not done him any favors. He felt... odd. "So do you. You look a lot like a housemaid I once knew. Her name was Rose. My Rose."

Her face swam in his vision, doubling and then coming clear again. Miles shook his head. He frowned at her "assistant," Miss Yates, who'd helpfully taken his valise from him and was now rummaging through its contents. Vaguely, that struck him as inappropriate. He had the impression someone may have riffled through his pockets, too. That beefy kid, Judah, who'd roughly taken his hat and coat after he'd come in? Had the bastard tossed him?

Miles was usually much savvier than this. Clearly, seeing Rose again had done him in. Despite her attempts to persuade him otherwise—despite the cat-and-mouse game they'd been playing thus far—he knew she was Rose, too. Rosamond McGrath Dancy. In the flesh. In a pretty pink dress. Her freckles still enchanted him. So did the sound of her voice.

He felt desperate to touch her, to reassure himself she was real. But after what had happened between her and that knuck Gus Winston earlier, Miles knew better than to touch her. Also, he wasn't sure he could stand up without toppling over. He might wind up facedown in her high-buttoned shoes.

Then it hit him. "You drugged me!" he accused.

Her virtuous demeanor didn't waver. "I think the stableman I knew was a bit…taller than you, though. Better looking, too."

"Better looking? Humph." He was "better looking."

"Yes." Another assessing, faraway look. "For one thing, my Miles had shorter hair. He was also clean shaven." She gave a dreamy sigh. "He always wore a clean, pressed uniform, too."

She was goading him on purpose. He knew it. But her musings didn't distract him overmuch. Partly because Miles knew damn well he was tall enough and "better looking" enough to suit any woman—especially one who'd haunted his thoughts for years.

Why hadn't he told her before how he felt?

His beard and hair and clothes could be changed. Not

that he truly believed Rosamond pined for braid-trimmed trousers and jackets with epaulets at the shoulders. Arvid Bouchard had dressed his staff in the most ostentatious livery possible.

He wanted to hear Rosamond call him her Miles again.

But there was the pressing matter of her recent misconduct to be dealt with first. He could not let that stand as it was.

Even if that, as much as anything else, assured him he'd located the right woman—the right redheaded runaway housemaid.

"You drugged me," he accused again, wishing he could strengthen his charge by standing. His knees felt rubbery and unfit to support him. "You tossed my coat and pockets looking for clues, and now Miss Yates is searching my valise."

"Yes. That reminds me—" Rosamond turned her attention to her partner in crime. "What have you found, Miss Yates?"

"Several train ticket stubs, today's copy of the Pioneer Press, assorted men's clothing, a battered old book and far, far too much money for any honorable man to possess in Morrow Creek." That traitorous woman aimed a sour look at Miles. "Furthermore, he only packed a single pair of underdrawers."

They both gave him patently scandalized stares.

"I'm wearing the other pair," Miles explained in his own defense, trying to ignore the additionally skeptical—and far more salacious—glance Miss Yates tossed him next. He'd have sworn she was imagining him naked. "I'm not made of money."

They stared pointedly at his valise full of banknotes.

Miles drew himself up with dignity. In his current state, he didn't know how to further defend himself without mentioning how he'd gotten all that money—and how much it had really cost him. He'd done his utmost not to spend much of it, but he'd had no way to search for Rosamond without it. He'd had to find out why she'd vanished from the Bouchards' household in the middle of the night without so much as a note. Couldn't she see that?

"Plus a wicked-looking knife," the strongman, Judah, put in from across the room, saving Miles a reply. "Don't forget that."

Stricken, Miles patted his leg. Beneath his trousers, the knife sheaf on his calf felt conspicuously empty. He squinted anew at his drugged teacup, feeling lucky not to be insentient.

At least he had the wits to recognize he'd been bested. Temporarily.

All the same, the notion made him feel perversely proud of Rose. She'd seen him as a threat. She'd dealt with that threat. Period. She was as capable and strong and spirited as ever. Those were all qualities he'd admired in her...once upon a time.

"Oh, we won't forget the knife," Miss Yates was assuring her hulking compatriot. "Or all that money, either." Her gaze skittered over Miles's black-clad form. "In fact, Mrs. Dancy, it might be wise of us to conduct an even more thorough search of his person. I'd be happy to supervise such an effort, if—"

"That won't be necessary." Rosamond's attention remained implacably fixed on Miles's face. She'd never even glanced below his neck, as near as he could tell. It was almost as though she didn't want to consider any of the overtly manly rest of him. But that didn't make sense. He'd never hurt her. He'd rather die than hurt her. "I think," she added, "we're almost done here."

"My Rose was never this devious," Miles complained.

"Your Rose is gone. And she isn't ever going back."

"Going back? Then you know that she left?"

At his question, Rosamond looked stricken. Because she'd been pretending not to know him. Because she'd been pretending—with admirable dexterity—not to know that she'd left Boston, left him…left everything in her old life behind.

Well, he was pretending, too. Pretending he had all the time in the world to sort things out. Pretending he had…anything to give her besides a charming tale and a pair of strong arms.

Near as he could tell, Rosamond wanted nothing from him—or from any man. Even if she was, as he'd learned, a widow now.

Determinedly, Miles leaned nearer to her. "You should know that I don't want Rose to go back." He had to communicate as much to Rosamond. It felt urgent. But the tea and the ale and whatever they'd dosed him with made it hard to say so. "I haven't come here to bring her back. Only to—" *See her. Proclaim my feelings for her. Save her, if necessary.* "—see her."

Hellfire. He still couldn't tell her. Not even drugged.

But there'd be time for sweet words and proper reunions later. All Miles needed now was to make Rosamond trust him. That was first. Later on, everything else would naturally follow.

"Well, I'm afraid you're stuck with me—Mrs. Dancy." She kept her hands folded in her lap, but her cheeks had turned a shade pinker. Her feelings were softening toward him already. Miles could tell. All the signs were there. "I'm sorry I can't help you find your friend, the housemaid you mentioned, but—"

"She was more than a friend. More than a housemaid, too."

"In any case, it was Miles Callaway you were looking for, wasn't it?" Placidly, Rosamond sipped from her own teacup, her gaze bright and intelligent over its rim. "How do you know him?"

"We worked together." He should not embroider this fabricated story. But what choice did he have? Miles was certain "Mrs. Dancy" was his Rosamond, no matter how unlikely it was. No matter how sophisticated and jaded she appeared. No matter how much she tacitly denied it. But he didn't want to spook her. That's why he'd pretended to be "looking for Miles Callaway" in the first place. He'd counted on Rosamond's interest in her former friend—and her intrinsic contrariness—to gain admission into her household. It had worked, too. She'd invited him inside, just the way he'd wanted. "Callaway left the Bouchards' household several months ago. He's been traveling ever since."

"Traveling? But he can't afford to—" Her eyes narrowed. "Traveling to what purpose?"

"He's been searching for someone."

Her gaze grew even more cynical. "For this 'Rose' person?"

A nod. "At times, he felt sure he'd found her."

A wobble of her teacup was the only sign he'd affected her. She set down her cup, then airily regarded her tidy parlor. "I suppose people in Boston were wondering where she'd gone?"

"Callaway wondered." Miles recalled the morning he'd learned she'd left. The confusion he'd felt then—the sheer disbelief and regret—still gnawed at him, all these months later. He and Rosamond had unfinished business between them. "He couldn't understand why she'd leave without saying goodbye."

"I'm sure she had her reasons."

"I'd like to know what they were."

A heartbeat passed. "I'm sure you would. So would Mr. Callaway and a few…other people, I'd imagine."

She was testing him. She didn't trust him yet. She was wise not to. Unwillingly, Miles recalled Arvid Bouchard's intense interest in "that housemaid's whereabouts." It was only because of something that Genevieve Bouchard had let slip during a carriage ride that either of them had had the slightest lead on tracking Rosamond. Equally unwillingly, Miles recalled that he was supposed to report his findings to Arvid. He was supposed to tell his former employer the moment he located Rosamond.

Miles didn't intend to do that. He never had.

He intended to find Rosamond, ensure she was safe, and then pay back every dime it had taken to find his friend…his Rose.

"If he were here now, I'd tell Mr. Callaway to forget about this housemaid," she said. "I doubt she's worth the trouble."

"She's worth everything. Everything to me."

"To you?" She gave him a contemplative, dubious look. "Without even knowing where she's been or what she's done?"

"None of that matters."

"It might." Her gaze turned pensive. "If you knew."

"It wouldn't," Miles swore, "as long as she's safe."

"Well, 'safe' is a relative term, isn't it? Coming from you, the man who dodged my guard, it's especially ironic."

"You don't need guards. Not against me."

"Humph." Her other protector, Judah, gave a disgruntled sound. With crossed arms, he regarded Miles.

"That's what all the low-down bastards say," he blurted, "right before they—"

"Language, please, Judah."

"—cheat you and leave you busted," Judah went on doggedly. "I should know. My brother is a cardsharp, meanest in the territory. Leastwise, Cade was a cardsharp, up until he got married to a prissy preacher's daughter. She's nice, but—"

"This really isn't the time, Mr. Foster," Miss Yates interrupted. She turned her attention to Rosamond. "Shall I bring in more tea, Mrs. Dancy?" She inclined her head toward Miles. "I may have underestimated his impressive size and strength. It appears the earlier dose is wearing off quickly."

"Yes." Miles brightened. "Come to think of it, I do feel more like myself." With vigor, he stretched. His big-booted feet came all the way beneath Rosamond's dainty table and out the other side. "I feel like a new man, ready to take on anything."

"What are your plans for the future, Mr...?" Rosamond broke off, wearing another wily look. "Oh, I'm sorry. It seems that in all my haste to learn about the intriguing Mr. Callaway, I neglected to ask you your name. I do apologize."

Her confident tone almost made Miles doubt himself. Was this his Rosamond McGrath? Or was this her more cultured double, living in a faraway town the likes of which Rosamond McGrath would not have had the resources or the know-how to reach?

He believed it was Rosamond. Otherwise, he wouldn't have persisted. But he dearly wished he knew why she was still pretending not to know him. The warier she was, the warier he felt he had to be. "I plan to stay in Morrow Creek."

Her pleasant expression didn't waver. "For how long?"

"For however long it takes."

Rosamond blinked. "I see. And your name…?"

"Doesn't matter." Yes. He felt markedly better. "Unless that's a requirement for admission into your marriage bureau?"

She frowned, clearly taken aback by his mention of it. "It's called the Morrow Creek Mutual Society. As far as admission goes, I should warn you, it's extremely rigorous."

"If it will help me woo the woman of my dreams, you can call it anything you want." Miles rose. He took his black coat from the coatrack, put it on, then grabbed his hat. "I've learned all I need to for now. I'll be back later to apply."

Rosamond seemed perturbed. "You might as well not bother. After all, you're off to a very poor start. You've already appeared here intoxicated, discussing your underdrawers! That's not behavior that's indicative of my approved members."

He couldn't help grinning. He turned to confront Miss Yates. "Miss Yates, do you agree with that assessment?"

That saucy woman whipped her abstracted gaze from the vicinity of his trousers. Caught, she grumpily shoved his open valise at him. Clothing and train tickets bulged from it.

"I agree that you're suspiciously eager to find a wife," Miss Yates told him. "You don't look like the marrying kind."

"I didn't feel like the marrying kind until I got here." Until I found Rose. He offered them both a raise of his eyebrow. "I guess I should thank the little something 'extra' in that tea you dosed me with. It's made me into a whole new man."

Rosamond's concerned gaze shifted to Miss Yates. Aha. Then her assistant was the one who knew how to drug a man and search his belongings, all while keeping him curiously complacent.

He'd already suspected what kind of women Rosamond had found herself keeping company with, given the line of business he'd learned Elijah Dancy had been in. Miss Yates's next words confirmed it. Because only a soiled dove would have known...

"A little laudanum never hurt a man," she grumbled in her own justification. Accusingly, she pointed at Miles. "I mean, yes, it can render a fella mostly harmless in a hurry. But it sure never made any man I used it on want to start proposing!"

"All right. That's enough, Miss Yates." Rosamond smiled at her assistant. Unrepentantly, she regarded Miles. "If you'd like to report our misdeeds, Sheriff Caffey's jailhouse is right down the street. I think you'll find yourself an ally in suspecting us of some rather serious wrongdoing in this household."

Holding his hat, unwilling to leave but knowing he had to, Miles angled his head. "Does that include the children?"

Rosamond lost a fraction of her self-assurance. Clearly, she'd believed he hadn't noticed the children who'd been playing in the house's yard. He'd heard them when he observed the place.

Arvid Bouchard would have been very interested in the children—in the possibility of Rosamond having had a child.

Miles was curious about that possibility, too. But not for Bouchard's sake. For his own sake. For his own future. For hers.

Just like Rosamond, Miles had left their former employer behind. All that bound them now was the sum of money Miles owed.

"It sounds as though they range in age. How old are they?"

"That, sir, is none of your business. I think it's time you left us." Briskly, Rosamond stood. "The door is this way."

Her manner was brusque as she passed him. Her rosy perfume haunted him, though. Again, he felt desperate to touch her.

In the past, he'd touched her, Miles remembered. Casually and only infrequently, but he'd touched her. She'd touched him. Their hands had brushed while exchanging apples for the horses or trading the burden of the coal bin. Once, memorably, Rosamond had brushed a hayseed from his cheek. When she'd done that, Miles had felt something. Something good. He believed Rosamond had, too. That was part of what had driven him here.

Two thousand miles was a long way to go not to touch a woman.

"I didn't mean to upset you," he told her.

"You haven't upset me." The new color in her cheeks told him otherwise. So did the firm line of her mouth. "I'm fine."

"In that case, you won't mind my calling again tomorrow."

"Tomorrow?"

"To collect all the details of admission to your society."

"You were serious?"

"About this?" Miles gazed directly at her, putting every ounce of longing he felt into his voice. "I've never been more determined to accomplish anything in all my life."

Their gazes met. For a moment, she seemed as affected by their unacknowledged reunion as he was. She seemed to remember their shared conversations, their shared laughter, their past and their friendship and all the rest. Then, "I think you'll find this is a more daunting task than you've counted on."

"I live for daunting tasks. And for conquering them."

"You sound entirely too confident."

"You must have forgotten exactly how intent a man can be when he's fixed on getting something he wants."

"No. I haven't forgotten that." Crisply, Rosamond nodded at him. She stepped resolutely away. "Judah will see you out."

As her guard approached, Miles felt bereft.

"And tomorrow?" he persisted.

"You won't be back tomorrow." Rosamond didn't so much as turn to face him again. Instead, she busied herself collecting the teapot and saucers on a tray. "You'll decide this is all too much trouble, and you won't come back. Most people cannot be relied upon, but their base selfishness can be. I know that much for sure."

"Then you don't know me."

At that, Rosamond did scrutinize him. Briefly. "Maybe I don't. Now that you're here…maybe I don't know anyone as well as I thought I did." She appeared on the verge of elaborating, then did not. Instead, she said, "Good luck to you."

"Good luck to us both."

A faint smile. "Now I know you won't be back."

"The devil couldn't keep me away." Miles aimed a sidelong glance at Miss Yates. "Nor could any of his minions."

That cheeky woman actually giggled. Despite everything, Miles began to believe he could succeed here, with Rosamond, in her new life.

"We are finished," Rosamond said firmly. "Please leave."

Then again, Miles concluded…immediate success might prove to be elusive.

The door had scarcely closed behind her visitor before Rosamond raced to the window to watch him leave. Bonita was only steps behind her, both of them battling to move the curtains.

As one, they watched him study the small Morrow Creek street upon which her house stood. Then he shouldered his untidy valise and moved confidently in a singular direction.

"He's headed for Miss Adelaide's boardinghouse," Bonita announced, her breath all but fogging the window glass. "That's odd. With all those greenbacks in his bag, he can afford to stay at the Lorndorff Hotel for a month, at least."

The stableman Rosamond remembered had not had that kind of money. "Yes, he did have an unusual amount of cash, didn't he?"

"'Unusual'? He had a king's ransom in that bag!" Bonita shook her head. "And that knife he carried, too. Hidden in a holster? That man is up to no good, whatever his name is."

"I know what his name is." But I don't know why he wouldn't admit it to me. Distractedly, Rosamond watched him stride away, his footsteps sure and his shoulders strong. He moved exactly the way she remembered. Drat it all, he even smelled the way she remembered, with traces of leather and soap clinging to his skin. "I knew it from the moment he took off his hat."

His long hair and dark beard had stymied her at first.

So had the sheer undeniable unlikeliness of them meeting again this way. But once he'd looked squarely at her...

Well, once Miles had done that, she'd known it was him. It had been all she could do not to give herself over right then.

"You did? Then why pretend you didn't?" Bonita protested, sounding exasperated with her. "If you knew you knew him, why did you ask me to dose him?"

I needed to protect myself. "I needed to know more," Rosamond hedged. The truth was, the warier Miles had seemed, the warier she'd felt she needed to be. It wasn't like him to be so evasive. So mysterious. Their mutual caginess had created its own unfortunate momentum. "Starting with why he's here—"

Bonita interrupted with a snort. "It sure as shootin' isn't to get himself married!"

"—and ending with where he got all that money. And why."

Rosamond had her suspicions, but she couldn't be sure. For her own sake—for the sake of the women and children depending on her—she'd needed to question him. She hated that she had cause to doubt Miles—to doubt anyone, in fact. She only hoped she wasn't overestimating her own intuition in this instance.

If Miles Callaway moved on after today, then she'd know he could have been trusted. She'd know he hadn't come in search of her at Arvid's or Genevieve Bouchard's behest. She'd know he'd only come to satisfy his own curiosity about a runaway housemaid, and, having done that, had moved on to more adventures.

But if Miles Callaway did come back to her mutual society tomorrow, if he did continue pursuing her...

Well, that was another situation entirely.

If Miles came back, it wouldn't be because he wanted

her or a wife of his own. Despite his claims to the contrary, Rosamond knew that could not be the case. The man she remembered had been an inveterate bachelor. And while she was a good person, she was not the innocent girl she'd once been. Once Miles realized that, he'd be finished with her. Worse, he'd be appalled at her.

He would see the gaping hole left in her.

He would pity her.

Rosamond didn't think she could bear that. She couldn't bear knowing that, in Miles's eyes, she would no longer be the lively and openhearted girl he remembered. She'd never be that girl again. If Miles knew that, too, it would be doubly real.

On the other hand, before today, she wouldn't have believed she could bear being in the same room with Miles Callaway and not acknowledging how good it felt to see his smile, to hear his voice, to experience the warmth of his protective nature, one last time. She'd succeeded in that already. So who knew exactly how deep her personal resilience really ran, after all.

Grit and determination had brought her to Morrow Creek. Those same qualities could bring her toe-to-toe with Miles. They could help her win—help her protect herself from…everything.

"He's very handsome," Bonita mused. "Very handsome."

Rosamond agreed. Silently. Her mind was still awhirl with all the potential implications of Miles's sudden appearance in Morrow Creek. She couldn't afford to go all swoony over his deep blue eyes, his Adonis-like dark curly hair and his sculpted features. Those transient qualities didn't matter anyway.

"Very charming, too," her assistant added leadingly. "Do you know, when the laudanum first hit him, he stared at you for a solid minute with a spoony, love-struck grin on his face? It was as if he'd waited years to see you, when clearly—"

"It's only been a little more than a single year." Forcefully, Rosamond dragged herself from her remembrance of Miles's euphoric expression. "And he was drugged, remember?"

"Drugged in a way that would remove all barriers to the truth," Bonita argued. Then her mouth dropped open. "A little more than a—then you do know him? Really? From Boston?"

"Home of rivers, bridges and a mother's love."

"I thought you only wanted to know about Miles Callaway."

"He is Miles Callaway."

"But you said— He said—" Bonita frowned. "I'm confused."

"So am I. But one way or the other, I won't be for long."

"Then you're 'his Rose'? The runaway housemaid?" Bonita sounded baffled—and a little bit hurt, as well. "But you've never told me any of that. I thought we were friends."

"We are friends." Tearing herself away from the parlor window—from fruitlessly wishing Miles Callaway had ambled back into her life with a smile and a laugh and wholesome intentions to help her shoulder her burdens once more—Rosamond sighed. "But there are things no one needs to know about me. Sometimes, I wish I could forget them myself."

Sympathetically, Bonita came nearer. Wisely, she stopped short of actually consoling Rosamond with a hug.

"Maybe it's best if he doesn't come back."

Rosamond gave a wistful smile. "I feel positive it is."

I only wish I could stop wanting him to come back anyway.

At least if Miles did return, she'd be ready.

Today, she'd been too taken aback by Miles's unexpected arrival to react properly—to consider all the potential ramifications and inconveniences of pretending not to be the Rosamond McGrath Miles clearly believed she was.

She'd never been a skilled liar. Probably, she still wasn't. Especially to someone who'd once known her well.

For a long time, her friend only regarded her. Then, "I guess you must be right." With forced jollity, Bonita added, "Anyway, you and I—we've got each other, don't we? In the end, that's all we need. Nothing ever needs to change. Not if we don't want it to. We've made things safe and secure and good."

"Mmm. We've certainly tried."

Absently, Rosamond smiled at her friend, hoping to reassure Bonita. But on the inside, she couldn't help wondering…if Arvid Bouchard found her because of Miles Callaway's visit, would she have anything at all left, for her or Bonita or anyone else?

Her so-called security had been tested and found wanting today. Her haven was no refuge at all. Not when someone like Miles could smash her security to smithereens with scarcely any effort at all. All this time, she'd been fooling herself, Rosamond knew now. She wasn't safe. Maybe she never would be.

But maybe she could start strengthening her defenses straightaway, she decided as she collected her tea set. That's exactly what she intended to do. Maybe she hadn't done it yet, but Rosamond knew she could find some security eventually.

After all, that was all she'd ever wanted.

That and a certain burly, blue-eyed stableman to call her own, of course. It was only too bad she could never claim him...

Chapter Four

The following morning, after a fitful night spent haunted by memories of Miles Callaway—memories that had been hideously interspersed with confusing recollections of Arvid Bouchard in her nightmares—Rosamond made several decisions.

The first was that she would conduct herself intelligently from here on out. The second was that she would protect the people in her household. The third was that she would stay put. No one else was chasing her from her home. Not again. Not ever.

To that end, there could be no more swooning over Miles's broad shoulders or raspy brogue, Rosamond chastised herself. There could be no more forgetting her own mission in favor of studying Miles's chiseled cheekbones and assertive nose. There could be no more wishing that she could be different—could be as carefree as she'd been before Arvid Bouchard and his odious demands on her. No matter what it took, Rosamond swore, she would remain calm. Composed. In charge and in control.

There was safety in control. She needed that dearly.

To that end, Rosamond smiled up at her newest potential employee, a man named Dylan Coyle who'd come recommended to her.

"Two years at the lumber mill, you say?" She craned her neck way up to examine his expression for truthfulness and integrity. "Before that, a year with the Pinkertons?" His nod assured her that her information was correct. Nonetheless, Rosamond pushed harder. "What made you leave the agency's employ?"

"I didn't like the way they ran things."

"The way they ran things?"

"With guns. They used guns." Coyle's steely gaze locked with hers. "I reckon if a man can't disable a criminal with his own two hands, he doesn't deserve to be called a man, does he?"

His hard demeanor both alarmed and reassured her. "I see."

"Yep. Most folks do, when it comes to me."

Rather than hurry onward, Rosamond deliberately allowed a long silence to fall between them. When faced with a silence, most people rushed to fill it. All she had to do was wait.

Eventually, Coyle rewarded her patience. The scarcest smile quirked his lips. "Also, about that same time, I met a lady."

"Hmm." Pretending not to have seen that telling smile, Rosamond looked down at her clasped hands. She didn't want to embarrass the man. As a private person herself, she respected others' privacy, too. It was only right. "Then you're married?"

"No, ma'am. I'm not married."

"But you just said—" Rosamond broke off, belatedly catching the hint of heartache in his voice. "Never mind. I have a job, and you have the ability to do that job. Marcus Copeland has vouched for you, and so has Cade Foster. With varied references like those—from a reputable lumber mill owner and a former cardsharp—I'd say you must be an interesting man, Mr. Coyle."

He gave her a direct look. "With an observation like that in your pocket, you must be a sharp-eyed woman, Mrs. Dancy."

"Please call me Rosamond. I insist." She didn't want to talk about her deep-seated need to be watchful. If he was going to risk his own well-being in her service, he deserved to be on a first-name basis with her. "All my men call me Rosamond."

"All my friends call me Dylan."

"Then we're settled." Rosamond stood. She felt better already, even before placing Dylan at his post. "Seth and Judah will brief you on your duties. I'm pleased to welcome you."

Undoubtedly catching her signal that their interview had concluded, Dylan stood, as well. His gaze swerved to her hand.

He plainly expected to find it outstretched for a welcoming handshake. Resolutely, Rosamond kept her position steady.

Dylan's brown furrowed. His astute gaze lifted.

"I guess a woman who hires three bodyguards has her reasons." He plucked his hat from the coatrack, then gave her a genial nod. "Thanks for the work, ma'am. You won't regret it."

"I trust you'll make sure I don't." Drawing in a breath, Rosamond smiled at him. "I'll show you where to find Judah."

She led the way, purposely taking the more impersonal long way around to avoid the house's living quarters. They passed through the front door, across the side yard, toward the gate.

In her house's small backyard, several of the children were already at play. Hearing the boys' chuckles and the girls' giggles made Rosamond feel more at peace immediately.

She may have given up on having a family of her own, but that didn't mean she didn't adore being with "her" temporary children. Along with her friendly "girls" and her own security, they were all she had. She needed to protect and cherish them.

At her side, Dylan went rigid. "Who's that?" He pointed. "You said there were only two men in this household. We passed Seth at the door and I see Judah right there, so who is—"

In the center of the crowd of children, a tall man rose from his formerly crouched position. He held something in his arms, but Rosamond couldn't tell what it was. She was too distracted by the realization that not only had Miles Callaway slipped past Seth again—and apparently bewitched Judah, too—but he'd also made a mockery of her Morrow Creek household haven.

This was why she'd needed to hire additional security. Miles had returned already, bearing…something.

"He's the thorn in my side," Rosamond finished for Dylan, briskly unlatching the gate. She couldn't look away from Miles…couldn't stop herself from wishing he hadn't come back. Because his coming back today meant that he couldn't be trusted. It meant that he wanted something from her—and it probably wasn't an introduction to a suitable candidate for a wife.

That was what most men in Morrow Creek wanted from her. They'd learned, quickly, not to hope for anything more.

"Do you want me to deal with him?" Dylan kept his

voice low, for her ears only. "Ordinarily, I wouldn't ask first, except—"

"Except Mrs. Dancy looks dumbstruck, as if she's found her long-lost love?" Miles strode toward them both with masculine bonhomie, obviously having overheard them. He didn't appear the least bit threatened by Dylan Coyle. Behind him, the children moaned in exaggerated disappointment at Miles's leave-taking. They tagged along in his wake like the devoted admirers they'd become. "Yes," Miles finished. "I've noticed that look, too."

His gaze met hers, then held. In it, Rosamond glimpsed all the caring, all the remembrance, all the teasing she'd missed.

Intentionally, she looked away. She knew she was guilty.

She didn't want him to know that. Because, more than likely, she did look at Miles as if he were her long-lost love. Rosamond heartily wished he had been hers once… or was hers now.

Her Miles. He was here like the answer to all her most heartfelt prayers…and she couldn't trust him one whit.

"Maybe you've had too much 'tea' this morning, and that explains that addlepated look of yours?" Miles guessed, his eyes sparkling at her with all the boyish audacity she remembered. "I understand your Miss Yates makes a mean brew."

Unwaveringly, Rosamond straightened. "If I look—" love-struck "—funny, it's only because I don't approve of trespassing. I usually don't entertain visitors at this hour of the morning."

Pointedly, Miles looked at Dylan. Her visitor.

"Except if they're employees," Rosamond amended. How did Miles set her akilter so easily? Drat him!

"I see. Well, it turns out that we both had the same idea today." Miles easily sized up Dylan. He nodded at him in instant affability, then switched his attention back to Rosamond. "You wanted more security, so you hired another 'protector.'"

Rosamond didn't like that Miles had guessed her motives so easily. She didn't want him to know that his presence had shaken her hard-won security so thoroughly. "How do you know Mr. Coyle isn't a proud member of the Morrow Creek Mutual Society?"

"I doubt the members of your society have arms like tree trunks, belligerent attitudes and a complete disinterest in the alluring way your bustle sways when you walk. Coyle does."

Rosamond felt her mouth drop open. She didn't know whether to be impressed by Miles's accurate assessment of her newest security man or appalled that she cared that Miles apparently did have an interest in what went on with her bustled backside. Otherwise, he couldn't have made that observation, could he?

Before she could collect herself, Miles went on.

"I wanted you to have more security myself, after I saw how feeble yours was yesterday," he was saying, "so I went with the most reliable and fearsome protector I could get for you."

Triumphantly, Miles lifted the thing in his arms.

It wriggled. Then it gave a tiny yip. A puppy.

The children went wild. "We want to play with it again!" Agatha cried out. "Please let us play with it again!"

"Can we name it?" Tommy pleaded. "I have a good name!"

"In a minute, you can play with it again," Miles assured them all, his voice a rumble of promise and possibility. "And no, Tommy, you can't. I'm afraid Mrs. Dancy has naming rights on this little rascal."

Rosamond stared. "You brought me a puppy?"

Miles blinked. "Oh. Is that what this is? I wasn't sure."

At his mischievous tone, the children guffawed. Tobe Larkin elbowed Miles in the ribs. They were obviously chums now.

"Aw, come on, Callaway. You knew what it was!" he said.

The bunch of them stared hopefully at Rosamond, awaiting her response. She swallowed hard, wholly unable to muster one.

This was a serious aberration from her typical morning.

If she turned away a puppy, the children would be crestfallen. Miles Callaway was devious, indeed. The only thing more irresistible than one of his smiles was this maneuver.

"She's not an Irish setter, like you've always wanted," Miles explained into the gap that fell, his voice as intimate as any long-lost friend's, "but the man I got her from last night promised me she'd be a good guard dog once she grew a little."

That didn't help. "An Irish setter? I've always wanted—"

An Irish setter. Rosamond broke off, her dreamy, innocent past colliding with her practical, safeguarded present. At one time, she'd thought her future would turn out so differently from this. She'd thought she could be safe and happy.

She'd also thought Miles hadn't paid much attention to the daydreams she'd shared with him. Evidently, he'd remembered.

She cleared her throat. "I do not need a puppy."

Miles appeared undaunted. "Everyone needs a puppy."

Having come closer now, Dylan agreed. He petted the creature's muzzle with his big, former-Pinkerton-man's hand. "She's a beauty, all right. Just look at those paws! Once she grows up, she's going to be a sizable dog." Dylan laughed as the critter nuzzled his palm. "Maybe not too fearsome, though."

"If I wanted a guard dog," Rosamond went on tightly, hoping to regain control of this situation, "which I don't, wouldn't I want a male dog? Male dogs are stronger. More aggressive."

"The right female can be just as ferocious," Miles argued.

Rosamond scoffed. "Until a bigger, meaner dog comes along."

"When it does, that's when we'll see how scrappy she is."

"Mmm-hmm." Dubiously, Rosamond watched the puppy as it wriggled in Miles's arms. Its tiny tongue lolled. Its small feet scrabbled for purchase against Miles's muscular, coat-covered forearm. The puppy yawned, then flopped onto its belly, gazing up at Miles through shiny brown eyes. It was so helpless, so ador-able…so trusting. "I don't think she stands a chance."

"She stands every chance in the world," Miles dis-agreed. "I'm betting on the underdog. All she needs is time and a little help. All those bigger, meaner dogs will be no match for her."

His meaning-laden tone referred to far more than the puppy and her care. Evidently, now Miles wanted her to believe he was there to help her. The irony of that was too much for Rosamond.

Before she could offer a rebuttal, Agatha piped up.

"He's right! She just needs you to take care of her!" The girl eagerly pointed at the puppy. Impatiently, she pushed up her wire spectacles. "Just like you take care of all of us."

Expectantly, they all regarded her, children and men alike. Even Judah had wandered over, arms crossed, to look at the puppy. He grinned, then scratched beneath its fuzzy chin. It was ludicrous to see such an intimidating man brought to his knees by a puppy. After all, it wasn't even an Irish setter puppy.

"I don't know how to take care of a puppy," Rosamond protested, feeling backed into a corner. Judging by Miles's still-sparkling eyes, he'd known this would happen. "I don't."

"You'll master it eventually," Tommy chimed. "You will!"

It was her catchphrase: I'll master this eventually.

Just like that, Rosamond's fate was sealed.

How could she go against her own oft-repeated motto? The children were counting on her. She had to set a good example.

She straightened. "Fine. The puppy's name will be Riley."

Tobe made a face. "That's a terrible name!"

"No, it's not." Miles shook his head, his attention shifting from the puppy. "It means courageous. Valiant warrior."

Uncomfortably, Rosamond looked away. She'd forgotten that Miles was every bit as Irish as she was. He knew the same folktales and Gaelic wisdom that she did. He'd grown up with them.

"I like the sound of it, that's all," she told him.

He didn't believe an inch of it. "Yes. And I'm here because I like the fragrance of honeysuckle on fence posts."

Miles's wry tone almost made her accept that. She'd missed this. She'd missed sharing jokes with him...smiling with him.

She gestured at those aforementioned flowered vines on her fence. "You'll have to thank Mrs. Jorgensen, Agatha's mother, then. She's the one with the green thumb in the household."

"Mama will love meeting you!" Agatha chimed. "She's always sayin' she's got a soft spot for handsome fellas, and you're—"

"He's sadly not staying for long," Rosamond interrupted. She gave Miles a straightforward look. "Please follow me."

"Anywhere. Anytime."

"To my parlor. Right now."

"Yes, ma'am." Obligingly, Miles crouched again. He deftly transferred the puppy to Agatha's waiting arms. Then, while all the children gathered around to take turns petting the tiny tuckered-out critter, he straightened again. "I'm all yours."

If only. Rosamond nodded. "Right this way."

Compliantly, Miles headed for the gate she indicated.

Alertly, Dylan stepped up. "I'll come with you."

"There's no need for that, Dylan. You stay here. Judah will fill you in on the way things run around here."

"The way things run isn't the same since he showed up," her other protector pointed out, jutting his chin at Miles.

"Yes, well…I'm about to take care of that," Rosamond told him crisply. Then she gathered her skirts and went to do precisely that—to take care of Miles Callaway and rid herself of him and all the dangers he presented, once and for all.

When Rosamond finally swept into her parlor, following in Miles's wake, and ushered him toward the settee, Miles knew he was in for trouble. All he needed was one look at her lively, determined face to know that Rosamond was in fighting spirits.

He needed a counterattack. Something more effective than a cuddly puppy. With unswerving deliberation, Miles found one.

"I have a confession to make." Still standing with his hat in his hands, he looked up. "I am Miles Callaway."

Rosamond's self-assured expression flickered. Only for a moment, but it did. The same as it had outside with Riley.

He'd known she'd love that puppy. He'd also known she believed he'd forgotten all the girlish dreams and hopes for the future she'd confided in him. But Miles hadn't forgotten a thing. Not when it came to Rosamond. His memories of her had driven him here. They'd kept him going on trains and on foot.

"I know that probably doesn't mean a thing to you," he went on, more disingenuously this time, "since you say you aren't the Rose he knew, and you didn't know him—I mean, me—yourself. But I heard how hard it was to get in to see you, so—"

"So you thought you'd lie to me?"

"No. I never lied to you." Miles thumbed his hat brim, buying thinking time. "Maybe some of what I said was misleading, and for that, I apologize. But this was important to me—"

"Infiltrating my household was 'important'? Sidestepping my guards and stealing the loyalty of my children was 'important'?"

"Interesting that you'd say they're your children."

Was, Miles wondered, one of them really her child?

It could have happened. Arvid Bouchard believed it had.

For the first time, Rosamond appeared flustered. She

flashed Miles an impatient look, then paced across the parlor's wide pine floorboards. "They're as much mine as any I would ever have. I love them just the same. And it's none of your business, besides. My household is my own, to run as I see fit."

"Of course. You've done an admirable job of it, too."

She stopped, her fingers trembling slightly as she reached for the armchair's support. She seemed...moved. "Yes. I have!"

Miles grinned. The sprightly housemaid he knew would have sounded exactly that proud of herself for her accomplishments.

"Most people don't say so, though," Rosamond went on. "In fact, you're the only one who has. No one here knows exactly where I started, how far I've come—" Her gaze met his, full of tremulous pride, then whisked away as she took up pacing again. Deliberately, she changed the subject. "If you're Miles Callaway, why didn't you say so yesterday?"

He'd already explained the difficulty in getting an appointment with her. Now, Miles added, "I can only blame the discombobulating effects of whatever you dosed me with."

"Hmm." Undeterred by his teasing, Rosamond surveyed him. She was indomitable, he'd give her that. "If you're that susceptible to intoxicants, I hope you'll stay away from the high-stakes faro games in town. You won't stand a chance against the cardsharps who arrive for the occasional tournaments we host here. Even Jack Murphy's saloon is full of men who'd as likely pick your pocket as share an ale with you."

"Don't worry. I can take care of myself."

As though evaluating that claim, Rosamond moved her attention southward. Her gaze encompassed his chest and his arms…and the region where another man would have worn a gun belt, too. The innocent housemaid he'd known would not have done that. Miles couldn't help wondering if she approved of what she glimpsed. Her friend, Miss Yates, certainly had. But before he could discern the same of Rosamond, she turned hastily away.

"You look it. Hale and hearty and strong. Probably this 'Rose' of yours would be glad to see you looking so well."

He hoped she was. He hoped she dreamed of him, the same way he dreamed of her. Last night had been…fitful, to say the least.

"Maybe. I've decided to give up on looking for her."

Rosamond wheeled to face him, her brows arched. "Really?"

Miles shrugged. "Sometimes folks don't want to be found."

A nod. "Sometimes they shouldn't be found."

"Sometimes a man's got to know when he's licked."

Another nod. She lifted her face to his. "That's true."

Had her chin just wobbled? Were those tears in her eyes?

Miles couldn't hesitate to wonder why his supposed abandonment of his search was affecting Rosamond so strongly. He pushed onward, knowing that he had to brazen out this encounter if he was to have any hope of succeeding. "That's why I came here today," he said. "To say goodbye."

Her mouth dropped open. Her brows knit. "Goodbye?"

"Yes. The puppy—Riley—was a goodbye gift."

"Oh."

"I didn't want to leave you unprotected in my absence."

"Of course."

"Also, you seemed as though you could use some uncomplicated affection in your life."

That revived her. "You don't know anything about me."

He remembered everything they'd shared and knew she was lying. "I think we both know that's not true."

Their gazes met. Rosamond broke that contact first. In the game of cat and mouse they were playing, she wanted to win.

"You're suggesting something that's preposterous. You don't know the woman I am. It's better for you if you never do." Rosamond squared her shoulders, then inhaled. "I asked you here to my parlor to tell you, privately, that you have to leave."

Her confident tone would have fooled another man.

Miles was different. He took a step closer. "Go ahead, then." He gestured with his hat. "Tell me I have to leave."

Rosamond wavered. He'd known she would. "I—"

"Tell me you want me gone, and I'll leave forever."

That appeared to stymie her. "If you're leaving anyway, why did you bother to tell me the truth about who you are?"

Because I wanted you to trust me. But Miles couldn't say that, so instead he shrugged. "I had to tell you. Just to see what you'd do. It's a bad habit of mine, being curious." For so long, he'd been curious about her. "I reckoned that any woman who's contrary enough to refuse a puppy would have an interesting reaction to a revelation like my name."

"I see. And have I satisfied your expectations?"

Not in the least. He still wanted to see her smile again, to hear her laugh, to know that she wanted him there simply because she wanted him, not because he'd maneuvered her into doing it. But since beggars couldn't be choosers...

"Partly. My expectations are partly satisfied," Miles conceded. "I guess we'll never know what could have been."

She was audacious enough to agree. "I guess we won't."

Against all reason, he admired Rosamond for her spirit. It turned out that she possessed even more resilience than anyone had credited her with. Given the conditions they'd put up with at the Bouchard household, that was saying a great deal.

"Take care, Mrs. Dancy." He put on his hat, then headed for the door. "I'm sorry I can't stay. I would have liked to have joined your society—to have courted one very special woman."

He meant her, of course. Rosamond divined as much and appeared flummoxed by it. Typically, she recovered quickly.

"If you mean me, I'm not a part of my mutual society," she informed him, turning toward the mantel. "I don't participate. And you're in no position to evaluate such a thing anyway."

"Too late. I believe I just did."

"And I'll be the one to say when you should leave."

He laughed. "Now, that's where you're wrong. I'm no woman's patsy, Mrs. Dancy. Not even yours."

She frowned. "I wish you'd quit calling me that."

"Mrs. Dancy? It's your name." Now.

"I thought you wanted to apply for membership in my mutual society." She gave him a clear-sighted look. "You said so."

"At this point, I might need convincing."

"No one needs convincing to join my mutual society."

He waited, clearly indicating otherwise.

He won. Rosamond rushed in to fill the space between them.

"It's a very reputable organization, where like-minded men and women can meet and converse under sociable circumstances. We engage in poetry readings, nonwagering card games, and dances and fetes of all kinds. All the members are properly vetted, ultimately by me, but also by my staff. My members possess good characters and fine hearts. They're capable of providing a reasonable living and a secure home for each other."

"Do the men in Morrow Creek know your 'girls' are former prostitutes?" Miles inquired. "Because it would be only fair."

Rosamond seemed surprised he'd guessed the truth. But only for an instant. "My friends' pasts are their own concerns," she told him, rallying to their defense without hesitation. "As far as anyone needs to know, they are upstanding women."

"Some with fatherless children to raise. Is that a bonus for your members? I'd imagine some might not see it that way."

Her eyes flashed at him. "There are many fatherless children in the West. I was a fatherless child after my parents' passing. If you are concerned about being saddled with an urchin that's not your own, then you should definitely not—"

"You've misunderstood me," he broke in, delivering her an assessing look. When had his Rosamond become so cynical? "I like children. I think you saw that yourself this morning."

In fact, he'd loved those little rapscallions. Being around them had reminded Miles of being in his own rollicking household in the tenements, with his beleaguered but loving mother trying to hang laundry, cook corned beef and change the diapers of his younger siblings all in quick succession. Mary Callaway had managed admirably.

At times, Miles had helped her care for the littler children. In a busy household with a strong woman at its head, everyone pulled their weight. Even his rascally father had done his share of bathing and storytelling and spoon-feeding porridge.

Unexpectedly, Rosamond gave a heartfelt smile. "Yes, they did seem to love you out there in the yard, didn't they?"

Her smile almost undid all of Miles's good intentions. Almost. He needed to be smart. He needed to be tough. He needed to be resolute. But when faced with Rosamond's sunny smile...

All he wanted to do was be beside her. Forever.

Nevertheless... "But you can count me out, all the same, Mrs. Dancy. I've decided that people who hesitate over caring for puppies cannot be trusted. So I'm rejecting your society."

She gawked at him, obviously at a loss for words.

"Perhaps we'll see each other in town someday," Miles went on with a tip of his hat. "Goodbye, Mrs. Dancy. And good luck."

Then, with a few thuds of his boot heels, he left the woman of his dreams behind—and, in the process, took the biggest gamble of his life so far.

Chapter Five

Rosamond was just finishing her third cup of strong coffee when Judah Foster strode into her breakfast room with his hat in his hands. Surprised by his swift arrival—since she'd only just sent him on his latest errand twenty minutes earlier—Rosamond clattered her coffee cup into its saucer.

"That was fast," she said. "Did you run all the way?"

She glanced past her security man with an instant smile on her face, half expecting to find Miles Callaway standing there, all tall and handsome and confounding. She'd sent Judah to fetch him—or, failing that, to deliver a note to him—but it wasn't beyond reason that Miles might impulsively decide to come for breakfast instead of simply answering her summons later.

After all, Miles had done several unexpected things so far, Rosamond mused—including arriving at her doorstep in the first place. His pretending not to be Miles Callaway—not to know her—had roused her suspicions. But when he'd told her his name two days ago, his unexpected truthfulness had gone a long way toward disarming her defenses.

So had his telling her he was giving up on his search

for "his Rose." It was significant that she'd nearly burst into tears upon hearing the news, Rosamond knew. She'd realized then that she didn't want to lose Miles so soon after seeing him again.

She wanted to trust him. She couldn't possibly trust him.

But if Miles wasn't in town at Arvid Bouchard's behest…

Well, if he wasn't, that changed things completely.

Rosamond so wanted to be herself with Miles—to be with Miles. It had been one thing to remain aloof when they'd both been pretending not to know one another. It had been another after he'd come clean.

If Miles was going to be honest…maybe so could she.

First, she needed to see him again. That was proving to be more difficult than she'd planned. But Rosamond was nothing if not confident in her capacity for rising above difficulties.

Almost from the moment Arvid Bouchard had cast his first lecherous glance her way, that was all she'd been doing.

"I've never known you to move so fast, Judah," she joked, spying no tall, dark-haired, bearded subject of her dreams in the doorway but holding out hope for a miracle nonetheless. She returned her gaze to the young man in her employ. "When your brother, Cade, recommended you for this job, he should have mentioned you could put a jackrabbit's pace to the test. He seemed to believe that your previous leg injury would hinder you, but that's clearly not the case, is it?"

Her lighthearted tone didn't budge the frown from her security man's face. Instead, Judah studied his hat brim.

It became clear that Miles was not waiting in the wings.

"I couldn't find Callaway," Judah confessed. "He wasn't at the boardinghouse. Miss Adelaide said he left all his kit in his room last night and didn't come back."

Hmm. It was unlikely Miles would have left behind all the cash that Bonita had found in his bag. Also, Rosamond couldn't help feeling it was unlikely Miles would have left her. Not after they'd just found one another. Not after all this time.

No matter that Rosamond had done exactly the same thing to him. She'd abandoned Miles back in Boston, too distraught to consider the consequences.

All she'd wanted was to find safety somewhere. Endangering Miles and his reputation hadn't factored in. That's what would have happened if she'd turned to him for help. She would have destroyed Miles's future as well as her own.

"You should have waited," she told Judah. "It's scarcely past dawn. He might have simply gone for a walk, that's all."

"A man who stays out all night isn't generally in a hurry to get back home again." Judah twisted his hat brim, sounding discontented. "A man who stays out all night isn't generally too fond of fresh air, either. I bet he's pulled foot."

"You think Mr. Callaway has left town?" Rosamond dismissed the notion instantly. Maybe because she didn't want it to be true. "No, he can't be gone already. He just got here."

"Maybe he knew he couldn't get what he came for."

"Which was…?"

"Well, not to put too fine a point on it…" Judah scowled at her wainscoting, obviously not wanting to say. "You."

"Pshaw. He wouldn't even join my mutual society."

That still irked her. No man had yet refused a direct invitation.

"He wouldn't? He turned down your marriage bureau?" Judah gawked at her, then smacked his hat-holding hand upside his head. "There goes five dollars I'd rather have kept to myself."

"Five dollars?"

"Seth told me Callaway turned down a membership to your marriage bureau. I bet him five dollars he was dead wrong."

Rosamond felt touched by Judah's faith in her and her society's supposed irresistibility. Also, troubled by Seth's apparent eavesdropping. She'd have to look into that. In the meantime… "Yes. Mr. Callaway did express a…reluctance to apply."

That was putting it mildly. The more Rosamond considered it, the more miffed she felt. How could Miles have dismissed her mutual society so readily? So easily? He had to reconsider.

She would have to make sure he reconsidered.

It was a matter of personal pride, wasn't it? Her pride. Aside from her friends and the children, what else did she have?

"But I've never heard of anybody refusing you," Judah protested loyally. "Most men are beating down the doors of this place wanting an introduction to one of your friends."

"That's true," Rosamond agreed, pleased that Judah had taken care to refer to them as her friends and not—as Miles had done—as former prostitutes. Miles's description had been accurate, but Rosamond didn't like to think about that fact. All of them—herself included—had moved on with their lives. "Most men are very keen for a membership in my mutual society."

"I reckon Miles Callaway isn't like 'most men.'"

Judah sounded disgruntled to say so. But the more Rosamond considered those words, the more she believed them.

After all, "most men" wouldn't have crossed several states and territories just to find a simple runaway Boston housemaid. Only that housemaid's old friend, Miles, would have done that.

Or a hired man working for the Bouchards. He would have done that, too. For a price.

Rosamond wanted her friend, Miles. She feared her potential pursuer, Miles. She didn't want to be dragged back to Arvid.

She knew all too well what Mr. Bouchard likely wanted with her. Miles's interest in the children playing outside the house—and their ages—had been far too obvious to misread.

But if Miles truly had had nefarious intentions, would he have given up on them so easily? He'd only spent a short while with her. What's more, he'd left empty handed, with little information and no definite conclusions. Arvid Bouchard did not like to take no for an answer. Rosamond—and everyone else in Boston—knew that. If Miles had been working for Arvid, if Miles crossed him…Rosamond knew there would be hell to pay.

Surely Miles wouldn't risk Mr. Bouchard's wrath merely for the sake of a few minutes with her…would he? Because if he had…

Well, if he had, that would be very telling about Miles's feelings for her. Could it be that Miles's feelings for her matched her feelings for him? That they'd both been unable or unwilling to say so back in Boston?

If that was the case, then Rosamond had some decisions to make. Because any man who cared enough about her to risk ruination, a beating—or worse—just for the sake of spending time with her, could not simply be dismissed. No matter what her suspicions about him might have been initially. That meant—

"Mrs. Dancy?"

Judah's voice broke into her musings. Rosamond glanced up to find her security man eyeing her worriedly.

"Are you all right? I guess you're thinking about Callaway and how much you want to see him, but you seem kind of…lost? Or something." He shrugged, unable to describe her demeanor more specifically. "My brother, Cade, is the eloquent one, not me."

Lost. That just about summed up her life so far. Judah didn't know the half of it —but he'd nearly guessed anyway.

Rosamond mustered a reassuring smile. "It's not the eloquence that counts, Judah. It's the caring. You've got plenty of that. So don't you worry."

Her security man seemed brightened by her praise.

"And I'm fine. Thank you for your concern, but I'm just a little tired. The puppy, Riley, kept me awake again." It sure wasn't thoughts of Miles Callaway keeping her tossing and turning. Oh, wait—it was that. Seeing Miles again had done her in. "The poor thing spends half the night whimpering."

"If you're angling to give her to me, you'll need a better selling pitch than 'she whimpers all night.'" Jokingly, Judah held up both hands. "I don't need a 'guard dog' of my own."

"Don't worry, I'm keeping her." *If nothing else, because she reminds me of Miles.* Also, because the puppy was eminently lovable. "There's no need to look so scared."

"I'm not scared. I just don't know how to look after a puppy, that's all." Judah shifted his massive feet. "I didn't sign on for detective duty, either. So if you're still planning on tracking down Callaway, you ought to ask Coyle. I reckon he'd know what to do. There isn't too much he doesn't know about."

Rosamond considered sending her newest security man in search of Miles, then rapidly discarded the idea. Both men were impossibly tough. Both were willing to go to improbable lengths to get what they wanted—at least if Miles's appearance here in Morrow Creek was anything to go by. Forcing Miles and Dylan Coyle together—especially at cross-purposes—would be unwise.

Besides, she wanted to talk to Miles, not vex him. She wanted to see him, to question him…to find out why he'd rejected her and her mutual society. Her pride demanded it, didn't it?

Bringing Miles to her own personal stronghold by force wouldn't endear her to him. Nor would it be easy to explain. Most women didn't have three burly bruisers at their disposal. Rosamond didn't particularly want to explain why she did.

She was fortunate that Miles hadn't asked her to.

"Maybe," she decided, "I'll send Miss Yates again."

"Exactly where are you going to send her?" Judah asked. "I told you, Callaway's gone from Miss Adelaide's place." He crossed his beefy arms. "If I were you, I'd give up on him."

"Has he left town altogether?"

"Miss Adelaide didn't seem to think so."

"Then I'll just keep sending people until I find him."

"Have you thought of going after him yourself?"

Of course she had. It was impossible. "No."

"Because I reckon he might show himself on your account."

"There's no reason in the world that he would."

Judah scoffed. "Then you haven't spent enough time around men, Mrs. Dancy. Because the way Callaway looked at you…let's just say, I reckon he'd come running if you did the calling."

She looked away. "You know I don't leave the household."

Everyone knew that. Everyone in town. The good thing about the West was, not many people questioned such things.

"Maybe it's time you did leave. Just for a spell." Judah gave a heartfelt gesture. "It might be good for you to leave."

It would be terrible for her to leave.

Rosamond shifted in her chair, full of resistance and wanting and maddening disquiet. She didn't want to abandon her sanctuary. Inside her house's four walls, she felt safe and secure. "I have everything I need right here."

Everything…except someone to share it with.

But that was nonsensical. She had her friends. She had her children. She had an adorable new puppy that still hadn't adjusted to its new home and thus kept her awake at night.

Just like thoughts of Miles kept her awake at night.

If she were honest with herself, that had been true for a long time now. Even during the days she'd spent with Elijah Dancy, Rosamond hadn't been able to stop thinking of Miles.

If what he'd said was true, he'd thought of her, also.

The realization made her feel downright exhilarated.

"The fact of the matter is," she told Judah to distract herself, "given another chance, Mr. Callaway will undoubtedly join my mutual society. That's why I sent you with that message for him today, to offer him another try

at it." That, Rosamond decided, had been as reasonable
an excuse as any to see him. "Speaking of which, let's
let Seth have a chance at delivering it next."

Judah looked exasperated.

"And then what? We'll start sending the youngsters
over one by one?" He tossed down the note he'd with-
drawn, knowing better than to refuse by pressing it into
her hand. "No, ma'am. These shenanigans have got to
stop. You've sent Miss Yates once, Seth once and me
twice to fetch Mr. Callaway. That's just in the last two
days!" He shook his head. "Something's got to give."

"Well," Rosamond said stubbornly, "it won't be me."

"It won't be Callaway, either," Judah warned her. "I
don't see it happening. Maybe another man would be
better—"

"Maybe." Dylan Coyle came into the breakfast room
wearing a somber look. He tipped his hat to Rosamond.
"Sorry, Mrs. Dancy, but I've got some bad news about
that thorn in your side."

He meant Miles. Rosamond recalled referring to him
as the thorn in her side on the day he'd brought over Riley.
The remembrance made her suppress a smile. She'd attempted more humor in the past two days than she had
in the past two months combined.

Maybe Miles had a positive effect on her spirits. Despite everything, maybe seeing him again had been good
for her.

"Bad news? About Miles? What is it?"

Neither of her hired men remarked on her familiar
way of talking about Miles. Probably, they'd already
guessed she had a past with him. Either that, or they both
believed Rosamond deserved the scandalous reputation
some of the townsfolk had accused her of having when
she'd arrived in Morrow Creek.

She had to do a better job of being ladylike. But first…

"Stop looking at me with woebegone faces and tell me!"

"He's locked up." Seth shouldered his way into the breakfast room, looking peculiarly triumphant about delivering his bad news—especially as compared with the other two men. "He's hunkering down in Sheriff Caffey's jailhouse right now. It doesn't look like he'll be seeing daylight anytime soon, either, on account of his being new to town."

Judah frowned. "Sheriff Caffey doesn't like strangers."

"Sheriff Caffey doesn't like anybody," Seth disagreed.

"Sheriff Caffey is a bad sheriff and a bad man," Dylan added, "but that doesn't change the facts. He's got your man."

Her man. Rosamond liked that. Unwisely. "What did he do?"

"Fix an election. Wrangle himself an underserved job." Dylan ticked off items on his fingers. "Gloat about both those things, impede the press who reported on his wrongdoings—"

"No." Exasperatedly, Rosamond waved at him. The vagaries of town politics didn't matter. Nor did Dylan's inside information as a former Pinkerton man. "What did Mr. Callaway do?"

Dylan shrugged. "I reckon you'll have to ask him."

"You didn't find out?"

"I thought it was more important to get here straightaway and tell you so you could rescue him."

Rosamond boggled. "What makes you think I'd rescue him?"

All three of her security men stared at her.

After a moment, Seth asked, "Isn't it obvious?"

"It's what you do," Judah explained, looking befuddled by her inaction. "This whole household is proof of it."

Still flummoxed, Rosamond stared back at them.

"They mean," Dylan said, "that you save people."

Rosamond didn't see things that way. "In the same circumstances, anyone would have done the things I've done."

"Not anyone."

"Not for anyone."

"Not the way you've done it."

The unified responses of her men made her laugh with disbelief. "I'm just one woman! One ordinary woman."

"Right." Seth nodded. "Now then...do you want company?"

"Company to go where?"

"To the jailhouse. To get Callaway."

"I'm not going to get Mr. Callaway." That would mean leaving. Leaving the safety of her household made Rosamond quake—quite literally—with fear. "However," she announced with sudden satisfaction, "we now know exactly where to deliver my note to Mr. Callaway, don't we?"

Miles hadn't intended to get Rosamond's attention by having himself thrown into Sheriff Caffey's jailhouse. But once he'd wound up in the hoosegow anyway—and once he'd recognized Dylan Coyle perusing the wanted posters—Miles realized this tactic might work out handily for him. Rosamond was far too softhearted to allow him to remain behind those cold black iron bars for very long. As soon as Coyle returned with the news of Miles's incarceration, Rosamond would likely skedaddle down to save him.

After all, back in Boston, Rosamond had saved several abandoned cats, finding them new homes as mousers among the staff in neighboring mansions. She'd nursed to health a pair of forlorn lost ducklings she'd found in the park while making a delivery for Genevieve Bouchard. She'd even taken the blame for other housemaids' mistakes, knowing that Arvid Bouchard would never voluntarily see her—his "favorite housemaid"—dismissed.

Because of that, Miles realized, it would be very like Rosamond to rescue him. Almost in the same way she'd rescued all the fallen angels in her care. Not that that's why he'd done what he'd done. Not in the least. But now that it was done…

Well, now that it was done and he realized the full implications of his supposed misdeeds, Miles didn't feel sorry.

He felt…hopeful. Despite everything. Especially when, lying on the lumpy jailhouse bunk with his arms crossed under his head and his heart full of bittersweet memories of Rosamond, Miles heard the first unmistakable feminine footsteps on the raised-plank boardwalk outside the jailhouse and grew instantly alert.

This was it. Rosamond was here.

Damnation, but he was lucky to have a woman like her.

Not that he had her. Not yet. But Miles knew it was only a matter of time. He and Rosamond belonged together. She was wary, understandably so, but he was determined. He knew he could win.

He could win Rosamond, and he could win love for them both.

Pretending not to feel as eager as a green schoolboy, Miles forced himself to remain still. He didn't want to draw the attention of his watchful jailer, Deputy Winston— no relation to Gus. He also didn't want to alarm Rosamond. Miles wasn't sure if she'd ever been in a jailhouse before. The place wasn't exactly the posh Lorndorff Hotel. It would be a shock for Rosamond to see him there. So Miles didn't move as he heard the jailhouse door open and close. He didn't speak as he inhaled the fresh air that blew inside to accompany the jail's visitor.

He didn't so much as blink as he anticipated Rosamond.

"Well, if this isn't a fine how-do-you-do, I don't know what is," came the sound of a feminine voice. "Deputy Winston, isn't it about time you chipped out a little self-respect and quit incarcerating honest people at Sheriff Caffey's whim?"

Surprised, Miles sat up. He stared.

An unfamiliar woman winked back at him from the other side of his cell bars. She had untidy hair, an invigorated glow and the most bizarre set of garments Miles had ever glimpsed.

She looked, it occurred to him, like one of the protesters for female suffrage who occasionally marched in Boston.

Deputy Winston groaned. "Grace Murphy. Missing us already, are you? I know you've spent a lot of time here, but we don't seem to have any charges pending for you. It must be a mistake."

Grace Murphy chuckled. "Give me time, Deputy. Soon I'll be raising a whole passel of rabble-rousers. I'm already capable of outthinking you. Soon, we Murphy women will outnumber you, too."

Another groan. Obviously distressed, Deputy Winston shot an annoyed glance at Miles. If he expected masculine solidarity, though, he was disappointed. Miles only shrugged.

He liked uppity women. Judging by her name and demeanor, Grace was saloonkeeper Jack Murphy's wife. He liked Jack Murphy, too. He doubted the man would wed just any conventional woman.

"Are you saying there's gonna be more of you?" The deputy shook his head. "That oughta be a crime, right then and there."

Grace smiled. "I believe, Deputy, that when a woman informs you of her impending motherhood, it's incumbent upon a well-mannered gentleman to congratulate her on her good fortune."

Another, much louder, groan came from the deputy.

But Miles perked up. "Congratulations, Mrs. Murphy."

Her intelligent gaze shifted to him. She beamed, obviously pleased. "See there?" She aimed her chin illustratively at Miles for Deputy Winston's edification, then went on. "I knew I was correct in taking on this request for my friend Mrs. Dancy. I'd say that you, Mr. Callaway, are worth bailing out of jail."

Miles's smile dimmed. "Rosamond isn't coming?"

"Of course not. It's not possible." Grace didn't explain why. Her omission concerned him. Brightly, she aimed an unnerving look at the lawman in front of her. "So, Deputy. Exactly how much brouhaha are we going to stir up today?"

Deputy Winston gulped. He glanced toward the door, undoubtedly hoping the sheriff would return. That didn't happen.

"Keep in mind," Grace added helpfully, "that I positively relish confrontations that help ensure the greater good." From her valise, she pulled forth a length of sturdy chain. It clanged as it hit the floor, followed by a robust lock. "Shall I chain myself to your desk? Or to Mr. Callaway's cell?"

Deputy Winston looked again for help. None arrived.

"You know that I have a long and glorious tradition of personal protests," Grace reminded him, straightening her unusual clothing and then busying herself with her chain. "Mr. Nickerson alone has brought charges against me at least twice per year for a decade. I'm not afraid. I am fully prepared to sacrifice myself until Mr. Callaway has achieved his freedom."

"You could just pay his bail," the deputy grumped.

"Pay unfair bail money?" Grace looked astonished. "I'd sooner smash my beloved bicycle to pieces than do that." Undeterred, she raised her chin. "You should know, of course, that editor Walsh from the *Pioneer Press* will be here at the jailhouse forthwith if he doesn't hear from me otherwise. Everyone will be most interested in the story he writes about Mr. Callaway's wrongful jailing. I've already turned in the first draft myself, in fact. It is my father's newspaper—"

Finally, the deputy had had enough. "You're...expecting, Grace! You can't start a protest!" Nervously, he shifted his attention from Grace's determined face to the chain she'd brought. "'Sides, you don't even know what Callaway's done!"

Calmly, Grace looked at Miles. She raised her eyebrows.

Clearly she'd been prepared to do whatever was necessary, purely on Rosamond's say-so. But since she was asking...

"I had a misunderstanding with a man," Miles told her, "about one of the dance hall girls at your husband's saloon."

Grace's eyebrows raised a fraction higher.

"He misunderstood that a dance hall girl isn't a prostitute. I misunderstood the law. Apparently, defending a lady's honor is a jailing offense." Miles shrugged. "Not that I wouldn't have taken a wallop at him anyway. He needed stopping."

"Yes." Grace nodded. "That explains the nasty bruise that's developing under your eye. One does as needs must, doesn't one?"

"You haven't seen the knuck who was misbehaving."

"Yes. I'm sure he doesn't look very fit today, either." She gave Miles an intense once-over, then nodded again. "Very well done." She withdrew a folded paper from her pocket, then strode to his jail cell. "Before I begin my protest, I should give you this. It's from Mrs. Dancy. She's gone through considerable difficulty to get it to you. Before, I was justifiably perplexed as to why. But now I understand."

Deftly, Grace passed the note through the bars. Miles fancied he could smell rose perfume wafting from the paper.

"Don't protest on my account," he told Grace. "I'm fine. I might be safer here than anyplace else." If Arvid Bouchard's men found him and realized he hadn't disclosed Rosamond's location, that would be true. "Thank you for coming, though."

"On the contrary. It's my pleasure!" Grace turned away, coming to a brisk stop at Deputy Winston's desk. She clanged her chain with evident zeal, then wrapped one length of it around the deputy's desk leg. "It's been ages since I've enjoyed a good old-fashioned civil protest. I can't possibly allow married life to make me complacent, now, can I?"

Miles could have sworn he heard Deputy Winston whimper.

"When motherhood enters its full swing, I'll undoubtedly be too busy to fully engage in the pursuit of justice," Grace went on. "At least for a while, that is. Also, my husband will be so disappointed if I don't follow through with this. Why, he's already looking forward to banning you from his saloon for life, Deputy Winston. The sheriff, too, of course. He said so." Grace aimed a delighted smile at Miles as she reached for the lock she'd brought. "My Jack is very supportive of my interests."

Miles laughed outright. He hadn't seen much of Morrow Creek yet, but so far, he liked it. He knew he could be happy here.

Then he unfolded the note Grace had given him… and realized he'd underestimated Rosamond McGrath Dancy yet again.

Tarnation. She sure did keep a man on his toes.

Chapter Six

"And one, two, three. One, two, three."

Rosamond's voice floated from a nearby window as Miles strode toward her house. Belatedly spying his approach, Seth moved from the side yard to intercept him. Miles waved off his interference and kept going inside. He headed down the hall.

No mere security man was stopping him from getting to the bottom of things with Rosamond. But the music he heard next, overlaid with the sound of Rosamond's voice, just might.

He recognized that song. He'd wager Rosamond did, too.

She gave no sign of it as she called out encouragingly in the distance, speaking loudly to be heard over the sound of a fiddle. "That's right, ladies! Keep going. Very nicely done."

Frowning, Miles followed the familiar lilt of her voice around the next corner. The lodgings Rosamond occupied were surprisingly large, with irregular twists and turns in the architecture and rooms added higgledy-piggledy next to other rooms. Miles couldn't help thinking those eccentricities suited the house's occupants. None of them were as expected, either.

As he neared the music's source, it grew louder. So did the shuffling of many feet. A dance lesson was under way, Miles surmised, with Rosamond at its head. The realization made him feel even more provoked than he had when arriving.

Catching flickering shadows moving against the hallway wall, Miles arrowed in on those telltale movements. He heard breathless exclamations and effortful footsteps. He reached the next room's threshold and glimpsed Rosamond herself at its far corner, keeping time. The room had obviously been pressed into service as an impromptu ballroom for Rosamond's mutual society.

Determinedly, Miles strode inside.

Women caught in middance parted in confused pairs as he came. As he passed the dancers—the saucy Miss Yates among them—whispers kicked up. They gained intensity as Miles reached Rose.

She didn't see him at first. She was concentrating on demonstrating the dance movements for her students, her arms outstretched to embrace an invisible partner. But once Lucinda Larkin, Tobe's mother, spied Miles and brought her surprisingly proficient fiddle music to a stop, Rosamond stopped. She looked for the cause of the silence. She found him immediately. Aha.

She seemed pleased to see him. "Mr. Callaway! You're back. You must have reconsidered your stance on my mutual society." Her gaze took in his rumpled clothes and hat, then landed on his face. "Not too worse for wear, I'd say. Although I think you're going to be sporting a black eye come this time tomorrow."

"You should know. You've seen a shiner or two in your day."

"Of course I haven't!" Rosamond issued an unconvincing titter, not letting on that she'd nursed Miles through a few of those bruises herself in the past. In fact, this whole situation was strongly reminiscent of their friendship… and their missed chances at having more, too. "I'm far too ladylike for that."

"Have it your way. My mistake, Mrs. Dancy."

"Indeed." She lifted her chin, then shifted her attention toward her waiting dance pupils. She found her assistant nearby. "Miss Yates, would you please take over for me here? I have something to discuss with Mr. Callaway."

"Of course she'll take charge." Miles wasn't in the mood to wait for that meddlesome woman to spoil his momentum. "If she can't, then I'm sure Miss O'Malley, Miss Jorgensen, Miss Scott, Mrs. Larkin, or any one of the others would be happy to do it."

Rosamond stared. "How do you know all their names?"

Miles smiled. "You'd be surprised how many of your friends found reasons to visit the backyard on the day I brought Riley. I think I've met…" He studied the room. "Everyone."

A general murmur from the women present confirmed it.

"Oh." Rosamond frowned, seeming taken aback. "I see."

"You're about to hear an earful, too," Miles assured her. Then he took Rosamond's hand and towed her out of the room, headed toward the silent—and much more private—hallway beyond, leaving all the ladies and a glowering Miss Yates in their wake.

Rosamond had forgotten exactly how tall and imposing Miles could be, especially when he had his dander up about something.

Well. She could be imposing, too, when she put her mind to it. Determined to do so, she tugged her hand from his grasp.

"Exactly what do you think you're doing, bursting in on my dance lesson this way? I have half a mind to call Dylan."

"Go ahead. Call him."

Whoops. She wished Miles would quit challenging her. No one else did. They didn't dare. They knew that of all the people in her household, Rosamond was the least likely to back down.

She didn't want to back down now, either. Because the truth was, she didn't want to call Dylan. Or Seth. Or Judah. She didn't want to put a stop to being alone with Miles.

Now that she had him, freshly jail broken, she wanted him all to herself. She wanted him to smile at her and talk with her. She wanted to know him, inside and out, the way she once had. That could only happen if they spent time alone together.

Urgently, privately, recklessly alone together.

She hesitated, trying to dream up a method to have it both ways—to preserve her authority while still being alone with Miles. Instead, all that flooded her mind were thoughts of how different he appeared today, with his longer hair and casual clothes and workaday boots.

He seemed so much…freer here in Morrow Creek.

She liked that about him. She liked the new easiness she sensed in him. In truth, she'd never approved of the gaudy livery that Arvid Bouchard had outfitted his male employees in. Miles had made it look better than most, but all the same…

All the same, she had to get down to brass tacks. She wanted Miles Callaway not to be the only man on record who'd refused a membership in her mutual society. She wanted…him.

She wanted him to stay until she made up her mind about him—which was taking much longer than she'd anticipated it would. In her experience, the best way to keep someone around was to keep them guessing. Hadn't that worked wonders to keep up her interest in Miles? She was certainly guessing about him. And the best way not to crack under pressure was to stand up straight—to forge brazenly onward, whatever the consequences.

Ready to do just that, Rosamond batted her eyelashes. "Why, Mr. Callaway, what's wrong? You look ready to breathe fire."

"Please call me Miles."

As if she hadn't done that a hundred times already.

"All right, Miles. What seems to be the problem? Are you having trouble thanking me for having you released from jail?"

"I think you'll find Mrs. Murphy did that."

"I promise you I was instrumental in the effort." Rosamond peered more closely at him, confused by his stern demeanor. Seth had filled her in—with relish—on Miles's supposed wrongdoings. His misdeeds hadn't been serious enough to warrant further conversation, but Rosamond had been glad that Miles had been wrongly jailed for doing something chivalrous. That was just like the man she remembered. This obduracy, on the other hand, wasn't. "All the same, you didn't have to burst into my dance lesson that way."

"Yes, I did." He sounded inexplicably aggrieved. "Did you know it was the same song? The song Mrs. Larkin was playing just now. It was the same song that you and I heard…that night."

Seeming undone by that knowledge, Miles ran his

hand through his hair. He paced a few steps down the hall. He turned and then gazed down at her, hard-faced and vaguely inscrutable behind his dark trimmed facial hair. If Rosamond hadn't known better, she'd have thought he found her dance lesson more distressing than his jailing or his impending black eye.

She raised her eyebrow, hoping to compel him to continue.

Thankfully, he did. He gave a gusty sigh, then confessed…

"I always thought I'd be the one to teach you to dance."

Oh. Relieved, Rosamond relaxed. Nothing dangerous was going on. Nothing threatening was happening. Miles was just…

Well, Miles was just being exactly as nostalgic as she was.

Maybe he felt just as lost these days as she did, too.

In that moment, with that lonesome stray thought, Rosamond mislaid another fraction of her resistance to him. When she should have been defending herself and her very reasonable dance lesson, she could only feel guilty for leaving Miles behind in Boston. When she should have been calling for Dylan to ensure her security, she could only take another step nearer to the man whose arrival had endangered her carefully built new life.

When she should have been moving away, Rosamond could only move closer. Because as soon as Miles mentioned dancing, she remembered the song in question… and she remembered the night during which they'd heard it, together, back in Boston.

They'd been sitting on a hay bale outside the stables, both she and Miles illuminated by the artificial light of dozens of distant dazzling gas lamps. They'd been listening to the music and laughter at one of Genevieve

Bouchard's innumerable society parties. They'd been pretending to have a highbrow conversation about investments and holidays, about summer homes and orchestras…about the kind of certainty and freedom that neither Rosamond nor Miles would ever enjoy in their lifetimes.

She recalled the two of them guffawing as they imitated Mrs. Bouchard's stuffy guests. She remembered Miles gallantly and elaborately bowing to her as he asked Rosamond's hand for the next waltz. She remembered her own heart hammering as she reached out, there on the mansion's grassy grounds, to accept.

She remembered Arvid Bouchard hollering in the moonlight for Miles to come hoist a heavy crate of whiskey for the kitchen staff, ruining the moment before it had a chance to blossom.

They'd both been so young then. It didn't matter that only a year or so had passed. She—and Miles—were much older now.

Looking into his face, Rosamond deeply regretted it.

"I tried to be the one to teach you to dance." Miles's gravelly voice reached all the way inside her, steady and familiar. "Remember? I was willing to risk you stomping all over my toes, just so you could know what it felt like to dance."

She'd so wanted that. She still did. Rosamond shut her eyes, just for a moment—just long enough to regain her composure and stop feeling the yearning that stretched between them.

"You could teach me now," she heard herself say. "We can hear the music from here. No one would need to know we did it. You could teach me now," she urged, "and we could—"

"We could go on pretending not to know one another?" Miles's sharp tone snapped open her eyes. Rosamond inhaled, ready to defend herself. She wished she didn't have to defend herself. But before she could formulate a coherent reply...

"I accept," Miles told her.

Her whole body felt glad.

It was a silly idea. Rosamond knew that. She felt it keenly as she gazed up into his handsome face, as she took in his outstretched arms and alert posture. Just then, she didn't care.

A part of her innocence had been stolen from her. A part of her vivaciousness was gone forever. If she could feel just a fraction of those things again, even for a single moment...

Yes. Willingly, Rosamond touched her hand to Miles's, her gesture as light as a summer breeze stirring the grass. She straightened her spine. She held her breath, feeling the anticipation between them grow as each moment ticked away.

Carefully, Miles placed his free hand at her waist. For an instant, feeling the gentle but unfamiliar pressure of his palm at her side, Rosamond thought she would panic. But then she looked up at Miles. She saw the certainty in his gaze and the caring in his face, and she knew she would be all right.

For this moment, with this man, she would be...

Held. She would be held in a way she never had been before, as Miles deftly danced them a few steps across the hallway. His gaze remained fixed on Rosamond's, his movements sure and his footsteps light. It was the dance they'd both been hoping for, however delayed it had been in coming, and it was...perfect.

Just for now, Rosamond didn't have to be on guard. She didn't have to be in charge. She didn't have to be afraid, the way she'd been afraid for all these months on her own. She didn't have to have all the answers for herself and everyone else who was depending on her to save them. All she had to do was let Miles clasp her hand and dance them both away.

He did, and Rosamond felt sure she was flying. She felt too carefree not to be flying. Higher and higher they went, and as that fanciful notion caught hold of her imagination, Rosamond couldn't help glancing down at their feet for reassurance.

She tripped over Miles's big boot. The spell was broken.

She laughed, releasing Miles's hand. "I'm sorry! It seems I'm the last person who should be instructing anyone in dancing, doesn't it? I learned from Lucinda, but she doesn't enjoy speaking in front of people. So the lessons fell to me and I—"

"It was a perfect dance." Miles's sparkling eyes told her he believed it. "Perfect. We could have another one. Right now."

His ready arms coaxed her to agree. So did his smile.

"I can't." Rosamond shook her head. "I shouldn't."

"Let's go outside, then. We can talk."

The abrupt change in his tone confused her. "About?"

"About your note."

Warily, Rosamond examined the angle of his head, trying to discern his plans. "You want to talk outside… in the yard?"

"Outside anyplace you want to go. I've heard the Lorndorff Hotel has a fine dining room. I'll take you to lunch. Or dinner. Or lunch and dinner." Miles aimed a mischievous glance at her. "After all, I still have far too much money for any honorable man to possess in Morrow Creek. I need to spend it."

"No." Rosamond shook her head, too preoccupied to

examine where that money might have come from. "I'm sorry. I can't."

Miles seemed disappointed. He crossed his arms. "Grace was right about you, then. She said you never leave here."

Uncomfortably, Rosamond shook her head. "I wouldn't say never. After all, I did arrive here at one time."

Miles wasn't fooled. "When she told me, I didn't believe her. The Rose I knew would never have hidden herself away." He examined her as he spoke, his tone sure and unrelenting. "She was too full of life for that. She was too strong, too bossy, too stubborn to keep herself hidden from the world."

His voice all but accused her of complacently letting herself be crushed by circumstances. Rosamond couldn't take it.

"Do you think that makes it better?" She whirled away, full of frustration and regret. Things had been so nice a moment ago. "Do you think throwing the past in my face will help?"

"No. I think telling you the truth will help."

Except it wasn't the truth. Rosamond knew that. Miles's assurances that she was somehow supposed to be better than she was—better than she'd turned out to be— only made her feel worse. They made her feel weak. She wasn't strong. Otherwise, she'd have found another way. She'd have found a way that didn't hurt Miles. Because now she knew it had hurt him to be left behind. Even though she'd been trying to protect him, she'd hurt him.

"I am not the Rose you knew," she said. "I never will be."

"But you danced with me."

As if that solved anything. Rosamond wished it did. Now she'd have to tuck away that memory along with her hopes for a husband and family of her own, an Irish setter of her own... With effort, she put aside those self-pitying thoughts.

"Of course I did. You're a good dancer."

"I had a good partner. You're a good woman."

Now, that's where he was wrong. For proof, Rosamond only needed to remember the note she'd written to him today. She'd purposely brought Miles back here. Now it was obvious that doing so would only disappoint them both in the end.

They couldn't recapture what they'd had.

She didn't know what she'd been thinking.

"I'm sorry. I'm not who you think I am."

Miles's gaze searched her face. "Are you sure?"

Rosamond wished she was. Her thoughts and feelings had never been more mixed up. Not even when Genevieve Bouchard had offered her that awful "choice" all those months ago.

"I'm as sure as I'll ever be." At the irony of it, Rosamond almost laughed. Because her certainty—about her life, about Miles, about love and right and wrong—was fading fast.

So were her opportunities to see Miles, if she didn't act.

"How can I make you feel sure?" Miles asked. "I'll do it."

Warmed by his audacious conviction, she shook her head. "If I told you that, I'd have to tell you everything."

"Then tell me." He leaned on the hallway wall, arms at his sides, studying her closely. "If someone in town has scared you or hurt you, I swear I'll see them pay for it."

He could do it, too. His presence assured her of that much. His attentiveness flattered her, his protectiveness touched her and his willingness to fight on her behalf alarmed her a little, too. The lighthearted stableman she'd known in Boston had been far less menacing than the man she saw today.

Maybe they'd both changed.

Maybe they'd both changed too much.

But the dance they'd shared—and everything else— made Rosamond hope that wasn't true. She…wanted Miles. He was the only part of her past that was good. He was the only part of her past that she could touch without wanting to scream. Or run.

That had to be some kind of miracle, didn't it?

"Let's just talk about the note I sent you." Hedging, Rosamond crossed her arms. "What do you intend to do about it?"

His mouth quirked in a half smile. Seeing it made her idly wonder if his beard would feel bristly to touch. Or soft.

She hoped it would feel soft. She was a foolish woman.

"Your note demanded that I come here and deal with Riley."

"Yes, I know. I wrote it."

"It said that your new puppy can't sleep through the night, and neither can anyone else within earshot."

Rosamond made a comical face. "Poor thing. She whimpers all night most pitifully. I think she bonded with you on the night you got her, and now she can't be satisfied with anyone else."

Miles nodded. "Sometimes I have that effect."

"No matter what I do, I can't comfort her."

"And you think I can?" Dubiously, Miles raised his brow.

"Yes. At least I expect you to try." Rosamond couldn't help grinning, knowing she was about to gain the upper hand, however briefly. "It's only reasonable. After all, people who hesitate over caring for puppies cannot be trusted. That's what I hear."

Undoubtedly recognizing his own earlier words to her, Miles laughed. He shook his head, looking at her with unearned fondness. "Some things never change. You always surprise me."

Rosamond let that reference to their shared past pass unremarked upon. "A good start would be for you to make frequent visits," she suggested. "Especially at nighttime."

"To comfort the puppy?"

"Of course. Why else?"

His gaze swept over her tight-bodiced, bustled dress and curly auburn hair, then rose to her face. "That's up to you."

"Believe me—if I didn't already know that, we wouldn't be here," Rosamond assured him. "In my household, I'm in charge."

"In your household, you're imprisoned," Miles disagreed. "No matter how willingly."

She frowned. "I think Grace told you a little too much about me when she got you from the jailhouse. Otherwise—"

"She didn't tell me." Miles stepped nearer. "You did. Just now. Mrs. Murphy told me you never leave, but she didn't tell me you feel imprisoned here." He seemed heartbroken at the thought. She'd never seen him appear so distraught. "Let me help you, Rose. Let me help you break free. I know I can do it."

For a heartbeat, Rosamond wanted to let him.

She didn't like feeling stuck. She didn't like trading freedom for security, didn't want to spend all her days tending to other people's romantic lives and children instead of her own. But then she remembered everything that had brought her to this place, this household, this decision…and shook her head.

"If I wanted to leave, I would," she promised him. "And that's enough said about that. When it comes to your helping to care for Riley, though, I think we should discuss the matter further. The most expeditious thing would be if you joined my mutual society," Rosamond added vigorously, "since that would ensure both our reputations and enable you to come here—"

"Prove it," Miles broke in.

Uh-oh. Immediately, Rosamond realized where she'd overstepped. Being with Miles muddled her thoughts and jumbled her priorities. Her pride and her longing had brought her to this place. Now she had only her wits to bring her out again.

"I'm sure I don't know what you mean," she bluffed as a starting point. "I don't have to prove anything. You, however, most assuredly do. As a potential member of my mutual society, you'll have to acquit yourself with honor, bedazzle the ladies with wit and prove to everyone that you're worth accepting."

"Prove you can leave here whenever you want to," Miles pressed. "Do it. Right now. Leave the house with me."

With faux jauntiness, Rosamond waved off his suggestion. She hoped he couldn't sense the moisture that rose instantly to her palms. Or detect the parched feeling that closed her throat and threatened to wreck her ability to speak as she rambled on. "You will have to acquire character references from respectable locals," she said hoarsely, "prove you have a reliable source of income and be assessed during social occasions on your deportment, abstemious nature and dancing abilities."

"I believe I already proved that last one."

Oh dear. He had. Now her knees felt wobbly, too. Surely that was a consequence of the dare Miles had issued and not a result of her all-too-intimate experience with his dancing.

"Those are all vital qualities," Rosamond strived to finish as serenely as she usually did. She wondered why Miles seemed so amused by her efforts. "They are qualities that the women participating in my mutual society demand. So until you satisfy me that you possess those qualities, I simply cannot admit you."

A pause. "You're going on as if I'm desperate to be admitted. Did you forget that I already turned down your society once? What makes you think I won't do it again?"

"Just one thing."

"And that is?"

"Your softheartedness when it comes to puppies."

His laughter made her heart feel buoyant, despite her sweaty palms, dry throat, weak knees and the overall anxiety brought on by his suggestion that she go outside with him.

"Nope." Miles shook his head, calling her attention to his dark hair. It fell over his collar in a most appealing fashion, combining with his beard to make him seem both manly and rugged. "I'm not anywhere near as softhearted as you think."

"Softheaded, then? I won't admit defeat, you know."

"I think I'd rather be thought mushy than simple."

"It's your choice." Brightly, Rosamond straightened. Another woman would have offered him a handshake. She merely tilted her head inquisitively at Miles. "Which will it be?"

"I need more time," he protested. "Choosing between mushiness and idiocy is more challenging than you think."

"I'm sorry." She pretended regret. "I wouldn't know."

His eyes sparkled at her with good humor. "Lucky you."

"I'm anything but lucky. Or patient. Well?"

"Well…let me get this straight," Miles said. "The deal is that my potential application to your marriage bureau—"

"Mutual society."

"—and my visits to your puppy go hand in hand?"

"Yes." Rosamond confirmed it with a nod. "They do. If you want one—" she left it up to him to decide which one most appealed to him "—then you'll have to accept the other."

She hadn't planned to bargain with him. But she would win either way. Miles would stay, help solve her problems with Riley and continue making her mutual society seem irresistible. Or he would leave, ensuring that her sanctuary was secure.

Too bad Rosamond really only liked one of those options.

"All right," Miles told her. "I'll give you everything you want and more." As he spoke, the fiddle music ceased. The society's members filed into the hallway, gazing curiously at the pair of them as they did. "All you have to do in return—"

Rosamond glimpsed a few of her friends veer toward them and knew she didn't have time to shilly-shally. If anyone heard her striking a bargain with Miles for membership in her mutual society, her reputation would suffer an awful ding. She didn't want to lose face in front of the women who relied on her.

Neither did she want to forgo any potential calming effect on Riley. The puppy really was forlorn every night.

And she very much wanted to get her way with Miles.

"Whatever you want," she said hastily. "It's yours."

"—is come out with me to help me buy food for my larder," Miles said at exactly the same time. "This afternoon."

Caught, Rosamond blinked. "Out? This afternoon?" Out. Outside. In the open. Where she would be at risk. At the very idea, her legs began to quiver.

"I've taken a job with Owen Cooper, the livery stable owner," Miles explained. "I'll be moving into Gus Winston's old quarters. While there's a cookstove and some tinned peaches left there, I don't think that will keep me going for long."

Rosamond couldn't concentrate on those mundane details. Not when she'd just committed herself to an outdoor excursion with Miles. Although she was impressed that he'd secured gainful employment already. Cooper's stable was a thriving business.

"I think my scalp is perspiring," she blurted. "It's the oddest thing!" She broke off, putting a hand to her head. She frowned. "My goodness, I feel quite dizzy, too." She peered at Miles as her friends approached. "Is it getting dark in here?"

He gazed into her face, then stepped nearer to her. His nearness and steady indigo gaze had wondrously calming effects.

The hallway even grew a teensy bit brighter.

"It will be all right, Rose. You can do this."

"Of course I can," she parroted automatically. It would not be like her to allude to any personal weakness. "I wouldn't have mentioned my physical symptoms—" which hadn't entirely abated "—except for their being so very unusual."

"I understand." He could not. "Have you had these symptoms before?"

Yes. Memorably. And not in a good way.

Rosamond fussed with her skirts, unwilling to say so. But she would never forget the first time that peculiar collection of maladies had struck her. She'd been strolling in the town square with her friend Molly Copeland, both of them making goofy faces at the Copelands' little daughter, when she'd glimpsed a heavyset man who resembled Arvid Bouchard in the distance.

Instantly, Rosamond had been beset with dizziness. Shakiness. Overall perspiring. Shortness of breath. Worst, with a powerful sense of imminent doom. She'd stuttered an excuse to Molly and then scrambled away, certain she was dying.

She'd made it home. Her condition had improved.

She hadn't ventured far from her house since that day.

"Let's just say you're a provisional applicant for membership in my mutual society and leave it at that, shall we?" Rosamond proposed, desperate to forget that incident. Hastily, she stuck out her hand to Miles to shake on their deal. "Congratulations, Mr. Callaway. I believe you've set a new record."

Chapter Seven

Miles stared at Rosamond's outstretched hand, struck both by its significance and by her fixed, fraught expression. She must be even more shaken by the idea of leaving her household than he'd realized. She'd forgotten to fear touching him.

Of course, she'd forgotten to do that earlier, too, during their dance—during their long-delayed, heart-stirring dance.

Years ago now, he'd begged his older sister, Colleen, to teach him how to dance in preparation for that moment with Rosamond. Now it had finally happened. He'd held Rosamond in his arms. Remembering it made a cozy sense of warmth curl up inside Miles's midsection and take up residence near his heart.

He was winning. He'd known he could win.

With the force of love on his side, how could he not?

"I'll need you to complete your formal application very quickly, of course," Rosamond told him in a clipped undertone. Her gaze darted nervously at the women who were about to encroach on their conversation. "As far as anyone needs to know, you're being evaluated on a probationary basis, pending your completion of all the mutual society's admission requirements."

"Right. So I'll need to be honorable, witty and worthy," Miles recited. "I'll need to wrangle character references, a job with a reliable income and an ability to dance well enough that your members will want to repeat the experience a second time." He paused, grinning meaningfully down at her. "That last one might be challenging."

"For you?" She smiled back. "I'm very afraid it might be."

Her pert expression belied her rueful tone, though, telling him she was teasing. That took away some of the sting from her earlier refusal to repeat their dance. Miles understood her reticence. If he'd put together the pieces from the Bouchards' dual accountings of things and Rosamond's reaction to Gus Winston correctly, then he understood all too dismally well.

"Worst of all," Miles said on a faux groan, putting aside that troubling concern for now, "I'll have to get ahold of an abstentious nature from someplace." He patted his pockets. He came up with nothing. "Not a single whiff of teetotalism in here. Do you know where a man can get something like that?"

"I wouldn't suggest Jack Murphy's saloon as a starting point. But I am impressed with your powers of recollection. You've remembered every requirement of my mutual society."

"Even a stableman can recount a simple list." He didn't like that Rosamond kept underestimating him. "Did you really think I came here to Morrow Creek—" to you "—without any idea of what you required of your mutual society members?"

"I didn't realize my society was so infamous."

"I didn't count on the secret puppy clause." Paying

nightly visits to Rosamond wouldn't be easy. The temptation to leap back into the camaraderie they'd shared would be immense.

The temptation to try for even greater intimacy between them would be even stronger. He'd have to proceed cautiously.

The problem was, Miles didn't have much time. Bouchard might be growing impatient for a report from him even now. Arvid didn't know Miles had never intended to deliver that report. He wouldn't be pleased when he discovered as much, either.

"Well, it's too late for regrets. You've already agreed. Riley will be glad." *So will I*, Rosamond's gaze said. She waggled her fingers. "Well? Shall we seal our deal?"

"Yes. No regrets." He'd never regret finding Rosamond, Miles knew as he accepted her handshake. He'd only regret not being able to find her sooner. He still felt gutted to know that she was struggling. It broke his heart to know that she felt imprisoned here in her own household. "I agreed gladly. So did you. Speaking of which, we should leave soon. My shopping—"

Can't wait. He didn't have an opportunity to say so. Miss Yates chose that moment to interrupt. She came forth at the head of a cluster of the household's women like a tugboat pulling a steamer, only to stop disapprovingly in front of Rosamond.

"That was not the best dancing lesson we've ever had," Miss Yates announced, "but it was adequate, given the interruption."

Her gaze centered in on Miles and Rosamond's handshake.

A vinegary look crossed her pretty face.

Seeing that look, Rosamond hastily pulled away her hand. She blinked at her palm, seeming surprised to have found herself touching Miles. Deliberately, pretending to be interested in the movements of the household's women who were wandering away to their next activities, Rosamond tucked her hand into her skirts.

The impact of her handshake wouldn't be easily forgotten, though, Miles realized. At least not by Miss Yates. He'd caught the way she'd looked when he'd initially touched Rosamond in the improvised ballroom. More importantly, he'd noticed the way Miss Yates had frowned when Rosamond hadn't shied away from him.

Rosamond's friend and assistant clearly didn't like Miles being there. Which was odd, given the interested— even blatant—way Miss Yates had assessed him during his initial visit.

He'd never been more openly ogled in his life.

Given the boisterous conduct of some of the women he'd met, that was saying something. There were reasons Miles felt comfortable with Rosamond's forthright behavior and her past in service. They were alike, the two of them—both from the same world, and now, at long last, both headed in the same direction.

He only wished he'd known, somehow, what Rosamond had faced in the Bouchards' household. He would never forgive himself for not divining what was wrong— for not putting a stop to it.

"Mr. Callaway." Miss Yates turned to him politely, her hands folded primly at her skirts. "Shall I escort you out?"

Rosamond frowned. "Our visit hasn't concluded yet."

"Oh. Of course. I'm sorry. I must have misunderstood your handshake." Miss Yates's censorious gaze transferred to Rosamond's face. "I thought it was a goodbye."

"Not yet," Miles told her cheerfully. "I'm going to be around for a while, working up proof of my worthiness."

"I see." Miss Yates looked away. "Good luck with that, Mr. Callaway. Given your ignoble entrance into our lives, I think you'll need an angel on your shoulder to accomplish that."

"There's no need to start calling on the Almighty already, Miss Yates. Mr. Callaway's own merits should be enough."

"I've seen his 'merits.' I didn't think he'd be using them to get admitted to your mutual society. That's a new one on me."

"Also, you should know that Mr. Callaway will be visiting us regularly. He'll be helping with Riley while I complete his admission into the mutual society." Rosamond's firm tone brooked no disagreement. Her authoritative demeanor was, in a word, impressive. "I assured him we would all welcome him."

For a moment, both women squared off silently. Then...

"Naturally," Miss Yates relented. "Welcome!"

Her stiff tone hardly sounded convincing. But Miles was fascinated that Rosamond had wrangled that much compliance from her balky assistant. Whatever Rosamond had endured during their time apart, it had changed her. It had made her into an even more resilient woman, one who commanded respect and admiration for her tenacity and her power of will. No matter what had happened, his Rose had done more than survive. She'd risen above her circumstances and helped others to do the same.

Not every woman, in her shoes, would have been capable of that. Miles wished he knew exactly what had brought Rosamond to this place. Had her brief marriage to Elijah Dancy altered her? Or had Bouchard caused all the changes he glimpsed in her?

He made a mental note to find out. Soon. In the meantime...

"...since you're here," Miss Yates was saying to him, "perhaps you can help us with a few chores. There are a great many things that need to be hoisted, fixed or seen to—"

"Mr. Callaway is not ours to command, Miss Yates."

"—and you seem to be just the capable man for the job."

"Mr. Callaway already has a job. At Owen Cooper's stable."

"Yes, but he's here now. And we need strong arms."

"We have Judah, Dylan and Seth. They can help."

"Not while guarding all the doors, they can't," Miss Yates reminded Rosamond. "You increased our security, remember?"

The two women's polite quarrel interested Miles, in terms of what Rosamond had accomplished here. But time was dwindling.

"I'm not sure your increased security is effective," Miles told them both. "Since when I arrived today, I'm sure I saw Seth in the side yard rolling dice with someone."

He didn't mention how easily he'd slipped past the security man. There was no point causing undue alarm. He was here now.

He intended to protect Rosamond with everything he had.

"Dice? Seth was gambling? During working hours?" Rosamond made a disbelieving face. "I know he complains of being short of money sometimes. Now I see why. He knows that's not allowed."

"No, it is not." Miss Yates tsk-tsked. "Things are getting very out of hand all of a sudden."

Her implication was plain. Miles was a distraction.

A distraction who should be sent packing. Or put to work.

"Still," Rosamond insisted, "I will not have Mr. Callaway treated like a servant. He's been through enough already."

Her determined tone was telling. Did she regret leaving him behind in Boston? Miles wondered. He didn't want Rosamond to be sorry for anything she'd done… but he did want her to want him here. If reminding her of their shared past in service to an unappreciative and demanding society family would do that…

"Whatever needs done, I'm your man." Meaningfully, Miles winked at Rosamond. Pleased by her blushing response, he shucked his coat. He offered it to a triumphant Miss Yates, then rolled up his shirtsleeves. "I'll make sure you're happy with my work."

His gruff assurance made Rosamond's blush deepen. Hmm. Maybe they could recapture some of the closeness they'd shared.

All he had to do was take things one step at a time.

Quickly. Before Bouchard or his thugs caught up with him.

"All right, then. What's first?" Duly prepared for manual labor, Miles glanced up. "Heavy lifting? Repairs? Cake baking?"

Both women fell silent, staring at his bare forearms. Puzzled, Miles turned over his arms. He flexed them. They were the same ordinary, well-muscled, hairy arms he'd always had.

That didn't explain why Rosamond and Miss Yates were so transfixed. Maybe the men they admitted to the mutual society were too well mannered. It wasn't a crime to take off a coat.

Rosamond blinked. "Cake baking?" she asked.

"In my previous job, I used to help the cook stir cake batter. Whenever she was making a fancy cake, the eggs had to be beaten hard for ten minutes, then the batter had to be beaten for another twenty before it was baked. If I helped stir—"

"You got to taste the batter," Rosamond surmised, smiling.

Miles nodded. "I just happened to be the best stirrer."

"I'll bet you were," Rosamond agreed. "I can imagine so."

He knew damn well she didn't have to imagine anything. Whenever he'd been able to—whenever she'd been free of duties—he'd shared those sweet batter swipes with her. Miles still possessed one cherished memory of watching Rosamond lick a big wooden spoon, her eyes closed in sweets-induced ecstasy.

Miss Yates harrumphed. "There won't be any special treatment of that sort here. Only a lot of work."

"And a lot of romance." Miss Jorgensen stepped up, looking like a grown-up version of her daughter, Agatha, right down to her blond hair and spectacles. "I'm sorry to interrupt, Mrs. Dancy, but that special appointment of yours is in your parlor."

What did that have to do with romance? Miles wondered.

He flexed his forearms again, this time in vexation.

"Ah." Rosamond smiled. She nodded. "I'll be right there."

"Appointment?" Miles prodded. "But you don't take appointments. Everyone in town was very clear on that fact."

"This one is special, as Miss Jorgensen said." Giving him an impudent look, Rosamond piqued his curiosity further. "Thank you for your help with Miss Yates's chores, Mr. Callaway. I'll just leave you to her authority, then. Until later?"

Later. When he could be alone with Rosamond again.

"Until later." He could endure anything with the promise of Rosamond's company as a reward. All he had to do was make himself useful, learn whatever he could about Rosamond—and so far her friends, like Grace Murphy, had proved very enlightening to him—and then use that information to help her break free.

If he had to apply for membership in her mutual society to do that, Miles reckoned, he'd be happy to. After all, he'd only pretended his initial reluctance to force Rosamond's natural contrariness to kick in. He couldn't believe she hadn't spied that tactic at work. He'd used it quite successfully so far.

Satisfied with his progress, Miles watched Rosamond sail off down the hallway to her romantic appointment in her parlor. Despite everything, she still possessed the same enchanting swing to her bustle, the same endearing assurance to her step…the same fearlessness to her demeanor as she always had.

Maybe Rosamond wasn't the same Rose he'd known before.

Maybe now, grown up and wiser, she was even better.

All the same, anyone who tried to hurt her would have to answer to him. They'd regret it. He'd make certain of it.

As Rosamond turned the corner, Miles transferred his gaze to the waiting Miss Yates. That doughty woman wore a smug look. From someplace, she'd procured a broom. She shoved it at Miles.

"So happy you're here, Mr. Callaway. Please follow me."

* * *

Rosamond dallied with her appointment for as long as she could. Partly that was because she wanted to delay the outing she'd agreed to with Miles. Partly that was because she wanted to savor the romantic nature of that appointment.

Appointments like these, she realized as she stood outside her parlor doorway—politely pretending not to hear any of what was going on inside—were some of her favorite things about the Morrow Creek Mutual Society and her role in it.

When Rosamond was successful, her efforts led to…

"Yes!" came the sound of Katie Scott's voice from within the parlor. "Yes, oh, yes, Mr. Robertson. I will!"

There were further muffled joyful cries, then a thump. Then a long silence. Outside the door, Rosamond gave a wistful smile.

Down the hall, Libby Jorgensen stopped. Her gaze swiveled toward the closed parlor door, then snagged on Rosamond's face.

She rushed forward. "Is it bad news?" Worriedly, Libby eyed Rosamond, wringing her hands at her skirts. "I'd never have thought Katie would turn down Mr. Robertson, but if she has—"

"No, it's not bad news. I feel fairly certain it's good."

"Then why do you seem so sad?" Libby pressed. "I know full well you take special delight in the proposals that go on here."

"I do." From within the parlor, Rosamond heard footsteps. She drew in a deep breath, prepared to set aside her personal melancholy for the sake of her friend. "Of course I do! This makes—" she paused to tally "—four proposals this year so far."

The society's proposals had begun with Gus Winston, her inaugural member, and his new bride, Abigail. But they hadn't ended there. Because of that, Rosamond cherished the success of her mutual society. In a very short time, she'd proven that Western men wanted more from their women than a bit of feminine company for a single sordid night. Contrary to Elijah Dancy's expectations, Western men wanted love. They wanted commitment. They wanted surety and sweetness and shared interests. With her mutual society, Rosamond helped her friends and neighbors in Morrow Creek—men and women alike—find all those vital things.

With each successful betrothal and wedding, she proved to the world and to herself that good men wanted to love and be loved. They wanted to give and receive, shelter and provide.

They wanted women who wanted those things, too.

It didn't matter that Rosamond had personally opted out of the romantic elements of her mutual society. She liked knowing that they existed for everyone else. She liked knowing that other people had hope. Foolish, irresistible hope.

The kind of hope she'd felt beckoning to her ever since Miles's arrival.

"Four proposals, three weddings, and more to come," Libby agreed. "When you had the idea to take Dancy's gambling winnings and lead all of us farther west, I'd never have thought—"

The parlor door opened, saving Rosamond an unwanted trip down memory lane. She didn't like thinking about her ex-husband. Their marriage had been fleeting...but not nearly brief enough.

"We're engaged!" Katie Scott shrieked, scurrying through the parlor door with a bashful-looking Clifford Robertson trailing in her wake. She grabbed his hand

and pulled him into the hallway with her. "Mr. Robertson proposed, and I accepted!"

"Congratulations to both of you." Warmly, Rosamond nodded at them. She wished she felt up to hugging Katie. "I'm pleased."

"I'm ecstatic!" Energetically, Libby did embrace Katie. They stood near Rosamond, beaming at one another. "I knew this would happen! When Mr. Robertson joined, I knew he was for you."

"I could only hope so," Katie confessed, blushing. "I liked him immediately, from that first dance we shared. Then later, when Mr. Robertson participated in our usual literary meeting…"

She went on, but Rosamond could only stand there, feeling peculiarly excluded. When she'd left Boston, she'd left behind the kinds of girlish hopes and dreams that Katie was describing. She'd almost forgotten she'd entertained them at all…

…until Miles had arrived to rekindle them.

Uncomfortably fussing with her skirts, Rosamond caught Mr. Robertson's reticent gaze. She smiled at him, then went on fidgeting while waiting for Katie to finish. Ordinarily, she loved celebrating with her members when they got engaged. Today, though, she felt unusually downhearted about the situation.

It would never be her who inspired a man to get down on one knee and pledge his heart to her, Rosamond knew as she watched Katie. It would never be her who inspired such love and commitment.

After all, how could a woman who feared touching, feared trusting, feared leaving her own home ever find love with anyone? It was beyond challenging. It was impossible.

It was impossible because of her and who she'd become.

It was impossible because of the four walls that guarded her. For the first time, as Rosamond stood there wanting to celebrate Katie's engagement, her cherished sanctuary did feel like a prison. Her walls served to keep out life, it occurred to her, as efficiently as they kept in solitude and security.

She hadn't intended to forgo her freedom for her safety. But what else could she do? People depended on her now.

Her newfound friends and their children relied on her. She couldn't let down her guard. She couldn't give in.

But she could, Rosamond realized, trade a fraction of her control to gain an immensity of strength. With effort and determination, maybe she could stop fearing that if Arvid Bouchard found her, she wouldn't be capable of handling him. Maybe she could stop fearing that she would once again be forced, against her will, to parcel out her soul.

Because that's what it had felt like every time Arvid Bouchard had groped her, and Rosamond had had to fight him off. That's what it had felt like every time he'd caught her unaware and whispered filthy things in her ear while she worked. That's what it had felt like on that awful sunny morning when Mr. Bouchard had found her making beds in an upstairs room in the mansion—when he'd locked the door behind himself and made sure Rosamond knew that he could take anything he wanted from her.

He could take her, anytime he wanted, and she couldn't stop him. Not that Rosamond hadn't tried. She had. She'd fought hard and often—only to learn that Mr. Bouchard liked her "spiritedness." She'd considered telling the housekeeper or the butler or even Genevieve Bouchard herself. But in the end, Rosamond had known she had to handle things on her own.

After all, no one else was ever there in the moments when Arvid Bouchard cornered her. And the things Mr. Bouchard had threatened to do to her if she ever told anyone...

Remembering those threats now, Rosamond shuddered. Even in hindsight, she couldn't blame herself for handling the situation on her own as best she could. But doing so had come at a cost. Every time she'd fought and lost, she'd sacrificed a portion of herself. Every time she'd felt Arvid Bouchard's hands on her, smooth and unwanted and unstoppable, she'd deadened herself more.

In the end, she hadn't felt much of anything at all.

Now Miles was the only one besides Rosamond who remembered the parts of her that Arvid Bouchard had stolen. Miles was the only one who could see them missing. That's why he pined for "his Rose." That's why he'd followed her to Morrow Creek.

That's why he'd said what he had about her being too strong and too bossy and too stubborn to hide herself from the world.

But because Miles knew her, he might also be the only one who could help restore some of those parts of herself, Rosamond mused now. In fact, Miles wouldn't even have to know that's what he was doing. Not if she proceeded carefully and intelligently.

She felt half convinced Miles had restored her faith by a few degrees just with a single dance. What more could Miles do, Rosamond wondered, if she gave him a greater opportunity?

If she spent just a little more time alone with him?

"...wouldn't you say so, Mrs. Dancy?" Katie was asking.

With effort, Rosamond roused herself from her thoughts.

"Wouldn't that sunny glade near Mr. Wilson's farmhouse be a lovely spot for a wedding?" Libby enthused, plainly helping Rosamond pick up the conversational thread. "That's where Adeline Wilson and Clayton Davis got married last month."

"Such a lovely ceremony!" Katie went on. "Wasn't it?"

It occurred to Rosamond that they'd already begun planning Katie and Mr. Robertson's wedding. Rosamond had attended the mutual society's first two weddings. She'd made excuses not to attend the third, on account of her upsetting spell in the town square on that day with Molly Copeland. And this, the fourth…

"I'm sorry. I'm afraid I wasn't at the Davises' wedding."

Katie looked perplexed. Libby looked doleful.

Mr. Robertson looked utterly out of his depth.

In that moment, Rosamond swore to herself that she'd missed her very last Morrow Creek Mutual Society wedding.

She'd be darned if she'd let the memory of Arvid Bouchard ruin a single additional day of her life. Starting that instant.

"But of course I'll be at yours, Katie!" Rosamond promised. She took a hesitant step forward, fully intending to bully herself into offering a laudatory hug. "Congratulations again!"

At her undoubtedly stilted tone, all three of her friends gave her puzzled looks. But Rosamond was determined.

Lift, arms. Lift! Doggedly, she tried to offer that hug.

Her arms flat out refused to cooperate. Instead, Rosamond wound up gesturing like a scarecrow whose heart wasn't really in the job at hand: awkwardly and ineptly. Everyone frowned.

All right, then. Sheer determination would not work.

She needed help in this endeavor, Rosamond decided. And she knew exactly the tall, dark and handsome cake-batter stirrer she could collect it from. If she spent just a little more time with Miles, she felt certain he could help restore her to the good person she'd once been. So, lifting her chin and forming her hands into fists, she said her goodbyes to her friends and then went to find Miles before she had a chance to reconsider.

She would master this eventually. She would.

Chapter Eight

Miles hadn't intended to bring along several children and a wriggly puppy while he carried in armloads of wood for the household's cookstove. But once the little ones spied Miles on the marriage bureau's premises, they began trailing him. One by one, they stuck to him like glue. Agatha Jorgensen had been the last to join, holding Riley in her arms. Within minutes, Miles had assembled a corps of pint-size helpers, each scampering around with all the grace and purpose of a newborn foal.

"Good job, Tommy." He nodded at the wiry child who'd just used his untucked shirt as an apron-turned-carrier for a pile of twigs. "Very inventive of you. Drop those right there."

The twigs clattered down alongside the bigger pieces that had already been placed in a pile beside the house's back door. Tommy grinned up at Miles, his face as grimy as his pride was huge. With a businesslike air, he dusted off his small hands.

"I'll go get more." He ran off to do just that.

"Mr. Callaway! Look! I got this big 'un." With a grunt, Tobe Larkin hoisted a split log. Red-faced, he carried it to the pile, then dropped it flat. It landed with a thud. "See?"

Miles squinted at him. "Are you sure you just turned thirteen?" Musingly, he squeezed the boy's scrawny arm. "I reckon you've got the strength of a sixteen-year-old in here."

"That's right. I do. And you ain't seen nothin' yet!"

Tobe ran off, his sights set on a ludicrously large piece of wood. Miles grinned, feeling fond of the boy already.

He'd been a lot like Tobe as a child. Tall, eager to prove himself and willing to talk up his own skills in the process.

Another child lurched into view, his face hidden behind a precariously balanced pile of wood. Miles recognized the red hair visible just above the pile, though. That mop top belonged to Seamus O'Malley. Even now, the boy was jabbering away.

Pretty much, Miles had learned, he never quit talking.

"...so that's how I got so many pieces of wood all at once," Seamus was saying now, his voice muffled. "I just stacked 'em up real good beforehand. I'm always thinkin' up stuff like that. It's just like playin' baseball. I'm real good at that, too."

With an elaborate grunt, Seamus dropped his load on the growing pile. At the rate they were all working— for Miles had done his share of carrying and stacking, too—it would be at least six months before anyone in the household would need to take more than three steps from the kitchen to gather wood.

His burden gone, Seamus chanced a glance at Agatha. He saw that she was engrossed in the puppy. His shoulders sagged. Evidently, he'd hoisted that heavy load hoping to impress her.

Miles's heart went out to the youngster. He knew what potentially unrequited love felt like for himself.

"I reckon that's enough wood for now." With due solemnity, Miles studied the pile they'd made, hands on his hips. Loudly, for Agatha's benefit, he added, "That last load you added plumb finished off the pile, Seamus. Well done. I'm impressed."

The boy perked up. He glanced at Agatha.

She smiled at him, her glasses twinkling in the sunshine.

Seamus all but bolted in her direction. Miles knew better. He clapped one hand on Seamus's shoulder, holding him back.

"Whoa, there, Seamus. Hang on just a minute."

"Huh? Why? Agatha just smiled at me! I've gotta go talk—"

"Just wait." Patiently, Miles watched Agatha.

Any second now...

"Hey, Seamus—do you want a turn holding Riley?"

"That puppy?" The boy humphed. He made an exaggeratedly disgruntled face. "What kind of fella holds a dumb puppy?"

Looking pleased to have presented himself as a tough, no-puppies-allowed kind of man, Seamus sneaked a peek at Miles.

A few yards away, Agatha looked crestfallen.

Miles shook his head. "When a lady invites you to do something," he instructed the boy, "you always say yes."

Forcibly, he tucked in Seamus's shirttail. He gave the boy's unruly hair a swift, mostly hopeless smooth down, then examined his freckled face for good measure. It was a dirt-smudged mess. Fortunately, Miles's shirtsleeve doubled handily as a scrubber. Within seconds, Seamus looked presentable.

Miles nodded. "I reckon you'll do. Go on. Start out by apologizing. Then think up a good joke. Keep it polite!"

Eagerly, Seamus headed out. Then, two steps in, he turned.

Beseechingly, he beckoned for Miles. Miles came over.

"Can you fix my sleeves like yours?" Seamus asked urgently.

Befuddled, Miles looked down at his rolled-up sleeves.

"Your sleeves look like somethin' a pirate captain would wear in a book," Seamus explained. "I think Agatha likes 'em."

Hiding a smile, Miles did as he was asked. He crouched to Seamus's level, fixed his shirtsleeves, then shooed the boy.

It made him feel downright satisfied to see Seamus approach Agatha with a little extra strut in his step.

"So that's how you do it," someone said from behind Miles, sounding amused. "You roll up your shirtsleeves and then unleash an irresistible onslaught on the nearest hapless female."

Rosamond. Miles turned to find her watching him. Smiling.

"Do you really think it's fair to pass on this skill of yours to the next generation?" she asked. "Look at Agatha."

He did. Now she and Seamus were jointly petting Riley, each of them cooing at the puppy as if they'd invented baby talk.

"She seems happy enough," Miles observed.

"She doesn't know Seamus had help impressing her," Rosamond pointed out. "As far as Agatha knows, Seamus never walks around with strawberry jam in his hair and cockleburs stuck to his britches. As far as Agatha knows, Seamus will love her forever."

"They're not even five feet tall. Give them time."

"You rolled his shirtsleeves at a rakish angle!"

"So? That's just embellishment. Women like embellishment. They're not gullible, though. Agatha eats breakfast with Seamus. She's probably wise to the strawberry jam problem by now."

"All I'm saying is, don't help him break her heart."

Miles gave Rosamond what he knew was a perceptive look. He didn't need miles of book learning to understand what she meant.

"It's not my intention for anybody to break anybody's heart." *Especially yours.* "Especially Agatha's." Miles pointed. "Look at her—she's single-handedly calmed down Riley."

"For that I'm grateful," Rosamond admitted. "For the rest—"

"You think I gave Seamus an unfair advantage."

"Didn't you?"

Miles shrugged. "Agatha smiled at him first. Seems to me the die was cast then. Now all Seamus has to do is meet her halfway. He didn't need help from me to do that."

"Well…she has a right to know his intentions."

At that, Miles chuckled. "You're funny sometimes, Mrs. Dancy. They're just practicing at behaving like grown-ups."

He saw her lips tighten at his use of her married name and wondered how long it would take Rosamond to let him address her less formally. It seemed to rile her every time he didn't.

Seeming irked even now, Rosamond put her hands on her hips. "How do I know you're not using these children to spy on me?"

"Easy. If I were, I'd know everything there is to know

by now." Miles grinned. "These youngsters love me to pieces."

She gave an impatient sound.

"Also," he relented, knowing she was wise to be at least partly serious about this issue, given his sudden arrival, "if I were spying on you, I'd want to know something else besides your favorite color and how much you like hotcakes for breakfast."

Rosamond seemed skeptical.

"Blue," Miles told her. "And a lot. Heaping plates full."

His bantering made her relax, just the way he wanted.

"If I were spying on you," Miles said, relaxing more now too, "I'd want to know a lot of things. I'd want to know—"

Whether that baby Lucinda Larkin is holding is yours.

Dumbstruck, Miles stared toward the upstairs window where Tobe's mother stood with a baby in her arms. He'd never glimpsed that baby before. Exactly why, he wondered, had it been hidden?

He couldn't be sure from this distance, but a baby that size might well be the correct age to be Arvid's bastard. It seemed significant that Miles hadn't glimpsed the child before now.

"You'd want to know what?" Rosamond's mischievous tone broke into his thoughts. "Go on. Finish what you were saying."

With effort, Miles swerved his attention back to their conversation. "I'd want to know if you'll help me today."

"Help you? With what?"

"With some of the chores I have yet to do." He gestured. "Inside the house. Upstairs. There's a stuck window up there."

"Really? Miss Yates hasn't mentioned it to me."

"Do you know how to fix a stuck window?"

Rosamond didn't seem to want to admit it, but... "Not yet."

"That's probably why she didn't mention it to you. Everyone knows you get tetchy at the idea you can't do something."

Rosamond harrumphed. "You must have me confused with some other Mrs. Dancy. Because this Mrs. Dancy can do everything."

That was just the Rosamond Miles remembered. It was a good thing, too. Because he needed to get inside the house quickly. If, as a bonus, he could watch Rosamond with that baby...

Well, it would be enlightening, was what he was guessing.

Not that Miles intended to report the results of his prying to Bouchard, the way he was supposed to. But as the man who'd admired Rosamond from afar for years—as the man who wanted more than mutual friendship and dancing from her now—Miles figured he had a right to know if Rosamond had run away to have a secret baby.

"Excellent," he said. "Let's go. You can hold my tools."

She gave him a chary look.

"I'll need more than brute strength to fix the window. I'll need tools. Expertise. Finesse." He shrugged. "The usual."

"Somehow, I doubt that." Rosamond grinned, seeming wholly unaware that Miles's attention had become divided among her, Mrs. Larkin and the baby in the window. "You look as if you could just smile at that stuck window and it would fly open."

"I'm glad you're so impressed by me."

"I'm glad we're not going to the market yet."

Hellfire. Miles had forgotten that was his plan. He

still wanted to help Rosamond face her fears of leaving the household.

"Don't get too smug, Mrs. Dancy. Our bargain still stands."

"I know." Determinedly, Rosamond lifted her chin. "I fully intend to hold up my end of our deal, too." She swallowed hard, then gave him a deliberately steely look. "I can't wait to leave here and help you kit out your new lodgings at the stable!"

For a long moment, Miles could only gaze at her with admiration. "I'm impressed. That almost sounded convincing."

"So did your dedication to fixing that window," Rosamond pointed out. "Yet here we are, chatting away instead."

Miles laughed, knowing he should skedaddle inside but wanting this easy closeness to last between them... the way it once had every day. "You're a hard taskmaster."

"I like to get things done, that's all. Now that I've decided what to do, there's no benefit to wasting time."

Miles disagreed. He crossed his arms, still studying her. "I think you'll find that some things are best done slowly."

Her brow arched. "Like window fixing?"

"Like kissing." And embracing, and stroking, and undressing...each garment following the next, until there was nothing left but skin on skin, warm and soft, coming together...

As if she could read his racy thoughts, Rosamond seemed uncharacteristically uncertain. "Kissing? I wouldn't know."

"Good." Miles couldn't help dropping his gaze to her mouth. It looked full. Soft. Pink and kissable and lovely.

"That was something else I was hoping to teach you about. Kissing."

Hazy-eyed, Rosamond examined his lips. He could have sworn he heard her give a regretful sigh. "I was hoping for that, too. Once upon a time, I was. Now…" She blinked and gazed up radiantly at him. "Well, now things are different, aren't they?"

"Not that different." Miles hesitated, then decided he didn't have time to squander. "I still want to kiss you."

Rosamond inhaled, eyes wide. Her gaze swerved to his.

"I would kiss you slowly," Miles clarified, needing to reassure her. Needing her to know how special she was. "I would hold your hand first, then maybe stroke your arm, like this—"

Deliberately transferring his gaze from her face to her arm, Miles brought his hand there in the lightest of touches. Using his fingertips, he savored the warmth of her skin through her long-sleeved calico dress. Gently, he wrapped his hand around her arm. Soothingly, he stroked her with his thumb.

"—then, when you felt very comfortable with that," Miles went on, leaning the slightest bit nearer, "I would come a little closer to you, just like this. I would wait a minute, just to breathe in that rose perfume of yours, just to remember that you're you, my Rose, the woman I've waited so long for—"

Rosamond stood stock-still. Raptly, she watched him.

"—and then I'd probably bring my other hand up to your face, like this," Miles said, raising his free hand to her jaw. He caressed her, feeling the space between them grow heated and languid and full of yearning. "I'd tell you you're beautiful—"

Rosamond swallowed hard. She swayed a fraction closer.

"—because you are, so beautiful," he told her, knowing that his whole heart might pound through his chest at any second with the intensity of the need he felt for her, "and then I'd remark on how very soft and warm your skin is, because it feels like heaven beneath my palm." Slowly, he caressed her, his voice growing husky as he went on speaking. "And I wouldn't be able to help looking at your lips, because I've imagined them on mine so many times now, and I know that kissing you will be so nice—"

Rosamond's gaze parted abruptly from his. Her attention flew from Miles's face to a point someplace over his shoulder, then returned. Skittishly, she took a step back. Damnation.

"I think it would be better," she surprised him by saying in all seriousness, "if I were the one to kiss you."

At the notion, Miles felt nigh on inflamed with desire.

He wanted that. So much. Especially now that he'd touched her so familiarly—now that he knew what desire really was.

"But since I can't very well do that in a yard full of children," Rosamond went on, sounding a little bit husky and bedazzled herself as she sought to gather her wits, "I guess we'll have to fix that stuck window instead, won't we?"

Miles frowned. Gradually, the overlooked sounds of the children playing nearby—of Seamus jabbering away to Agatha—penetrated his awareness again. "Fix the window? What window? I don't remember any window."

Gaily, Rosamond smiled at him. "Come on now. Time's wasting." She gestured. "Get your tools and let's go."

"You know, the children don't care what we're doing out here," Miles said. "Maybe you haven't noticed, but some of them wandered off when we started talking. The rest started a game over yonder near that tree. So I think we're safe."

Rosamond shook her head. "We're anything but safe."

"I meant—"

"I know what you meant." Boldly, she took his hand. She tugged, pretending she could haul him her direction. "Quit dillydallying and start demonstrating your usefulness."

Not giving in, Miles persisted. They'd been so close…

"I won't ever hurt you, Rosamond. I hope you know that."

Her handhold went slack. She examined him for a minute, recalling what he'd said. Her hard gaze almost made him shiver. An evaluative stance like hers would have made a lesser man give up. But Miles wasn't just any man. He would never give up.

Rosamond would be a difficult woman to get close to. But Miles meant to try, all the same. If it took his dying breath, he meant to help Rose break free of all her restraints. He meant to help Rose be happy. He hoped her happiness would include him.

"That makes us even then," Rosamond told him. "Because I don't intend to let you hurt me. So…shall we get started?"

The window. Miles had never wanted to perform handyman duties less than he did in that moment. He wanted to get closer to Rosamond instead. He wanted to touch her again, to kiss her…

"Yes." He nodded. Then, because he wasn't a man who backed down easily… "You're going to be awed by my prowess. Let's go."

* * *

Following Miles's broad-shouldered lead as he directed their way back inside her household, Rosamond knew that she already was awed by Miles's prowess. Who wouldn't have been?

Already, her onetime favorite stableman had managed to accomplish more in a few days in Morrow Creek than another man could have managed in...well, forever. Because no other man had ever tempted Rosamond to stand close, close, closer to him. To breathe in the musky male scent of him. To look at his lips, to watch him speak, to soak in the good, familiar lilt of his voice and the sure, comforting promises inherent in his words.

I won't ever hurt you, Rosamond. I hope you know that.

She did. More and more, with each passing moment, she did.

Otherwise, why would she have allowed Miles to touch her? To caress her cheek, to speak so shamelessly, to tempt her into almost raising on her tiptoes and pressing her mouth to his?

Frankly, Rosamond realized as she stepped into the cooling shade of her kitchen with Miles ahead of her, she'd gone considerably beyond wondering if Miles's beard was soft or scratchy. Now she'd begun wondering if Miles's mouth would feel as gentle as his words did, if his touch would feel as stirring as his declarations of feeling for her did, if being with him, intimately, would scare her half as much as the notion of being without him had already begun to.

You're you, my Rose, the woman I've waited so long for.

Honestly. How could any woman be expected to resist sweet words like those? Rosamond was only human.

She was only one woman. She already knew she needed Miles. In the space of a few days, she'd again been lured into relying on his kind nature, his laughter-inducing ways, his strength and his integrity. To know that he felt similarly about her…well, that was almost enough to make Rosamond throw caution to the wind altogether.

In fact, she had abandoned reasonable prudence for a few dangerous moments. All because she'd been trying to distract Miles from the view of Lucinda Larkin and the baby he'd obviously caught in the window. Rosamond had seized upon the one opportunity she had to divert Miles's attention and place it squarely on herself…only to succumb to his attentions for real.

She had sidetracked him long enough for Lucinda and the baby to disappear safely from sight in the upstairs window, but Rosamond's strategy had nearly backfired. By the time Miles had stroked her cheek and gazed into her eyes and drawn ever so nearer to kissing her, Rosamond had forgotten her initial intentions completely. Instead, she'd found herself growing immensely curious about Miles. And his mouth. And his kiss.

Because she truly hadn't ever been kissed before.

That was one thing the despicable Mr. Bouchard hadn't troubled himself with. He had never touched her gently, never kissed her, never said anything kind. Later, when Elijah Dancy had come into the picture…well, that had been more of a business dealing than anything else, courtesy of a vengeful Genevieve Bouchard. There had been all the other "girls" present, too—the ladies who were now her friends and mutual society members. So Rosamond had been saved Elijah's lustful intentions. Certainly, Rosamond had been unique, since she was the unlucky one who'd been all but sold into marriage to Dancy. But aside from that…

No. She wouldn't think about any of that now, Rosamond told herself as she forced her gaze onto Miles's overlong hair and jovial gait. She'd think about Miles, and her deal with him, and the opportunity she now had to delay fulfilling that deal.

After all, he needed her help with those chores. He'd said so. If doing that prevented Rosamond from taking her first brave leap into the scary, panic-inducing world outside, so be it.

At least she'd successfully deterred Miles from asking about Lucinda and the baby. She'd dallied with him long enough for Lucinda and that precious child to disappear from sight.

Now if Rosamond could simply steer Miles to another area of the house, far away from Lucinda's room, she'd be home free.

"There hasn't been a handyman here for some time," Rosamond said by way of accomplishing exactly that. "I'm fairly certain I noticed a broken riser on the stairs this morning. Maybe you should start by repairing that before you tend to the window."

"I'll do both."

But the window might be upstairs, with Lucinda. "But the riser is more urgent." If she had to, she'd kick it into smithereens herself. "Someone might trip and fall."

"Someone might need fresh air."

"Safe stair-climbing is more important."

"I have time to do both." Miles paused. He tossed Rosamond an over-the-shoulder wink. "Especially with your capable help."

"I don't know, Miles." Absently, Rosamond nodded to her friends in the household as she passed by them in Miles's wake. Everyone was busy with their individual tasks and mutual society business. "I'm inexperienced.

I might not be as helpful as you think. Let's go tend to the stairs, then fix the window."

At that, Miles stopped, almost causing her to collide with his big, powerful backside. Rosamond had to put out her hands to keep herself from bumping into him. She only succeeded in treating herself to an up-close-and-personal tour of Miles's back muscles. He felt notably sturdy and surprisingly warm.

She whipped away her hands, her face heating.

He turned. His expression said he knew darn well the effect he might have on a woman who was encountering all that manliness for herself. His eyebrow rose. He waited for her to breathe.

She did. With effort. But she felt powerfully intrigued, all the same. If a man like Miles used his strength for good...

"If I didn't know better," Miles mused aloud in a shrewd tone, "I'd think you were trying to deliberately steer me away from upstairs." He crossed his arms, examining her. "Are you trying to deliberately steer me away from upstairs?"

"Only as much as you're trying to avoid working."

He grinned. "Touché, Mrs. Dancy. You're a clever one."

She didn't want to be. She wanted to let down her guard completely. But she couldn't do that—not with Lucinda and the baby at home. Instead, purposely, Rosamond pretended to be impatient. "You're clever enough to recognize that. Does that mean you're finally ready to work on fixing that stair riser?"

His smile told her the only thing he wanted to work on was an introductory kissing lesson. With her. Right there in the small space between the household's pantry and the hallway.

Sensibly sensing that she wasn't ready, Miles gave in. "The tools I've been using are over here, in the back stairwell."

Resolutely, he marched to retrieve them. Left behind momentarily, Rosamond danced a victory jig. She liked it when she persevered with Miles. It made her feel secure with him.

"Are you coming or not?" Miles called, already ahead of her. "For someone who's so antsy to work, you sure are slow."

Sobering, Rosamond wheeled around…only to come face-to-face with Miles. He hadn't gotten very far in his search for tools.

In fact, he'd stayed close enough to watch her dance.

His face said it all. He'd viewed every uninhibited move.

"Evidently," he remarked, his gaze full of good humor and affection, "you became quite a dancer while we were apart."

"Yes, I did. I'm happy you think so." Rosamond gave a cheeky curtsy. "If you want, I'll give you lessons on that particular dance." That particularly gawky and jubilantly celebratory dance. "I'll begin slowly, just the way you like."

"I would like that." Miles went on looking at her. His wicked expression made her doubt he was thinking of dance lessons anymore. He looked the way he had when he'd been talking about kissing her. "I'd like that very much. So would you."

"I'm nothing if not eager to take charge."

"I'm nothing if not capable of being a good student."

She had the impression they definitely weren't talking about dance lessons anymore. "And if I couldn't teach you?"

Miles didn't hesitate. "I would wait for you."

She couldn't hope for that. Yet, "For how long?"

"For however long it takes." His answer reminded her of the cocksure reply he'd given on the day he'd arrived—the day she'd questioned him in her parlor. "You're worth waiting for."

Rosamond couldn't help it. She had to know... "Even...now?"

A nod. "Now. Then. Later. Forever. No matter what."

She was a fool for relying on that.

She was an ever bigger fool for believing it.

All the same... "Then I'm doubly sorry this is necessary," Rosamond said, catching sight of a movement to the side and just behind Miles. She lifted her arm to give a signal to Dylan—who'd been waiting unnoticed in the hallway—and watched him send Miles, all unaware, go crumpling toward the floor.

"Catch him before he gets hurt," Rosamond demanded.

Without questioning her, Dylan did as she'd asked.

From the shadows, Lucinda stepped forward with the baby. She'd thrown a small blanket hastily over the child's head, but Rosamond didn't need to see the tyke's face to know the truth.

What she'd just instructed Dylan to do had been necessary. She was only sorry it had come to this. For Miles's sake.

And maybe, a teensy bit, for her own sake, too.

Chapter Nine

After four more days' worth of steady part-time work in Rosamond's household, Miles was no closer to getting the answers he wanted than he had been when he'd first awakened, woozily cradled in Rosamond's lap on her hallway floor, confused and disoriented and yet oddly comforted to be held by her.

"You're awake!" Above him, Rosamond's tearful face had greeted him. She'd stroked his bearded jaw, then given a strangely enlightened sigh. "Thank heavens."

Groggily, he'd blinked. "What happened?"

"I don't know. I was helping you get your tools—"

"You were dancing. I remember that much."

"—after I finished dancing," Rosamond had hastily amended, "when I heard something thud. It was you!" With her skirts, she'd fanned his face. "You're lucky you're not hurt worse."

"I'm lucky you like me. I'd hate to think what you'd do to someone you weren't fond of." Miles had sat up, wincing at a pain in the back of his head. He'd probed it with his fingers. He'd definitely been walloped with something. "Why do I keep winding up insensible in your presence?"

"Isn't it curious? I certainly can't explain it." Rosamond had shrugged. "It's as if your body just plain gives up whenever I get the upper hand with you in an argument."

"You've never had the upper hand with me in an argument."

"But I have the upper hand right now. Can't you see?" She'd given him a consoling pat on the knee, along with a galling tsk-tsk. "You can't even tell when it's happening—until you keel over. I'm afraid your head's going to get all lumpy."

"Your reasoning is what's all lumpy."

A grin. "That is a distraction and a defense, not a worthy argument. You'd better try harder next time, Miles." She sighed. "You weren't out for long, just a few seconds, but who knows what might happen? It's not good for a man to be so contrary."

"I suppose it's excellent for a woman to be contrary?"

"Why, that's just a lady's birthright, isn't it?"

Upon offering up that absurd theory, Rosamond had widened her initial grin to a beatific smile. Miles had harrumphed, knowing full well that she was keeping something crucial from him. Something about the baby he'd seen with Mrs. Larkin. Then Miles had gotten to his feet. He'd looked around fuzzily, expecting to see one of her security men lurking nearby.

Neither Judah nor Seth nor Dylan had been in sight.

"I could have sworn I caught a glimpse of someone," he'd managed, squinting as he pointed, "right there. With a baby."

Rosamond's forced laugh had told him all he needed to know. She was definitely hiding that baby from him. But why?

"If there were a baby in this house," she'd hedged,

"don't you think it would have taught itself to walk by now, just so it could toddle after you like all the rest of the children do?"

"Hmm. I just can't argue with that logic."

"See?" After graciously accepting his chivalrous hand up from the floor, Rosamond had helped brush off his clothes. She'd studied him through concerned eyes, appearing genuinely worried about his welfare. "Once again you've found yourself outmatched. Now you know better than to argue with me, don't you?"

"Now I know better than to turn my back on you, you mean."

He didn't like thinking that Rosamond was desperate enough to have her security man clobber him. Miles guessed he hadn't made as much progress with Rosamond as he'd hoped. Either that or Rosamond was truly determined not to have that baby found.

All the same, that's exactly what Miles meant to do—and quickly, too. He hadn't said so. Not then. Not now, four days and innumerable chores later, either. Instead, Miles had only carried on with his work, mending doorknobs and fixing hinges and scaring away bats from the attic, doing all the assorted odd jobs that Rosamond and Miss Yates dreamed up for him.

But he would learn whose baby that was, Miles swore to himself. He would find out why Rosamond had hidden the child, too. Although he thought he knew that already. Then he would…

Well, he didn't know what he'd do. Not yet.

"Now, a mallet." Keeping his gaze fixed on the broken ladderback chair he'd been repairing, Miles held out his hand.

His assistant was decidedly tardy in assisting him. Holding the chair steady, Miles shifted his attention to Rosamond. She sat on the floor beside him, dreamily looking at his hands. She held the mallet he'd entrusted her with at a cockeyed angle, leaving it sticking out from beneath her face while she rested her chin in her hands and watched him work.

She didn't look like a woman who'd coldcock a man just to hide a secret baby from him. She looked sweet and innocent.

"Woolgathering again, Mrs. Dancy? Much more of this, and I'll start thinking you aren't really interested in helping me."

Rosamond snapped to alertness. Her gaze swiveled to his face, then held. Her cheeks colored pink. "Can I help it if your work pace is so slow I feel like napping in between jobs?"

"Very funny." He waggled his fingers. "Mallet, please?"

She handed it over—not the least bit docilely, either.

Perversely, Miles was pleased he couldn't intimidate her. He was pleased that Rosamond felt in such high spirits, too. Not that he wanted to bully her or ever would—just that he knew another man might. He wanted Rosamond to be ready for anything.

He gave the chair a few whacks, placing its loose leg more firmly in position. Then he turned to Rosamond again.

"You've had your way long enough. It's my turn."

"Your turn?" She blinked. "Your turn for what?"

"I want to go riding with Mrs. Murphy's bicycling club."

Rosamond blanched. "Bicycling? You can't be—"

"Serious? I'm not." Miles grinned at her. "It was worth it to see the excitement and disbelief fight for supremacy in your face, though. You could sell tickets to that show."

"As someone once said to me…very funny." Playfully, Rosamond shook her head. "What do you really want to do?"

"Free you." Miles set aside his mallet, put the newly stable chair upright again, then stood. He held out his hand to Rosamond. "Come on. You've delayed me long enough with these chores. It's time for us to take that sojourn outdoors."

Rosamond balked. "Delayed you?" Her tone was beyond disingenuous. "However in the world would I ever begin to—"

"Nice try, Mrs. Dancy, but you can quit batting your eyelashes at me. I'm already good and hooked on your beauty and charm. That doesn't mean I don't intend to get my way."

Obviously spying the grit in his expression, Rosamond relented. Grudgingly, she accepted his hand. "All right. I'm coming. But don't go getting up your hopes. When it comes to accomplishing miracles, even you must have your limits."

"I don't accept that." He squeezed her hand, glad she felt safe enough to touch him now—glad they'd recaptured that much of the companionship they'd once shared. "Neither do you."

"Pshaw. How do you know that?"

"I know because you're still holding my hand. Let's go."

Rosamond wanted to make a point about how much she did not need Miles by her side. She wanted to take away her hand from his, deliberately, and prove that she wasn't relying on him. Especially after spending only days in his company. But the moment she spotted her yard fence's wide-open gate, looming ahead of her, with

Judah at the latch, Rosamond found herself clenching Miles's hand hard enough to crush it in her fingers.

Manfully, he didn't give more than a muffled "oof!" as her grip tightened. He only smiled encouragingly at her.

"No worries," Miles promised. "It's only a little shopping. It's only a few of your neighbors. You can do this. If you feel faint or sweaty or at all strange, I'll be here for you."

Rosamond wondered if he'd be there if she swooned. That was her most worrying fear. That and the distinct possibility that her peculiar malady might be lethal. It certainly felt debilitating enough to kill a person. It felt scary and unstoppable. But since she didn't want to admit as much…

"Sweaty?" Rosamond scoffed. "Ladies glow, Mr. Callaway. I'll thank you to employ the proper terminology with me."

"I'll thank you to quit stalling," Miles returned.

"I'll thank you to quit goading me."

"I'll thank you to keep your feet moving." Deliberately, Miles moved his hand to the small of her back. Gently, he steered her down the front walk toward that dreaded gate.

He seemed heartened, though, as they went, that her vivacity hadn't deserted her completely—that she was still capable of joshing with him. Rosamond was, too. She needed all the verve she could get just then. She'd spent the past several days trying to drum up courage for this excursion.

She still wasn't ready.

On the plus side, though, she doubted she ever would be ready. So there was no reason to delay any longer, was there?

Besides, if she postponed this excursion anymore,

Miles would know the true depth of her fear. She couldn't allow that.

"Afternoon, Mrs. Dancy." Judah offered up a nod, then tugged his hat brim. If he was surprised to see her leaving the household, her security man didn't let on. "Just let me get Seth to watch this front gate, and I'll be with you lickety-split."

"Thank you, Judah, but that won't be necessary." Rosamond raised her chin, trying to ignore her increasing heartbeat. "Mr. Callaway will be accompanying me. I won't be gone long."

Judah's gaze narrowed. He shifted his attention to Miles.

"I'll take good care of her," Miles promised. His hand still lingered reassuringly at her back. "Don't you worry."

"I do worry." Judah gave Miles a menacing look. "I worry quite a lot, in fact. If anything happens to Mrs. Dancy—"

"It won't."

Judah did not seem mollified. He softened his expression, then leaned conspiratorially toward Rosamond. "If he's taking you by force, ma'am, you just give me our secret signal."

He waited, doubtless expecting Rosamond to do so.

She'd prearranged several such signals with her staff. If worse came to worst, they would need every advantage. It was because of such signals that she'd been able to drug Miles with laudanum-laced tea and question him. It was because of a similar signal that she'd been able to instruct Dylan to lay out Miles long enough for Lucinda and the baby to sneak off undetected. Even now they were hiding, secreted away at the Lorndorff Hotel.

Hmm. Put bluntly, it occurred to Rosamond, her actions didn't seem terribly kind. But they had been justified.

She'd have to make up things to Miles later. Somehow.

"Ma'am?" Judah's gaze probed hers. "I'm here to protect you always. So if there's any little thing I can do for you—"

Gratefully, Rosamond patted Judah's hand. "I'm fine. Thank you, Judah. I'll be back directly." *If I survive, that is.*

Judah's gaze dropped to her consoling hand. He gawked.

Vaguely, it occurred to Rosamond that was the first time she'd touched Judah since she'd hired him. That was progress, wasn't it? Next thing she knew, she'd be hugging people.

"That's enough dillydallying," Miles broke in. "Off we go."

He whisked away Rosamond through the gate before she had a chance to anticipate and fear those first few steps. Before she knew quite what was happening, she found herself walking along the side of the street with Miles. The breeze toyed with her upswept hair, teasing tendrils from her chignon. The sun shone on her shoulders, warming her suddenly rigid neck muscles.

After all the time she'd spent sequestered inside her safe household, it felt decidedly unreal to be outside again.

"Well," Miles said cheerfully as they walked onward, "Judah will never let soap and water touch that hand of his again."

"Hmm?" Focusing on completing one wobbly step after another, Rosamond looked up. "What do you mean?"

"I mean, ma'am, that your youngest security man has gone one hundred percent spoony over you."

Rosamond laughed, distracted from her racing heart-beat for a minute. She even forgot to concentrate on prac-ticing regular breathing, the way she had been doing. In, out. In, out.

"Judah? Don't be silly." She and Miles passed by a few houses, rapidly nearing Morrow Creek's main street. Rosamond's neighbors waved. Shakily, so did she. "He's not sweet on me."

She wasn't entirely certain she could do this. Already, as the false-fronted buildings and busy streets of Morrow Creek closed around her, Rosamond felt a rising sense of trepidation.

"I'm not being silly." Miles moved his fingers from her back to her hand. He gave a comforting squeeze. "As a man myself, I guess I can recognize all the signs."

Oh. That was intriguing. But, more pressingly, "We have to go back," Rosamond said urgently. A wave of nausea swept over her, making her feel clammy and cold. "I can't do this."

She was defenseless out here. It was getting darker.

Miles kept going. "You can do this. You already are."

"That's where you're wrong." Stiffly, still moving, Rosamond shook her head. "I'm only pretending to do this."

"Well, you're being remarkably convincing." Hearten-ingly, Miles led them both through the alleyway that led past Molly Copeland's small bakery. Its elaborate gables and sweets-filled windows beckoned, reminding Rosa-mond of happier times.

She absolutely adored Molly's cinnamon buns. Even now, she fancied she could catch a whiff of spicy cin-namon in the air.

"Where should we go first?" Miles asked in a brac-ing tone as they emerged onto the street. Jovial and gallant, he helped her onto the raised-plank boardwalk. "The mercantile?"

"It will be full of people." I won't be able to escape.

"The general store, then. I'll need pots and pans."

As if he could cook. She doubted he could open a tin can.

"I can't." Inundated with rising terror, Rosamond clenched Miles's hand. She turned to him, longing to bury her face in his shirtfront and pretend they were safe in her parlor. "I can't!"

"You already are," he protested. "Everything is fine."

"It's not fine!" All at once, she wanted to smack him, to kick him, to pound her fists against his big, dumb, outlandishly strong chest. "Can't you see? I'm faint, I'm seeing stars—"

"I sometimes have that effect on women."

"—and my heart is about to gallop straight out of my chest." Fretfully, Rosamond tugged at her dress's collar. She glanced around, convinced her friends and neighbors could see her distress. "This isn't good for me, Miles. I might be dying."

At her doomed but stoic tone, he actually chuckled.

"You are not dying." He framed her face in his hands, giving her a determined and magnanimous look. "I won't allow it. Not after I spent so long finding you."

"That's wonderful. I'm dying, and you're worried about having wasted all your westward traveling time."

"A man's got to have his priorities."

"I can't believe I trusted you to bring me here."

"I can't believe you ever doubted you could."

He had a point there, given all they'd shared. Still, "It hasn't been easy for me, Miles," Rosamond protested, momentarily distracted from her perspiring palms and tunnel vision by the need to explain exactly how wrong he was about this. "I've been through a lot, you know. First I had Arvid to worry about—"

Beside her, Miles instantly went alert. She scarcely noticed. She was too absorbed in her near-hyperventilating breath, her trembling knees and her overall looming demise.

"—then I had Genevieve offering me the preposterous choice of either being blackballed from Boston service or being sold into marriage to a man who was really no better than a common brothel owner." She waved her shaking arms, channeling all her anxiety into indignation. It felt better than helplessness. "Elijah Dancy liked to call himself an 'entertainer,' but it was his 'girls' who were expected to entertain people." Rosamond gave a bitter laugh. "I don't know how he was connected to Mrs. Bouchard, but he definitely understood what she wanted."

Miles stood near her, not speaking, just…being there. Comfortingly, he took her hand again. He held it in his securely.

"She wanted revenge, plain and simple," Rosamond assured him with another unhappy laugh. "She thought I'd seduced Mr. Bouchard, but I swear nothing could be further from the truth."

Staunchly, Miles nodded. His grip tightened on hers.

He said, "I can't believe you didn't thrash them both."

This time, Rosamond's laugh was genuine. It was hoarse and full of disbelief, but it was real. She loved Miles for that.

She loved him for standing by her this way.

"Well, I wasn't always the woman I am today." Ironically, she gestured at her trembling posture, her sweat-dampened dress and her breathless, heart-palpitating demeanor. "I used to be much less assertive and composed than I am right now."

"You were always capable of speaking your mind," Miles disagreed. "As far as being composed goes..." He studied her, fully taking in every inch of unsteadiness, wooziness and irrational fear. "Well, I guess being brave beats being poised."

"Brave?" she scoffed. "If wanting to run from this place and never come back counts as brave, then yes. I'm fearless."

Someone brushed past her, coming from behind. Rosamond jumped, her heart rate instantly tripling. She clutched Miles.

"You are brave." Gently, he maneuvered them both safely out of the way of the foot traffic. All around them, dust kicked up and horses clip-clopped past and the noon church bells rang, but Miles only had eyes for her. "You are the bravest woman I've ever known. To have endured what you did, to have come all the way out here to Morrow Creek...it's nothing short of amazing. You saved all those 'girls.' You gave them a home—"

"That wasn't bravery. That was common-sense survival," Rosamond argued. "After Dancy got shot over that faro game, we had one chance to skedaddle. So we did, one step ahead of the sheriff." She frowned, remembering it. "In the kerfuffle, I thought to take Elijah's winnings. Because they were rightfully his, and I was officially his wife. I didn't have any other way to get by anyway. I convinced everyone else to come with me—"

"I know they were relieved you did. They've told me so."

"—but it wasn't to save them," Rosamond confessed. "It was just so I wouldn't be alone! That's all it was." She was ashamed to say so, but it was the truth. "I was far from Boston by then. You know I don't have any family left anymore. It's hard to get a job in service without a reference—at least to anyone who'd treat a housemaid decently, that is. What else could I—"

Rosamond broke off, her semidistracted tirade coming to an abrupt conclusion. Cautiously, she eyed Miles. She frowned.

"You questioned the women in my household?"

"You look a little less pale," he pointed out approvingly—not to mention distractingly. He didn't want to answer her. "That's excellent, Mrs. Dancy. You must be doing better."

Mrs. Dancy. It bothered her every time he addressed her that way. But as long as she kept Miles calling her by her married name, she retained a necessary distance between them.

"I'm not 'doing better,'" she argued. "I'm merely too preoccupied to think about my imminent collapse right now."

"That seems like progress to me."

"What about my question? You were spying on me?"

Miles held up his palms in an ostensibly innocent pose. Unwisely, Rosamond wished he hadn't. She missed his hand on hers. It had been nice when Miles had been holding her hand.

Also, it occurred to her, she'd survived at least five or six minutes outside in town. That was improvement. Wasn't it?

"I didn't have to spy on you. The women in your household couldn't wait to sing your praises to me." He gave her an artless look. A smile. "I think they're trying to pair us up."

"I think they've lost their minds."

He appeared offended. "I'm not such a bad catch."

"I'm not a part of my mutual society, remember?"

"Then I no longer want to be a member."

"You're not a member yet. You're a provisional applicant."

Miles waved off that technicality. "I'm in. I know it."

"I hold your fate in my hands. So you'd better please me."

His gaze swerved to hers. Held. "I'd be happy to. Just tell me where and when. I have a few ideas how to please us both."

"I'm not as naive as you think." Sadly. She wished that wasn't true. "But if you're implying I'm going to kiss you—"

"I'm ardently hoping you're going to kiss me."

"—then you're in luck. Because I just might, one of these days." *I think I would like to.* "Just as soon as I—"

A flash of movement caught Rosamond's eye. In the distance, she spied a mustachioed, stocky man wearing a fancy suit.

Arvid Bouchard. Arvid Bouchard was walking this way, coming from the direction of the Morrow Creek railway station.

Catching her undoubtedly fearful expression, Miles looked around, too. He seemed unbothered, though, except for...

"I recognize that look of yours. If you're fixing to have someone clobber me or drug me again, here's fair warning," he said. "I'm getting fed up with all this. I'm a patient man, but pretty soon I'm going to have to fight back. And when I do—"

"It's Arvid Bouchard." Automatically, Rosamond put her feet in motion. She stumbled off the raised sidewalk in the opposite direction, twisting her ankle in the process. Limping, not caring that it hurt, she kept going. "He's here. He's found me."

"No. He hasn't found you. He can't have found you."

"This was a terrible idea." Waves of nausea rolled over her. Panting, Rosamond veered into the alleyway. She braced her hand on the exterior wall of Mr. Nickerson's Book Depot and News Emporium, fully expecting to spew her guts. When that didn't happen, she made herself start walking again. Blindly, she kept moving. It wouldn't be long now before her shaky legs gave out.

"Wait!" Miles trailed her, sounding confounded. "Stop!"

If he thought she could do that, he didn't understand a thing. Rosamond lurched away from the town's clustered central businesses, headed for the quiet district where she lived.

Casting another watchful glance over his shoulder, Miles followed Rosamond down the alleyway and onto the next street.

Mindless of his pursuit, she just kept walking. As he watched, she staggered unseeing into the path of an oncoming wagon. He saw its team of horses bearing down on her, heard the driver's surprised shout and felt nothing but terror seize him.

If Arvid Bouchard killed Rosamond without even being there…

Miles couldn't let that happen. Not the least because Bouchard could not be there. Miles had had a telegram from his former employer just a day ago, delivered surreptitiously from Boston via the adjunct telegraph office located outside Morrow Creek and run by Savannah Corwin and her husband Adam. That missive from Bouchard had been terse and threatening, but it had been evidential, too. Arvid Bouchard was home in Boston.

Miles still had time. He had time to be with Rosamond. At the last second, he heaved forward and pulled her to safety. She landed in his arms with a yelp and a whoosh of exhaled breath. Her whole body trembled uncontrollably. She twisted, trying to get free. Then she just started whaling on him, kicking and yelling and pounding her fists on his chest.

"Get off! Get away!" Rosamond cried in a frightening raspy tone. It was evident she didn't know who'd grabbed her. Even as Miles tried to comfort her, she punched him. "No. No!"

"Stop it. Stop," he soothed. His heart broke a little bit more at her distress. "It's just me. Everything's all right."

She didn't listen. She squirmed harder, her motions making her hair come partway undone. Those red strands flew in his face as he fought to hold her, still speaking calming words. As he did, the errant wagon and its driver clattered past, joining the traffic coming to and leaving town. Birds chirped in the trees.

The ordinariness of it all contrasted sharply with Rosamond's pain and distress. Miles wanted to fix all of it.

"Get off me!" She wriggled, then stomped his foot.

Ouch. Reflexively, Miles released her. She ran.

"Rose!" He chased her. He caught up but was afraid to touch her again, lest he frighten her even more. "Rose, wait."

Somehow, his voice breached her panic. She stopped. Her face turned to his, dusty and tear streaked.

Her eyes were wild, her expression mulish. "If you brought him here, Miles," she said, "I swear I'll never forgive you."

At her words, something inside him gave way. In that moment, Miles felt a fraction of what Rosamond must have experienced in town when she'd been overcome by dread.

Because Miles had an overwhelming fear, too, he

learned in that moment. His fear was that Rosamond's threat would come to pass. That she would find out how he'd come to be there. That she would never forgive him. That he would have followed her for nothing.

That he couldn't save her after all.

What else did he have to offer her besides his help? He couldn't give her the security she needed. That was in her power to grasp. Or not. No one else could make her feel safe again.

But Miles sorely wanted to try.

"How could I bring him here?" He didn't need to clarify who they were talking about. Miles spread his arms wide in surrender, trying for that second chance he needed. "Why would I bring him here, when you're not even yourself? When the runaway housemaid I was looking for never even came to Morrow Creek?"

Her stubborn expression only intensified. If he'd thought to force her hand…well, that was plainly impossible to do.

She crossed her arms. "You don't believe that."

"You can't say for sure that I don't."

"I believe I just did."

"Ah, but you're not sure, are you?" Deliberately relaxing his shoulders, Miles meandered a little closer. "You think maybe you're clever enough to pull off your deception. You think maybe that stableman you knew could no more tell who you are than he could remember a list of arcane rules for your marriage bureau."

"Mutual society. And you did remember the rules."

"That doesn't prove much except that I want to be with you." Miles reached her. He stood with his hands at his sides, defenseless and serious and full of yearning. "I want that so much that I'm willing to act like a house servant, polishing silver and fixing chairs for you. I want that so much that I left behind my whole life. I want that so much that I can't think of anything else. I sleep with it and wake up with it."

Her eyes flashed. "I'm sorry if you're disappointed."

"Not disappointed. Frustrated. I'm frustrated, Mrs. Dancy." He observed the irate way Rosamond glanced away and knew that he still understood a few things about her. "Either I have a chance to be with you…or I don't. So why don't you tell me which it is, before I make myself into an even bigger fool for you."

Still looking belligerent, Rosamond hesitated.

A million years crawled by while Miles waited.

Then, unbelievably, she chose that moment to do something he didn't expect. "Please," she said, "call me Rosamond."

Miles was so pleased and so surprised that it took him a second to realize… "You didn't answer my question."

Did he have a chance with her? Or didn't he?

Would he ever?

But Rosamond had already hobbled down the street, leaving Miles alone to watch Judah rush to help her, still limping, inside her yard. The security man scowled in Miles's direction, but once Rosamond was safely inside the fence, she waved.

She seemed to believe she had the upper hand. Again.

Damnation, but she was an extraordinary woman.

Luckily for Miles, she seemed halfway clear to trusting him, too. For now, that was all the encouragement he needed to persevere.

Chapter Ten

Rosamond glanced up just as Bonita Yates carried in another cool compress for her twisted ankle. She couldn't help grinning.

"I declare, Miss Yates. You're going to spoil me rotten with all this mollycoddling you're doing." Rosamond set aside her account book along with her financial worries. She waved for her friend to come forward in the lamplight and give her the compress she'd brought. "It's a hurt ankle, nothing worse."

"Humph. At least you finally agreed to prop it up the way I told you to do. But you still don't have enough pillows there." Helpfully, Bonita provided another cushion. "That's better."

"Thank you. But it'll be fine in a day or two."

"That's what you said after you came back from town…four days ago." With an ease borne of their long-standing friendship, Bonita took a place on the chair nearest to Rosamond's settee. Suspiciously, she asked, "Are you sure you only tripped?"

"Of course I tripped. What else would I have done?"

Darkly, Bonita looked away. Rosamond remembered her friend's calamitous past—remembered how Bonita had come to be included in Elijah Dancy's unlikely cadre of "entertainers"—and felt awash in commiseration. For Bonita, joining up with Mr. Dancy had been a step up from the "businessman" who'd profited from Miss Yates's former work in Boston's red-light district.

"I don't trust that Mr. Callaway of yours." Bonita wrung her hands with concern. "I know you said you knew him—"

"I do know him." Rosamond also knew that her imagination had likely gotten carried away with her on the day of her outing in town with Miles. She couldn't have spotted Arvid Bouchard. She'd merely conjured up his likeness out of fear. She'd turned some unknown mustachioed, thickset stranger into the spitting image of the man she feared most. She'd run from a specter.

Even Miles had bolstered her theory when they'd talked later.

"—but in my experience, men cannot be trusted," Bonita was saying. "Especially men who are willing to care for puppies."

Fondly, Rosamond smiled, reminded of the nighttime visits she and Miles had shared over the past week or so. She'd expected him to abdicate his duties on the evening of their disastrous outing, but Miles hadn't. He'd arrived promptly, carrying a paper-wrapped package from Mr. O'Neil, the butcher.

"For me?" she'd gushed, knowing full well it wasn't.

"If you want it," Miles had said doubtfully. "It's yours."

The meaty bone he'd brought for Riley had been almost as big as she was. The puppy had been delighted, all the same.

Rosamond had found herself softening even further as she'd watched Miles playing with the mutt afterward, too. As silly as it was, his gentleness and patience with her puppy—and his willingness to engage in the charade of comforting it days after the tiny critter had quit whining at night—endeared him to her.

"Mr. Callaway would disagree with you about that supposition," she told Bonita, distractedly tracing circles over the leather-bound face of her account book. "He has several theories about puppies and the people who care for them."

"I'll just bet he does." Bonita frowned. "He's too slick by half. And you're falling head over skirts for him. I can tell."

I am. I have. "It wouldn't matter if I did."

"Humph. That's not a denial."

"I'm sure I don't know what you mean." Rosamond sneaked a glance at the mantel clock. It was nearly time for Miles's nightly visit. Anticipation fluttered through her. "Aside from which, it's not as if you haven't had your share of suitors."

Bonita only grumped. "I like things the way they are."

"You're too picky."

"You're not picky enough."

"I'm not a member of my mutual society," Rosamond pointed out reasonably. "You are. We were supposed to be finding happy lives for everyone, remember? We were supposed to be settling down where the past couldn't catch up with us."

Her friend looked away. "That's all I ever wanted."

"It's all I wanted, too!" Rosamond had known she couldn't hope for more. At least she had...until Miles had arrived.

Once she'd had a chance to think calmly after their outing, she'd understood that Miles had sacrificed a great deal for her. He'd left behind a steady job—even if it was for a ghastly household—a loving family and a horde of giddy housemaids who would have taken up with him in a heartbeat, if he'd asked.

And how had Rosamond repaid him? With threats and suspicion. With drugging and distracting and a pounding of fists. But she'd strived to do better since then, and she had.

"Is that all you still want?" Bonita asked. "It seems like things are changing around here. I don't take kindly to—"

The front door opened. Bonita jerked upright. She stood.

"To what?" Rosamond asked, frowning in bafflement at her friend's abrupt silence and acerbic mood. In the distance, she heard footsteps. "You don't take kindly to what, Bonita?"

It was obvious something was bothering Bonita. If her concerns had to do with doubts about Miles…well, Rosamond knew from her own experience that those doubts might abate with time.

After all, she hadn't asked Miles to call her Rosamond just on a whim. She'd done it because she'd decided to trust him.

There on that dusty street, with her ankle hurting and her pride smarting and her heart still hammering away with the aftereffects of her unreasoning terror, she'd decided to give Miles the benefit of the doubt. Maybe because she'd realized, almost too late, that she'd nearly pushed him too far.

Here's a fair warning. I'm getting fed up with all this.

Miles might be easygoing, but if he reached his breaking point, a team of horses couldn't drag him in a direction he didn't want to go. Rosamond had seen it before back in Boston.

She didn't want to create a similar reaction here.

"I'll say good-night," Bonita blurted. Then, casting a scathing glance at Miles as he entered the parlor, she left.

"Good night!" Rosamond called, puzzled by her behavior.

But then Miles was there, just as he was every night with her lately, looking tall and handsome and dependable and good, and Rosamond simply couldn't sustain her interest in anything except the way his dark hair shone in the lamplight. The way his chiseled features tensed with momentary guardedness when he passed by Bonita. The way his bluer-than-blue eyes lit up when he saw Rosamond waiting there for him on the parlor settee.

His beard was soft, she'd learned on the day she'd hidden away Lucinda and the baby. She'd stroked it during those brief moments when Miles had been insensible. It had been irresponsible of her, at best, but she'd been unable to resist.

"Hmm." He stopped at the foot of the settee to examine her injured ankle, all broad shoulders and big muscles and willingly given competence. He was utterly at her disposal. "You're posed like an injured woman in a refined parlor, but you look like a self-satisfied lion tamer lounging in a lion's den."

"It's interesting you should say so. I have been feeling there's nothing I can't lick lately." Rosamond wondered why Miles's eyes flared with interest at her admission... then decided she was better off not knowing just then. "I guess there's something to be said for confronting your fears. It wasn't easy going to town, but I did it. I'm proud of myself for that."

"You should be." With nimble hands, he tested the swelling in her stocking-clad ankle. His nod suggested he was satisfied with her progress. "You made it through with flying colors."

"That's an overstatement, don't you think so?"

"No." In the midst of adjusting her cool compress to whatever exacting specifications he had in mind, Miles locked his gaze with hers. "I don't. You stood up to your fears—"

"I ran away from them, you mean."

"Before that you stood up," Miles reminded her. "You don't have to be perfect to start traveling in the right direction."

"Yes, I do. I'll settle for nothing less than excellence."

"Then you're going to be disappointed with me," Miles joked as he came to sit on the ottoman opposite her settee. He settled in, earnest and dazzling. "Because I'm chockablock with flaws."

He looked perfect to her. "I don't believe a word of it."

"For instance, I hate tinned peas. That's one flaw."

Rosamond laughed, reminded that they hadn't yet ventured out for another shopping expedition on account of her sore ankle. Miles had been around, though, nonetheless. Owen Cooper had been understanding about Miles's split duties between his livery stable and her ramshackle household. They'd managed to feed Miles capably between repasts at the mutual society and meals shared with the Cooper family. But Miles still needed to outfit his quarters with his own foodstuffs and supplies.

"Still eating Gus Winston's leftovers?" she asked.

"The pictures on the cans look good." Miles made a face. "The vittles inside taste bad. I had half a mind to gnaw on that juicy bone I brought over for Riley. Speaking of that mutt—"

He stopped as Seth broke in, a flustered look on his face. When Seth saw the placid scene in the parlor, he stopped short.

Coolly, Miles looked up. "Is something wrong?"

"The front door was open!" Seth blurted. "I—"

I left it unguarded, was what he didn't need to say.

He caught Rosamond's disapproving look and tried again.

"—I wanted to make sure it was just you, Mr. Callaway," Seth said, "who'd come over for that nightly visit of yours."

Rosamond shook her head. She guessed that Miles had left open the front door as a warning to Seth and was dismayed that such a maneuver had been necessary at all. Lately, her security man just wasn't the dependable protector she knew he could be.

"I'm fine, Seth." Rosamond met his gaze squarely. "Since Mr. Callaway is, as you've pointed out, here to keep me company, everything is fine. This time." Providentially, Arvid Bouchard had been an illusion. But that didn't mean she could relax. "However, if I have to count on random guests to protect me—"

"Stop right there," Miles protested. "I'm not 'random.'"

"—then I might as well reconsider my security needs."

Seth caught her intimation immediately. "Yes, ma'am. I'm awful sorry." He clenched the door frame, clearly torn about something. He yanked his hat brim. "It won't happen again."

"Thank you. See that it doesn't."

Contritely, Seth nodded. He took his leave from the parlor.

In his wake, Miles whistled. "That dressing-down was a sight to behold. Remind me not to make you mad."

Rosamond sighed. "Ordinarily, I wouldn't be so hard on him," she admitted. "But I can't have Seth abandoning his post—especially if he's gambling. I know he's strapped for funds right now, but playing dice is not the way to come up rosy."

"Ask Tobe about that." Miles grinned. "He might disagree."

"Tobe? He's just a child."

"He's a junior sharper, and make no mistake. He might even be the one who's been throwing dice with Seth. Tobe could have turned a tidy profit from Seth by now." Easily, Miles rested his elbows on his knees. "Haven't you met Cade Foster?"

"Judah's brother? Of course I have. He and Violet attended the mutual society's dances early on, before I had a full contingent of members. I invited a few townspeople to sample the services I was offering. The Fosters offered to help me."

"Right. The thing is, Cade's a professional gambler," Miles reminded her. "And Violet and her father watched over Tobe for a while. None of them ever mentioned Tobe's...skills to you?"

"If you're suggesting that child is a miniature swindler—"

"I absolutely am."

"—then you're crazy. I know Tobe's mother. Lucinda Larkin is the sweetest, most kindhearted woman you'll ever meet."

Miles raised his eyebrow. "Good women can raise dastardly sons. Just look at me. My mother is a saint."

"Hmm. I guess I'll consider that a warning."

"I only mean that sometimes people surprise you," Miles said. "For instance, you didn't know that Tobe has a wily way with a pair of dispatchers."

Rosamond angled her head in bewilderment.

"Dispatchers are weighted dice," Miles explained. "They're used to 'dispatch' suckers who risk playing with them."

"Like Seth." Suddenly, Rosamond felt even less

pleased about her security man's gambling. She leveled Miles with a look. "Exactly how do you know all about cheating devices?"

He grinned. "A man has to know these things, or he'll be taken advantage of. Just like a woman has to know all she can about the people she trusts." Miles leaned forward, his tone turning low and intimate…ideal for inviting confidences. "You didn't realize the truth about Tobe, but that's all right. Maybe you haven't known the little knuck and his mother for long."

"I've known them for more than a month!"

"A month? Well, if that's enough for you…" Miles raised his shoulder in a casual shrug. "Who am I to disagree?"

On the verge of opening her mouth to defend herself and her good judgment, Rosamond thought twice. Already Miles had cajoled her into telling him how long she'd known Lucinda. He'd convinced her to confirm that she thought Lucinda was a good person. She could guess—however belatedly—exactly where this conversation was leading.

Miles hadn't forgotten the glimpse he'd had of Lucinda and the baby. He meant to inveigle more information from her.

Purposely, Rosamond nudged her account book off her lap. It landed with a resounding thud on the pineplank flooring.

"Oh dear! Butterfingers." She delivered a coquettish look at Miles—one she'd learned from the ladies who'd become her friends. It was enormously effective at snaring his attention. "Would you mind picking up that ledger for me, please?"

He did. Then he turned it over interestedly.

"Looks well worn." Another eyebrow lift. "Money troubles?"

Whoops. Now she really did have butterfingers. Stupidly, Rosamond hadn't counted on the possibility of Miles's interest.

Eagerly, she tried another round of that flirtatious look.

This time, it had a less predictable effect on Miles.

"If you do have financial worries, you should tell me." He sat on the ottoman again, her account book still held worryingly in his big, clever, capable hands. He stroked its leather spine, noticing all the worn places where she'd rubbed away the finish while studying her uncertain income flow. "Maybe I can help."

"You're a stableman. You can't help."

"Aha. Then you do have financial worries."

Inwardly, Rosamond gnashed her teeth. Why did he have to be so observant? So insightful? So helpful and so…appealing?

A part of her wanted Miles to help. It might be nice to temporarily lay down the burden of responsibility for a change.

The rest of her knew that counting on him would be a mistake. It would only enmesh her with him more thoroughly.

"I thought you had money," Miles remembered. "Elijah Dancy's gambling winnings. You said you took them."

"I did. Along with all the money Genevieve Bouchard paid him to take me out of Boston and off her hands." Defiantly, Rosamond raised her head. "I deserved that money. I combined it with all the similarly ill-gotten gains from all the other ladies, and we came here. Dancy had already purchased this house to be a brothel."

"Well…at least your home is free and clear."

At his wry, optimistic tone, she chuckled. "That's true."

"Mrs. Bouchard said you fell in love with Dancy. She said you ran away in the middle of the night to marry him."

"What?" Rosamond stared. "I would never!"

"I know that." Miles's straightforward gaze met hers. "It devastated me, all the same. Waking up. Finding you gone."

Caught up in his obvious remembered despair, Rosamond shook her head. "I'm sorry. That must have been awful for you."

"It was." Miles stood with her account book in hand. He strode over to place it back on the shelf nearby—a motion that would have relieved her under less guilt-stricken circumstances. When Miles faced her again, he wore a forced smile…doubtless for her benefit. "If I'd known you were flush with gambling winnings and crooked brothel-owner payouts, I would have come sooner."

"You think I would have shared my plunder with you?"

"Of course. Nothing's good with no one to share it with."

Reminded of her earlier despondent thought that she had everything she needed in her Morrow Creek sanctuary except someone to share it with, Rosamond found she could not make another joke. Not about that. It struck too close to home.

"Well, you're about to be disappointed, because most of that swag is long spent," she told Miles. "I've had expenses, investments in lessons and supplies, handouts to members—"

"Handouts?"

"I'm supposed to turn away my needy neighbors?"

Huffily, Rosamond shook her head. "I won't. Anyway, the real problem isn't expenditures. It's income. Plainly put, I don't have any."

"But you require your members to prove that they earn a reputable income."

"That's so they can support a spouse, not so they can pay admission," Rosamond clarified. "I decidedly don't want to give the impression that anyone is paying for companionship here."

Miles nodded, understanding at once. She'd succeeded in distracting him from talking about Lucinda, that was for certain. But in doing so, she'd started a tangled-up conversation that she didn't want to continue. Not tonight.

"I'm not trying to turn a profit," Rosamond explained to Miles as a way to button up this subject. "This endeavor was only supposed to last until the initial group of girls who came west with me found husbands. But then it snowballed. People started coming in from Landslide—from all over. My mutual society took on a life of its own. A life I wasn't ready for."

"Maybe you just need help."

"If you mean you, the ladies won't appreciate that. I mean no offense, Miles, but some of us are wary of 'helpful' men."

She thought of Bonita's past—and her comments tonight—and knew she was right about that. None of them wanted to be beholden to a benefactor. All of them wanted independence.

"I don't mind a bit of struggle," Rosamond assured Miles with a smile. "After all, I come from humble beginnings. It doesn't take much to make me happy. My friends are the same."

"If you're saying I should be content to watch you scrape by, worrying and praying..." Miles frowned. "I won't. Not ever. You deserve more than that, Rosamond. You deserve…everything."

"Pish posh." She waved. "It's not as dire as all that."

He didn't give in. "But it is serious."

"It's none of your concern."

"Everything about you is my concern. I care about you."

"I…" She hauled in a deep breath, wanting this conversation done. "I care about you, too." Of course she did. She always had. Her feelings had only intensified after Miles had followed her to Morrow Creek. "But that doesn't mean you're supposed to—"

Catching sight of the uncommon look on Miles's face, Rosamond stopped. She tilted her head, feeling baffled.

"Are you all right? You look…unusual."

He looked, it occurred to her, markedly loopy. He looked the way he had while gawking at her, euphoric on laudanum, the day they'd first met in her parlor. It felt very long ago now.

He managed a crooked smile. "You care about me."

Oh. That. Filled with joy at the truth of it, Rosamond smiled at him. Trying to tamp down her feelings, she nodded.

"Of course I do." That was an understatement. "I do. We've been friends for a long time, haven't we? Friends care about—"

"Say it again." He didn't seem bothered by her last-minute attempt to present her feelings for him as merely friendly.

She inhaled, slightly giddy, knowing her feelings weren't merely friendly…but unable to risk more. "I care about you."

Miles's grin could have lit the room. "One more time?"

"You're so demanding."

"I'm not certain I heard you."

"Then maybe I should come closer." Wanting to laugh with sheer hopefulness and audacity, Rosamond swiveled on the settee. She leaped to her feet, knowing there was only one thing that would truly convince him. She hurried all the way until she stood toe-to-toe with Miles. She looked up at him. "I care about you."

Gruffly, he said, "I care about you, too."

Their exchange was a drastic understatement, given all they'd been through together. Still, joyfulness stretched between them, warm with familiarity and alive with the possibility of something more. For so long now, she and Miles had danced around the notion of being together. Romantically being together. But tonight, with so many secrets already shed...

Rosamond found herself feeling positively liberated.

"I might need to hear you say that again," she said.

"I care about you, Rosamond. You're in my heart all the time."

"Well." It wasn't quite a formal love declaration, but it was near enough. Pleased, she blinked back a few incipient happy tears. "Isn't that the most romantic thing I've ever heard."

"Wait until I get started."

"I doubt my mutual society members could do better."

"I know they couldn't do better."

"In fact, I reckon that statement might deserve a fitting reward of some kind." Feeling her belly somersault with delight, Rosamond put her hands on Miles's sturdy chest. Bravely, she stroked him, feeling the warmth of him through his shirtfront.

His eyebrow rose rakishly. "A reward? From you?"

Rosamond nodded. She looked at his mouth. She liked it.

Miles's tone became suspicious. "If this is some sort of premembership test designed to gauge whether I can acquit myself with honor…" His gaze roved over her face, full of affection and yearning. "Damnation. I don't think I can hurdle it."

She smiled. "It's not a test. You're already honorable." Rosamond knew that as surely as she knew her courage in this matter would never feel more robust. "That's why I can do this."

Before Miles could protest, she took aim, used her palms on his chest for leverage, then lifted herself to his level. Carefully, she pressed her lips to his. Once. Then again.

"Mmm." She flexed her fingers against his shirtfront, holding herself a little steadier. "Interesting."

A hoarse exhalation escaped him. "Interesting?"

"I like it. I like kissing. Your mouth is soft and your lips are nice." Daringly, Rosamond reached up to stroke his beard. "Your beard and mustache are a little tickly, though."

"I'll shave right now. I'll borrow a razor from Dylan." Miles made a comedic face. "I doubt Judah or Seth shave yet."

Rosamond didn't care about her protectors or their potential lack of maturity just then. She gazed up at Miles wonderingly. "It seems a bit intrusive, though. Kissing you does. I'm not sure—"

"Believe me, I want you to do it."

"You sound convincing."

"There's only one way to find out."

Rosamond knew what he meant. Musingly, she tried again.

This time, Miles kissed her back. He caught her head

in his palm and held her close, and he kissed her back, very sweetly.

She leaned away, feeling starry-eyed. "That was…"

"Nice?"

"Better than before. I like that we're doing it together."

His gaze darkened. "I would never force myself on you. I swore I'd never hurt you, and I meant it. So if you mean—"

"I don't mean anything of the kind. If you're thinking about me and Mr. Bouchard, please don't." Rosamond shook her head. "What he did to me was an attack. It was violence, plain and simple." She looked away, shaking her head, finally feeling crystal clear on the issue. "It wasn't what people think. It wasn't what Mrs. Bouchard thought. It wasn't like this, between us. It wasn't gentleness, and it wasn't you." She couldn't help adding, "It was barely even me. The whole time, I was scarcely there. I was scarcely myself." She looked up at Miles, grateful and resilient. "I'm starting to come back together now, though."

"I wish you hadn't gone through that at all." Sounding remorseful, Miles stroked her hair. He brought her closer, cradling her against his chest. "I'm so sorry, Rosamond. I'm sorry I didn't know. I'm sorry I didn't help you! If I had—"

"It's all right. You're here now." She savored his embrace, loving its warmth. Its closeness. Its burgeoning and bewitching familiarity. "That's all that matters, isn't it?"

"No." Miles looked murderous. "Retribution matters, too."

"Stop. I won't hear of it."

"I mean it. If Bouchard were here right now—"

"That name is banned from here." Her tone allowed no argument. Miles tried anyway. She kissed him to make him stop.

He did stop. Kissing, she realized, was a handy argument winner. Thus distracted, Miles quit talking almost immediately.

"I'm still sorry," he slipped in hastily afterward.

"Stop!" Rosamond insisted. She gave him another kiss.

"I don't ever want to leave you again," he went on.

Another kiss. "No one is asking you to. I like that you're here. I like seeing you every night." She saw him open his mouth to add another rebuttal and triumphed by kissing him before he could. She was truly starting to enjoy this. "I like you."

"I like you. I've dreamed of you. My Rose."

He stroked her face, then pulled her nearer with his other arm. It felt almost like dancing…only better. It was better because Rosamond didn't need to think about keeping time or practicing the correct steps or begrudging the moment when the music stopped. All she had to do was be in Miles's arms.

"You're very handsome," she said. "I've always thought so."

"Humph. You hid it well enough."

"What?" Eyes wide, Rosamond pretended to be outraged. She couldn't sustain it. She smiled at him. She cupped his dark bearded jaw in her hand, intimately, just because she could. "I couldn't hide a thing. Didn't you see me blushing? Stammering? Tripping over my own feet every time you came near me?"

"I thought you were just clumsy."

"Miles!"

"I liked it. I liked you. I wanted to tell you—"

A confirming nod. "You should have told me."

"But I didn't have enough for you. Not by far." Miles glanced at the parlor's shadowy interior, undoubtedly blind to its fancy furnishings just then. "I couldn't give you the secure life you wanted. I couldn't take care of you."

"I don't need to be taken care of. I can manage."

It was true, Rosamond realized with a start. She could take care of herself. She'd been doing so for more than a year.

She didn't have to be afraid. She was strong. Despite the mistakes she'd made and the regrets she had, she was strong. She had Miles partly to thank for helping her remember that.

Feeling practically invincible now, Rosamond turned Miles's face to meet hers again. She needed to tell him something more. "I'm sorry I left you behind. I thought it was for the best."

"I'm sorry, too. Otherwise, we could have gotten here sooner." He dropped his gaze to her mouth. "Together."

She grinned. "By 'together,' do you mean 'kissing'?"

His eloquent gaze lifted to hers. "When you kiss me," Miles confessed, "it feels as if everything is right in the world."

There was nothing Rosamond could say to argue with that.

"Then let me give you the world," she offered, broadening her smile. She brought her mouth to his again. The whole room spun. "I think kissing makes me dizzy," she murmured.

"Hold on to me," Miles instructed. "Don't let go."

Rosamond never wanted to let go. She did hold on to Miles, even as he lowered his head, even as he pulled her closer, even as he delivered the first kiss he'd initiated between them.

It was gentle. It was full of caring. It was…

"It's as if you love me…with your mouth!" she exclaimed when they'd parted. She brought her fingers to her lips, feeling astonished and moved and very, very reassured. "I was worried that I'd be afraid, when it came right down to it. Afraid of this, of us, of being together. But now that we're here…"

She knew this was like nothing she'd ever experienced.

"I'll stop if you want me to." Miles seemed concerned. Also a little dreamy-eyed for such a big, strong man. She couldn't believe she affected him that way. "I don't want to push you."

"You're not. I'm the one who kissed you first, remember?"

"Besides," Miles continued, adding a scoundrelly lilt to his brogue, "I am loving you with my mouth. It's trying to say what my poor addled stableman's brain can't manage. Like this."

He cradled her jaw in his hands, then tilted her face upward. A heartbeat later, his mouth met hers. Gently, his tongue traced the seam of her lips. Willingly, Rosamond parted them. The kiss that followed nearly made her melt against him.

At her swoony reaction, Miles smiled. "You are innocent, Rose. You're innocent to genuine feeling. To gentleness. To love. You deserve to know what that's like. If I can show you—"

"If you keep on talking, I won't be able to concentrate on what it feels like." She smiled, too. "Let's try again."

"I'm pleased to indulge you." Miles kissed her. Expertly.

Rosamond frowned. "Have you kissed very many women?"

"None who mattered. Until you."

"Come on now, Miles. You did not become so skilled at kissing without having a little practice, did you?"

"I became skilled because I became inspired. By you."

"Oh. That sounds nice." She felt her cheeks heat as she blushed. "Miss Yates was right about you. You are a charmer."

Rather than agree, Miles kissed her. That was when she realized that the conversationally diverting qualities of a kiss could serve him as readily as they had her. Caught up in Miles's arms, in his next kiss, in the soft, low moan he gave as their mouths opened and then came together in an even more erotic fashion, sweetly and wetly and stirringly, Rosamond found that she couldn't dredge up a solitary sensible thought. All she could do was kiss Miles back…and then hope for more.

Or abandon waiting and use Miles's shirtfront as a pulley to draw herself upward, taking more for herself. Mmm. Kissing…

"Oh! I've manhandled you. Is that all right?" Suddenly worried at her own unthinking boldness, Rosamond smoothed Miles's wrinkly shirt. "Are you all right? Did I hurt you?"

"Hurt me?" His chuckle reassured her. "It hurt more to wait for you to kiss me than to have you climbing all over me that way." He gave her a twinkly-eyed grin, deepening her blush. "You're an agile climber, that's for sure. In fact—"

He broke off, head tilted, giving her a suspicious look.

"In fact, I'd swear you never hurt your ankle at all."

"Uh…" Trapped, Rosamond fidgeted. Maybe she could bluff her way through? She brightened. "Your kiss must have fixed it!"

Miles did not appear convinced.

"You are terribly handy at fixing things, Miles."

"Not that handy, I'm not. A few minutes ago, I distinctly recall you throwing aside your foot-propping pillows, getting up from the settee and practically galloping over here."

"That proves it!" Elaborately, she waved. "It's a miracle!"

"All of that happened before I kissed you."

"A...preemptive miracle?" Rosamond shook her head, pretending to be immensely impressed. "My, you are powerful, aren't you?"

"Mmm-hmm." Miles crossed his arms. "While I am powerful—"

Oh, good. Her flattery was working. Maybe because it was very close to the truth. That made it especially persuasive.

"—and every man likes to believe his kisses can work miracles, I don't think that's what's going on in this case."

"You don't?"

"No."

"Hmm." Rosamond gave up. "Well, I wonder where Riley is."

She disentangled herself from Miles—for she truly had all but climbed his body in a quest to get closer to him—and crossed the parlor. Idly, she stacked her foot-propping pillows into a corner of the settee, the better to forget what she'd been using them for. She bent over, pretending to search for her puppy.

"That's a very alluring pose," Miles said from behind her, his voice louder as he neared her, "but I won't be deterred."

"I'm sure I don't know what you're talking about." Rosamond straightened, breathlessly patting her chignon. "Do you think Riley might be in the kitchen finishing off that bone?"

"You were playacting, Rosamond."

"I swear, that puppy has slept so much better since—"

"How long has your ankle felt better?" Miles asked.

"Was it healed that very night, or did it take until the next day?"

"Be serious, Miles. Why would I pretend to be hurt?"

"To avoid going to town with me again."

Yes. There was that. Disinclined to admit as much, Rosamond employed another tactic. "I think we should try more kissing."

His gaze sparked with interest. Still, "Tell me the truth."

"That is the truth! I do enjoy kissing you."

His mouth crooked with a satisfied smile. But Miles was nothing if not persistent. "We're going out again tomorrow."

"I'm so sorry, but I'll have to give you my regrets. My mutual society has a poetry recital tomorrow afternoon."

"We'll go in the morning."

"I have a members-only literary meeting then."

"You might be obliged to miss it."

"I'm not sure if Miss Yates would agree to replace me."

"Do you remember what I told you about my patience wearing thin?"

Exasperated, Rosamond faced him. "I don't want to go. The first time might have been a fluke. This time, I might die."

"You won't die."

"Or keel over! Or scream or lose control or run away."

Any number of awful things might happen to her.

"We'll go as many times as you need. I'll be there."

"Why would you do that for the woman who purposely misled you about her injured ankle? Maybe I'm not worth it."

"You're worth it."

"Maybe I'll refuse." She crossed her arms. "I do refuse."

Miles came closer. His expression appeared dangerously attractive. How did he manage to keep doing that?

"After we finish shopping, I'll show you my quarters at Owen Cooper's livery stable," Miles promised. "We'll be alone. I'll let you stroke my beard just as much as you want to."

Oh dear. Her eyes widened. "You knew about that?"

He shrugged. "It was all I could do to hold still."

Rosamond whirled around, deeply embarrassed. She'd thought he was conked out cold when she'd touched him. Why had she had to indulge her fascination with Miles's beard? Why?

"Also," he said, "I'll let you kiss me just as much as you want to. You can kiss me all over my face. Whatever you like."

At that, some small, traitorous part of her perked up.

"You will? As much as I want to?" Contemplatively, she eyed him. "What if I wear out your lips? I can be very curious."

"So can I."

"That doesn't answer my question."

"You won't wear out my lips." Smiling, Miles pulled her into his arms again. "But I'd like to see you try. I'm yours, Rose. Now and forever."

Despite being on the cusp of losing her fight not to go outside again, Rosamond couldn't help sighing. She liked that Miles allowed her to be in charge. It reassured her mightily.

"You're a hard man to say no to, Miles."

"Then say yes, Rose. Just say yes. And kiss me again, too."

Gladly, Rosamond did. For now, she had everything she needed. Just as long as Miles didn't snoop around too very much...

Chapter Eleven

It took a while, but Miles truly began to believe he was helping Rosamond. Every day they met at the mutual society. Every day they followed the same street into town, walking hand in hand. Every day Rosamond managed to linger just a little longer there in town, walking up and down Morrow Creek's raised-plank sidewalks and chatting with the townspeople she knew.

Right alongside her, Miles got to know Marcus Copeland, the lumber-mill owner, out on an errand to advertise for workers in the *Pioneer Press*. He got to know rancher Everett Bannon and his intrepid journalist wife, Nellie Trent Bannon. He got to know Thomas Walsh, the newspaper's editor, and his ladylove, Mellie Reardon. He met schoolmarm Sarah, the wife of jovial blacksmith Daniel McCabe, and several members of Grace Murphy's ladies' baseball league, too, including her three sisters-in-law who'd arrived from the States. He encountered Judah's brother, Cade Foster, and his wife, Violet. He even met the reclusive and wealthy Griffin Turner, owner of the Lorndorff Hotel, who was fixing to start up a newer and even fancier hotel in town.

"I think that's nearly everyone in this part of the territory," Miles told Rosamond as they parted from Turner. He watched the hotel magnate stride away, his unforgettable visage lifted to the sun. Miles faced Rosamond again. "Everyone except for Jedediah Hofer."

"The mercantile owner?" Busily, Rosamond strode down the sidewalk, arm in arm with Miles as she glanced into the windows of the shops he hadn't yet been able to encourage her to enter. "Mr. Hofer is a lot like most mercantile owners. Aproned. Businesslike. Constantly sweeping the front steps of his shop."

Miles refused to be deterred. "I still need supplies."

Rosamond balked. "But I'll be trapped in there! The mercantile is crowded. It's full of people and packed wall to wall with merchandise. If I feel an attack coming on—"

"Maybe you won't."

"—I won't have anyplace to go. Everyone will see what's happening to me. I'll be even more gossiped about than when I came to town—and that's saying a lot, given that I was taking over a supposed brothel with a passel of attractive ladies."

"It's not as bad as all that." Miles tipped his hat to a passing group of parasol-toting women. They tittered, then entered the apothecary shop. "It's far worse for you. No one else can tell what's happening. We'll go in for only a minute."

"Wouldn't you rather meet Olivia Mouton?" Clearly having been struck by that idea just that instant, Rosamond clutched his arm. She attempted to steer him toward the Lorndorff. "Her father manages the hotel. She's engaged to Griffin Turner, but if there's any man who can turn her head anyway, it's you."

"That's very loyal of you, but I don't want to meet Miss Mouton. I want to take you into the mercantile.

I want to buy flour and pans and at least two spoons. I want to scoop out about ten pounds of crackers from the barrel. If I'm feeling especially optimistic, I might even buy a tin of beans."

"Olivia Mouton is the prettiest girl in Morrow Creek."

"I heard Adeline Wilson was the prettiest girl in town."

Rosamond waved off that assertion. "Depends who you ask."

"Either way, that's got nothing to do with our up-coming visit to the mercantile." Miles sighted its store-front a few yards off and veered them straight toward it. "There it is."

"Yes, it does! You'll see Olivia Mouton's image at Hofer's mercantile, but you'll see the woman herself at the hotel."

Her tone suggested that doing so would be a treat beyond compare. "I'm hardly going to gawk at a stranger, Rosamond."

"We could be discreet. We could have tea!"

He thought about it. Rosamond was dogged, he'd give her that. "Why would we see Miss Mouton's image at the mercantile?"

"Her picture is lithographed onto every single bottle of Milky White Complexion Beautifier and Youthful Enhancement Tonic. It's a bestseller all over the world. She's famous!"

Miles hesitated, trying to make sense of a town that was packed with so many unlikely types of people. All of them seemed to like Rosamond, though. He found that encouraging. Maybe her future here was brighter than he'd originally envisioned.

"Well, then, I have to see that tonic bottle." Tenaciously, Miles steered Rosamond onward. "Look at that. We're here."

Undoubtedly unhappy that her diversionary tactics hadn't worked, Rosamond bit her lip. Appearing full of foreboding, she stared up at the mercantile's hand-painted sign. Its flourish-filled font and colorful background didn't seem to reassure her.

Glumly, she said, "There won't be any cups of tea here."

As if that was the worst part of coming there. With empathy, Miles studied her. He knew this was difficult for Rosamond. He also knew that she was up to the challenge.

"Remember, as soon as you've spent at least five minutes in a shop and purchased something, we'll go back to the livery stable. I'll show you my quarters. You can kiss me plenty."

Her eager-to-delay gaze shifted to collide with his. "That's a fine idea. Let's just do that right now, shall we?"

Miles wanted that more than anything. But he hadn't been convinced Rosamond had. So he hadn't thought she'd call him on his bluff. He'd been having a few second thoughts about it.

Dangling the promise of uninhibited kissing in front of her as an incentive was one thing. Fulfilling it was another.

"Aren't you worried about ruining your reputation?"

"Aren't you?"

"Women have finer, more valuable reputations to protect."

"Not me. I'm a potentially scandalous widow. Besides, I've been nothing but full of decorum ever since I came here. It's time to benefit from the goodwill and virtue I've built up." Still looking panicky, Rosamond reexamined the mercantile sign. She gave an unconvincing airy wave.

"I'll tell everyone I'm helping you bring in supplies. No one will think twice. I'm unimpeachable."

"I'm not."

"You're dawdling."

"You're trying to sidetrack me." Pointedly, Miles nodded at Hofer's sign. "We have to go inside for a while first."

"No." Very politely, Rosamond added, "Thank you, though."

Shakily, she turned. He stopped her. He put his hand under her chin, then tipped up her trepidation-filled face to his.

"Please don't give up. Don't let Bouchard win."

Rosamond's expression turned steely. "I haven't given up. I've been here every day, haven't I? I've spent longer and longer in town. Every time I try, I succeed a little more."

Patiently, Miles went on watching her. He nodded.

A long moment passed. Rosamond's face scrunched up.

"Ah, I see what you've done there." Her expression eased into a grin. "You tricked me into giving myself a pep talk."

"I'm getting a little hoarse after all the ones I've given lately," he teased. "I don't mind giving you a turn."

"I see. Well, I can't very well contradict myself, can I?"

"It would be very unlike you if you did."

"Then I guess I'm going in." Shifting him another anxious look, Rosamond straightened. She clutched her woven shopping basket's handle. "If I do this, will you quit pestering me?"

"If you do this," Miles assured her in a low, private tone, "I'll kiss you all over…just as much as you want me to."

That stopped her. Her cheeks turned pink. Her mouth made an O. She seemed almost as perplexed by the notion of being kissed all over as she'd been a second ago by his wrangling to get her to encourage herself. It was evident that Rosamond had no experience in real lovemaking—no concept of how remarkable it could be between two people who truly cared for one another.

Damn Arvid Bouchard for stealing that from her. Miles almost wished his former employer had come to Morrow Creek, just so he could make the man pay for hurting Rose the way he had.

Then Miles realized that Rosamond had finally divined what he meant. Her blush spread all the way to her neck. But her shaking stopped. So did her breathlessness. She leaned nearer.

"All over?" she asked in a quiet voice. "Really?"

Hellfire. She seemed entirely...thrilled by the idea.

Miles swallowed hard. He wished he hadn't kicked up this naughty conversation in such a public place. Beset by thoughts of himself kissing Rosamond's mouth, her neck, her breasts and her belly and her knees and every-place in between, he felt himself ache. For a heartbeat, he couldn't speak at all.

Manfully, he cleared his throat. He nodded. "Really."

"Well, then. I think I might like that. I can pretty well imagine what that might be like." She gave a pert nod. "Have I ever told you what an extraordinary imagination I have?"

Sweet heaven. If she kept on talking like that—looking like that—he was the one who might die. From unfulfilled longing and unrequited desire. Didn't Rosamond know how she affected him?

When she was nearby, it felt as if Miles was better than he'd ever been. Then she tempted him to kiss her...

and all his better intentions flew out the window. He simply needed her.

"No." He shifted. "I don't think you told me that."

"Yes. Well, I do." A nod. "My imagination is as big as the territorial sky, and it's broadening every second, thanks to you." She delivered him a chiding look. "Why didn't you say all-over kissing was an option before?" Appearing emphatically revived, Rosamond gave him an eager smile. "Let's get cracking."

It was at that instant that Miles finally realized he'd underestimated her again. Rosamond McGrath Dancy was nothing if not full of surprises for him. He loved that about her.

He loved her. Because of that, he'd do anything.

Even stand in a crowded mercantile with a headful of ribald thoughts and a heart full of need and a soul full of secrets.

Rosamond caught him dawdling on the sidewalk moments after she'd already sailed inside. She doubled back to haul him in after her. "Come on, slowpoke! We've got shopping to do!"

Lord help him. Rosamond had fully set her sights on him.

He had no chance at all to defend himself now.

It didn't take Rosamond long to realize that she'd made a terrible mistake. One minute, she was strolling along, just one of many nearly shoulder-to-shoulder customers inside Mr. Hofer's mercantile, feeling blithe and authoritative and absolutely ready to just get finished with her shopping and get on with kissing Miles…or with having him kiss her in that intriguing all-over way he'd mentioned. The next minute, she was seized by a powerful wave of lightheadedness and fear. Just like always.

She knew she was doomed. Now. Again. Forever and ever.

She'd been a fool to think she could force her way through this. She'd been a fool to leave her nice safe sanctuary.

The mercantile darkened precipitously around her. Rosamond grabbed a pickle barrel, feeling wobbly. Her heartbeat kicked up. Her mind raced. Her throat closed, giving her the simultaneously heartening and terrifying thought that at least she wouldn't embarrass herself by screaming at the top of her lungs.

Miles saw her stop. He was beside her in an instant.

"Just breathe," he instructed, taking hold of her hand. "Don't think about what might happen. Just breathe with me."

Ludicrously, he demonstrated for her. Making sure she was watching, Miles inhaled mightily. He blew out that breath while puffing his cheeks, his gaze holding calm and steady on hers.

It might have been silly to demonstrate something as elementary as breathing, but Rosamond felt grateful, all the same. Miles's presence—and his breathing— anchored her amidst a sea of emotions and fears and noise and thoughts and dizziness.

She clutched his hand for dear life, then breathed in.

Her first inhalation helped. Her second was even better.

Dimly, Rosamond began to feel calmer. Then, hopeful.

Instantly, as though in punishment for her paltry success, a heat wave overtook her. Her body broke out in a sweat. Her hands trembled. Her knees shook. This wasn't working. It wasn't.

"I can't." Rosamond shook her head. "I have to leave."

"You are," Miles disagreed with his usual contrariness. "You're here and you're holding steady, just like always."

"No, I'm not. Most of the time I run away. Or I don't come in the first place." She eyed him doubtfully. "I know what you're trying to do. You can't distract me with an argument."

He lowered his gaze to her mouth. Tellingly.

"Or with thoughts of kissing, either," she added shakily.

Although the idea did have merit, she found. Her terror eased a fraction as she considered it. That was encouraging.

Someone nudged her from the side. Rosamond jumped, holding back a strangled shriek of alarm. Frustrated, she grit her teeth. She stared up at Miles in consternation. "When will this end? I'm doing all I can, but this feeling is still there."

"What feeling?"

"That something awful is going to happen to me."

"I see." Miles nodded. "What does it feel like?"

"Like impending doom. What do you imagine it would feel like?" She hauled in another breath, detecting the familiar scents of pickling brine, dried meat, crackers and tobacco and vaguely musty fabric. "I can't explain it. It's just there."

"So are you. You're still here. You're all right."

She scoffed. But Miles had a point. Grudgingly, Rosamond admitted it. "I haven't crashed to the floor yet, if that's what you mean. I guess I ought to have a party to celebrate."

He smiled. "That's the Rose I know." He squeezed her hand again, ignoring the inquisitive onlookers who passed them while coming and going from the mercantile. Miles behaved as if they were all alone. "Do you still feel shaky? Dizzy? Queasy?"

"If you're trying to bring on those symptoms—"

"I'm not. I'm trying to make you see that you can survive them. Nobody ever died from a little sweatiness."

"Glowingness, I'll have you know." She wanted to withdraw her hand from his but didn't dare. Not yet. "And I resent your implication that what's happening to me isn't serious."

"You think I'm belittling you?"

"Only because you sound as if you're making fun of me."

"Never. I'm not." To prove it, Miles put his free hand on his heart. His repentant expression drew stares and knowing nudges from Mrs. Sunley and Mrs. Archer, two die-hard romantics and two of Morrow Creek's most meddlesome matchmakers, who were shopping nearby. Paying no attention to them, Miles peered in thought at Rosamond. "Maybe if you try to withstand how you're feeling for long enough, it will go away on its own."

If Rosamond's throat hadn't felt so parched, she would have used it to laugh outright at that. "What makes you think that?"

"I'm hoping the same strategy will work for me. To vanquish the feeling I have that I might die without you in my arms."

Oh. That pulled her up short. Rosamond eased her grip on the pickle barrel a little. "You do have a way with words."

"It's a family trait, passed down through the generations. Like blue eyes and stubbornness." He grinned, proving both those assertions in a single go. "So…are you game to try?"

"I'm not sure. Have we already been here for five minutes?"

If they had, she could escape this situation and still fulfill Miles's harebrained requirements…if she somehow found the wherewithal to make a purchase from Mr. Hofer first.

Rosamond's spirits sank. She couldn't possibly accomplish a retail interaction in the state she was in. But she wanted to experience that special kissing Miles had talked about before.

"Fine." Rosamond relented. "What do I have to do?"

She could always search for a getaway route while Miles formulated and described whatever plan he had in mind. It was always good, Rosamond reasoned, to have a secondary plan ready.

"First," he coached her, "close your eyes."

"Here? In the mercantile?" She shook her head. "I'll look like a lunatic." Although given the state she was already in…

Cooperatively but skeptically, Rosamond closed her eyes.

"Now, feel your heart racing. Is it racing?"

"Are you trying to make it race harder?"

"No." Miles held her hand. "But is it?"

"Yes. My heart is racing. I'm afraid it's going to overtax itself. You know that Doc Finney says we only have so many heartbeats in a lifetime, don't you? If I use up all mine now, I'll have less of them to spend later, with you."

Miles went silent. Possibly—if she didn't die now—he was savoring the notion of being together with her in the future.

She hoped he was savoring the notion of being together.

Then, "Don't make up a story about how awful it

is," he suggested. "Just feel it. Really feel it. Feel it and trust me."

She frowned. "Are people gawking at me yet?"

A second passed. Then, "They're all too busy shopping."

That was a relief, at least. Rosamond turned her attention to her pounding heart. She concentrated as hard as she could.

To her surprise, her thundering heart slowed a little.

Astonished, she opened her eyes. "It's better!"

Miles smiled, too. "How about your breathing?"

"I haven't thought about it for at least a minute or two." It was a verifiable wonder. "My breathing is much better."

"Good. Do you still feel unsteady?"

Tentatively, Rosamond let go of the pickle barrel. She waited to see if she'd crumple and prove Miles's theory wrong.

Honestly, she did feel a little shaky still. But as soon as she paid attention to that feeling—instead of thinking about how dire it was and worrying about how much worse it might become—her shakiness began to subside. Full of relief, Rosamond smiled.

"Maybe I'm not going to die today!" Or anytime soon, either.

"Maybe you're not." Smiling, Miles went on supporting her. "Maybe all the times you've come to town, over and over again with me, have gotten you more ready than you knew. You're not trembling anymore, either. Are you too hot? Too cold?"

As hard as she could, Rosamond considered how she felt.

She felt…as though the worst had passed. Her dress, dampened by perspiration, still stuck to her underarms. Strands of hair clung to her rapidly cooling neck. But her dizziness had gone. Her pressing sense of imminent doom had faded, too.

"I'm fine." Jubilantly, Rosamond realized it was true. She was fine. For months now, she'd feared this happening. She'd feared having her bizarre malady's symptoms overtake her in a place she couldn't escape from. But now that they had—now that she'd come successfully through the other side of it all—she felt perfectly well. "I could dance another victory jig!"

"Another victory jig?" Miles raised his eyebrow. "That's what that was? The other day? At your house?"

"Of course. I was happy to have beaten you."

"Beaten me?" He seemed baffled. "In what contest?"

In the contest of whether I could distract you from Lucinda and the baby, Rosamond recollected too late. Whoops.

Why did she keep letting down her guard with Miles?

Easy. Because she loved him, a part of her replied, and Rosamond knew that was true. She did love Miles. She'd loved him in Boston and she loved him now—not least of all because he'd stood by her and helped her through her frightening experience.

Nonchalantly, she waved away his lingering question, hoping he wouldn't pursue it more diligently. "All this time, I've been accidentally making things worse, not better, for myself," Rosamond confided. "All this time, I've been running away—even when I was at home, safe behind my gate and my protectors."

"You were only doing what you thought you had to."

She nodded. "What I felt each time was so real. So scary!" Rosamond shook her head, growing curious about her situation. "I just knew I had to take it seriously. Intense feelings like those couldn't just exist for no reason,

I thought." Idly, she moved aside to let someone pass. "But now I'm wondering…"

"You're wondering whether the ten pounds of crackers I want will fit in that little basket of yours?" Jokingly, Miles nodded toward another nearby barrel. "I enjoy a good cracker."

Lightheartedly, Rosamond grinned. "Now I'm wondering if maybe sometimes feelings do come over a person. Like memories do. Like the weather does. After all, rain isn't a problem on its own…unless you're worried about ruining your brand-new shoes. It's all in what you tell yourself, isn't it?"

Miles shrugged. "I'm just a stableman. All I know is that you look like you've put down a hundred-pound load someplace."

"I have." Proudly, Rosamond straightened. Thanks to Miles's steadfastness—thanks to her own resiliency and willingness to trust in him—she felt stronger than ever. "If this problem tries to sneak up and ambush me later, I'll know exactly what to do."

"You'll let me help you. That's what you'll do."

"You might not be there."

"I'll damn well be there."

Rosamond pacified Miles with a pat to his brawny arm. "But if you're not, I'll know I can handle things myself."

"You won't have to handle things yourself." Miles frowned, seeming gravely perturbed. "Why do you keep saying you'll have to handle things by yourself? I'll be there!"

"Of course you will. But if you're not—"

A mutinous scowl was Miles's only reply this time.

"—I'll just borrow your effective technique of thinking about what's actually happening instead of telling myself a terrible story about what I'm scared might happen."

He perked up. "That was my idea. It worked, too."

She loved it when Miles showed off his confidence and manliness. On him, those qualities were a natural fit.

"I reckon your dizzy spells are just another outcome of that oversize imagination you mentioned having." Miles steered her assuredly toward the cracker barrel, seeming doubly determined now to get into it. "Maybe if you apply your fanciful thoughts to other areas, you'll feel a lot better."

"'Other areas'? Such as?"

"Such as me. You. Us, together, putting away the twenty pounds of crackers I aim to buy just as soon as you quit dawdling and step up to Mr. Hofer's counter."

"I see. And after we've stowed your provisions?"

"I believe you can recall our plans for after that."

"Yes." Rosamond could. She recalled that those plans were meant to involve kissing and closeness and all-over love. Wholly unbidden, a smile came to her face. "I can. I can hardly wait."

Chapter Twelve

While in the mercantile with Rosamond, Miles had realized two important things. First, that Rosamond had known darn well that he'd seen Lucinda Larkin and that unaccounted-for baby at her house, because she'd all but gloated over having distracted him from his glimpse of them. Second, that Rosamond had grown even braver and stronger than he'd expected her to—and in a very short time, too. She wouldn't need to close herself off behind her locked doors and security men and secrecy for much longer.

He was glad he'd been able to help her break free.

That afternoon, after they left Hofer's mercantile, there was no sign of the woman he'd first encountered in Morrow Creek—the woman who was self-possessed but wary, direct but hidden away, intelligent but afraid. That afternoon, a transformed Rosamond McGrath Dancy left the mercantile as a woman who could handle anything that life and its vagaries could throw at her.

For proof of it, Miles only had to watch her move.

"Well, I think that's that." Smartly, Rosamond strode across Miles's quarters at Owen Cooper's livery stable, looking for all the world as if she owned the place.

"All your purchases are safely stowed away. Except the crackers, of course. All twenty pounds wouldn't fit your cupboards, so you'd better get eating." With a smile to accompany her teasing exaggeration of his love of crackers—because they'd only purchased two pounds, not an outrageous twenty—Rosamond took in his living area, his corner kitchen, his narrow bed with its two piled-up pillows and neatly spread coverlet. "You've kept things tidy here. I approve."

He approved of the way she looked just then, all auburn hair and sparkly eyes and unconquerable demeanor. In her calico dress and high-button shoes, Rosamond was the very image of a proper lady. But in her sidelong mischievous glances and willingness to "accidentally" brush against him as they put away tinned beans and cornmeal, Rosamond was one hundred percent alluring woman. She knew what she wanted. It involved those kisses he'd promised her. Kisses that would roam all over her body…

No. He'd better not think about that now, Miles admonished himself. Otherwise, he'd prove a very poor host for Rosamond's first visit to his new home. He wanted her to feel comfortable.

"I trained a long time to be a stableman. I learned that everything has its proper place." Miles shrugged. "Plus, Mrs. Cooper comes up here sometimes for a visit with Élodie and the baby. She brings me things she's baked when she wants to test a recipe. I don't want this place to look a mess when she does."

"Yes, I understand Mrs. Cooper is a marvelous cook." Languidly, Rosamond traced her hand over the arched back of his kitchen chair. "Her cookery books are sold all over. Poor Mr. Nickerson can't even keep those volumes in stock at his shop."

"I can see why. Her baking rivals Molly Copeland's."

"Mmm. That's certainly saying something." Rosamond fiddled with her hair, drawing Miles's attention to the elegant curve of her neck, the slender gracefulness of her arm…the feminine curve of her bosom. He doubted she knew the nature of his thoughts. "I imagine little Élodie and the Coopers' baby daughter must adore you, just the way all the children in my household do."

"I reckon they do." In truth, those adorable little girls' adoration of Miles held no bounds. When they came to his quarters, Élodie wasted no time requesting piggyback rides, proclaiming that Gus had been "too old" to indulge her. The baby, Fleur, only drooled and babbled and grinned, but Miles imagined that she was crazy about him, too. "Fleur hasn't been too happy lately, since her first tooth started coming in."

Rosamond gave him a distracted glance. She licked her lips, inciting in Miles an urge to taste her lips. Very, very slowly.

Damnation. Why was he rambling on about baby teeth?

Why, when Rosamond looked so pretty and so inviting…when she seemed so hell-bent on testing his strength of character?

Aha. That was it. Because Miles still wasn't convinced this visit wasn't some sort of test designed to gauge his resolve and his better nature and his determination to get into Rosamond's mutual society. After all, she had seemed annoyed when he'd initially refused. It would be like her to want to push him.

"Mrs. Cooper keeps the girls entertained with those get-togethers she has, though," he went on, just in case Rosamond was testing him and his underlying desire for her was showing. "Every morning, some of the Morrow

Creek ladies show up with their little ones to take part in her mothers' meetings."

"Hmm. Isn't that enterprising of her?" Rosamond didn't seem entirely enthralled by Miles's attempts at polite conversation. Instead, she seemed interested in Miles himself—in the fit of his shirt and the shape of his hands and even the fly of his trousers…which felt ever snugger with each glance she gave.

"I do admire Mrs. Cooper," she said abstractedly. "Gus Winston told me that Daisy's risen above some very challenging circumstances. She's proven without a doubt that happy endings can prevail, even for someone with a difficult past."

"I wouldn't know about that." Miles turned away, pretending to be absorbed in the correct placement of his valise near the woodstove. In fact, he scarcely saw that traveling bag of his. In his mind's eye, all he could see was Rosamond smiling at him. Rosamond kissing him. Rosamond coming nearer while unbuttoning all those millions of buttons on her dress… With effort, he cleared his throat. "Would you like a cup of tea?"

Yes. That was masterful. He congratulated himself for having come up with such a courteous offer—especially while most of his attention and a fair quantity of his imagination had headed south on him, leaving him at the mercy of his wayward yearning.

"No, Miles. Thank you, but I would not like a cup of tea."

He sagged with momentary disappointment. That had been his best effort at masculine decorum. Now all he had left to think about was Rosamond's intoxicating nearness, her remarkable poise, her tempting femininity… and the fact that they were utterly alone just then. They wouldn't be disturbed by anyone.

"What I would like, instead," Rosamond said as she came closer to him, her gaze trained on him with what he would have sworn was sweet seductiveness, "is what you promised me."

"Promised you?"

Rosamond could not look purposely seductive. Could she?

She was kind and caring, not overtly sensual.

Yet she seemed, just then, to be all those things at once.

"You promised me kisses," she reminded him. "All over."

At that, Miles almost groaned with needfulness. He had promised Rosamond kisses. All over. At the time, he'd been trying to encourage her to overcome her fears. He hadn't truly expected to be asked to deliver on such an indecent offer.

"I also have coffee." Miles blurted out that fact in a burst of saving inspiration, knowing he had to keep trying to hold himself in check. For Rosamond's sake. "I only have to roast it and cool it, grind it and brew it, and then—"

Rosamond took his hand. "I want those kisses, Miles."

He couldn't stand it. "I could make lemonade! Mrs. Cooper told me how it's done. I was only half listening, on account of playing checkers with Élodie at the time, but I think I can—"

"Miles, stop." A pause. "Are you worried about me?"

"Always." But he hadn't been thinking about that. About everything Rosamond had been through and all the ways she might be scared of Miles's more wicked impulses. Until now. Now he was worried. Hellfire. He had twice the reasons to behave himself.

"You don't have to worry about me." Reassuringly,

Rosamond squeezed his hand. It was funny that she thought she had to comfort him. Miles knew damn well he was stronger than she was. "I want to be here, Miles. I want to be here with you. Alone."

Her low, private intimation made everything clear.

His Rose had come to collect her kisses. She was not taking no for answer. Just as in all the rest of her life, Rosamond meant to conquer Miles and his meager sense of propriety, too.

He didn't stand a chance holding out against her.

His only hope at maintaining any propriety at all was that she might be bluffing. Sometimes Rosamond liked to bluff, Miles recalled fuzzily. Maybe this was one of those times.

Maybe now, while she stood there with her calico-covered hips curving alluringly next to his kitchen chair and her smile smiling enticingly up at him and her fingers absently stroking his pine tabletop in a way that all but forced him to wonder what her fingers would feel like sliding over his skin…

Maybe now Rosamond was only pretending. So she could win.

So she could perform another endearing victory dance.

Dredging up every ounce of fortitude he possessed, Miles faced Rosamond. Her eager, affectionate expression was nearly his undoing. All he wanted was to be with her, in every way.

But he needed to make sure she wanted that, too.

"All right. Kissing." He hitched up his britches, preparing for the outrageous bluff-calling to come. "That's fine."

"You mean it would be fine if it ever got started."

Her laughing eyes convinced him she was bluffing. If he hadn't thought so before, looking at Rosamond then would have persuaded him. She didn't really want his all-over kisses.

"The first step," Miles said, "is that you get naked."

"What?"

His shrug cost him half the resolve he had left. Because saying so had made him imagine it happening... and the idea of Rose, his Rose, nude and willing before him made him shake.

"You'll have to get naked," Miles explained hoarsely, "before all the kissing can start. That's how it's done."

Skeptically, Rosamond eyed him. "It's full daylight out."

"It's easy enough to draw my curtains." Miles did so.

Behind him, Rosamond spoke up. "You'll light a lamp though, right? I mean, there's enough light in here as it is, but—"

"You want it to be light?"

"Of course. That's how I'll know it's you." She gazed at him with certainty and love. "I want to savor every moment."

God help him. Miles wanted that, too.

His bluff-calling wasn't working. Not sure what else to do, he went to his bureau. He lit the oil lamp. "There. Better?"

"Much better." Rosamond wrapped her arms around him from behind. She rested her chin on his back. "I swear, if I didn't know better, I'd think you don't want to do this."

He closed his eyes, desperately wanting. "If you hug me much lower, you'll find out how much I want to do this."

At that warning, to Miles's surprise, Rosamond did not wrest away her arms in a panic. Instead, she squeezed him tenderly. "I'm not afraid of you, Miles. I've never been afraid of you. I'm not afraid of anything else, either. Not today."

That's when he understood. Rosamond's success in conquering her fears had made her even bolder than usual. She was drunk with a sense of fearlessness, willing to do things she otherwise wouldn't. That explained everything…including the way Rosamond brazenly pushed her breasts against his back as she hugged him.

She felt so good. He'd dreamed of her for so long.

"And I'm proud of you," he managed to say, hoarsely and with effort, "for all you accomplished today. But you can't do something you might regret. Maybe now isn't the right time."

For a moment, there was silence. Rosamond didn't move.

Then she wriggled confusingly behind him. She reached her hand over his shoulder. She dropped something. It fluttered toward the floor in a curl of palest blue. Miles caught it.

It was the ribbon she'd used to adorn her dress's neckline.

"Is now the right time?" Rosamond asked.

Miles fisted that ribbon, loving its silkiness. Its feminine delicacy. Its significance. Rosamond had removed the very first barrier between herself and complete nakedness.

Maybe more would follow. Miles didn't dare turn around to find out. How could he? How could he…and still maintain control?

But Rosamond was even more certain than he'd bargained on. While he stood motionless, trying to be as respectful as he could, Rosamond stepped away from him, still behind him, and went on with whatever tantalizing plan she'd come up with now.

For several long moments, Miles wasn't sure he'd be able to stand upright. His blood pounded, making him feel hazy. He frowned and flexed his arms, trying to divert his attention.

All he could see was that blue ribbon in his hand.

"Miles, turn around," Rosamond said. "Look at me."

Her voice reached inside him, lovely and sure. He could no more resist its call than he could tear down the walls of his new quarters, here at a new stable, here in a brand-new life.

That thought was what helped Miles do as she asked. Because now he had started a new life here in Morrow Creek, as surely as Rosamond had. Maybe, between the two of them, both of their new beginnings could be the start of something unified and real.

Something loving. He hauled in a breath, then turned.

Rosamond stood with her dress partly unbuttoned. The curve of her breasts was fully revealed, beckoning him with smooth skin and wonderful roundness and bold, impertinent femininity.

"Is now the right time?" she asked him.

Miles swallowed hard. The ribbon fell from his hand.

"You don't know what you're doing, Rosamond."

"I'm counting on you to teach me." Keeping her gaze locked trustingly on his, she lifted her hands to her bodice. She undid another button. Another. The gap she'd made widened, showing him her corset. Just visible above that garment's lace-trimmed edge, he caught a scandalous glimpse of her pink areolas.

Miles drank in the sight of her, feeling nearly undone.

"Now?" Rosamond asked, cheekily continuing. Another button slipped free of its buttonhole. "I confess, Miles, I can't go much further. Not in this dress. But if I lift it up here…"

She bent to collect her dress's hem. She lifted it with audacity, showing him her shoes, her stockinged ankles...

"Stop." Miles rushed to her before she could show him more—before she could go too far. He covered Rosamond's hands tightly with his, depriving himself of everything she was offering.

That didn't stop his imagination from delivering it to him, though. That didn't stop Miles from envisioning Rosamond's long, shapely legs, her stocking-clad thighs... even the junction of those thighs, warm and sweet and waiting for him. He wanted her. She seemed to want him. But was it too soon? Taking a ragged breath, Miles made himself focus on her cherished face instead.

"Maybe we should reconsider this."

"Reconsider? Now?"

"Yes."

"No."

Miles was losing this fight. He looked at their joined hands, absurdly holding her dress half up and half down, then regrouped. He had already warned her that his mother had raised a dastardly son, hadn't he? "Are you sure, Rosamond?"

"Don't I look sure?" Her saucy gaze met his. Meaningfully, she directed his attention toward her gaping dress's front. Her partly raised full skirts. "I honestly don't know how much plainer I can make things."

Miles relented. He had to. "Maybe an inch plainer?"

He refused to be the man who reawakened Rosamond's awful past. But those hurtful events seemed to be years and years behind her as Rosamond smiled victoriously at him...as she raised her dress an inch higher. Another inch higher. With his hands still atop hers, Miles implicitly cooperated in her unveiling.

Under other circumstances, he would have already

undressed her by now—and she would have willingly let him. In a different world, he would have already wooed her, married her, taken her to his bed and pleasured her. "I should be undressing you."

Rosamond shook her head. Trust and love shone in her gaze. "Those aren't the rules," she reminded him. "Besides, I want to do it myself. This way, there can be no doubt what I want."

There was even less and less doubt as she proceeded. Miles released her hands, giving in completely.

Rosamond rewarded him by pulling off her dress altogether. It fell to the floor, faster than he could have hoped. Her shoes and untied bustle came next, followed by her drawers, her stockings and her frilly white petticoats. Duly discarded, those garments made a frothy, lacy pile on his pine-plank floor. They left Rose standing before him with just her chemise and corset to cover her.

Defiantly, she tilted her chin. That one gesture, so uniquely hers, was Miles's final undoing. His breath left him. His knees quivered. He felt positively overheated.

"You're beautiful," he said. "And I'm a little dizzy."

"Ah." Her smile was both shy and exultant at once. "Well, you know what you should do if you feel dizzy, don't you?"

Miles couldn't remember. Because he could see almost all of Rosamond now. He could see her breasts, mounding demurely above her corset. He could see her waist, nipping in above her rounded hips. He could see her legs, outlined beneath her chemise's sheer fabric. If he'd tried, he could have glimpsed even more. Silently, Miles blessed all the light in the room. He gave thanks for his glowing lamp and for the absolute joy-causing, brightening effect of Rosamond's presence.

"I don't have the faintest idea about dizziness," Miles confessed huskily. "I've never felt this way before."

"I see." While he watched, Rosamond pulled a hairpin from her upswept auburn hair. She tossed it aside. A few more pins followed. *Ping. Ping.* Luxuriantly, her hair tumbled down

She took his hand. "You're supposed to just feel what you feel. Like this. Like you showed me before. Remember?"

Utterly bedeviled, Miles let her take his hand. He let her place it on her smooth silken shoulder. With his heart pounding, he watched as Rosamond drew his hand down, lower and lower...

"How about those all-over kisses?" she asked, twining her fingers with his as she looked up. "Is now the right time?"

The faith in her gaze made it impossible for him to refuse her again. Miles simply didn't possess the stamina.

Not for that, he didn't.

"Soon," he promised, feeling himself leap to new and even more rigid alertness at the idea of what was to come. "There."

He looked to his waiting bed with its downy coverlet. Rosamond did, too. She swallowed. She nodded.

With her hair tumbled free around her shoulders, she looked to him like another, even more bewitching woman. She looked like the private version of herself—like the woman only the man who loved her could see. Miles liked that idea. He loved her.

"I'll need your help with my corset," Rosamond said.

Lithely, she strode to his bedside. Alluringly, she lifted her hair from her neck. Invitingly, she turned her back to him.

Miles studied those miles of corset laces. He took in

the shapely curve of Rosamond's derriere, just discernible through her fine chemise. He wanted that damnable teasing garment gone.

"I'm yours to command." He reached her within his next breath. His fingers plied her corset laces with a deftness that would have shocked a lady's maid. Her undergarment came undone with satisfying speed, leaving Miles with two hands full of hooks and eyes and whalebone stays. "Are you sure about this?"

He couldn't help asking again. He needed to know.

But Rosamond only nodded. She released her hair. "Maybe…you could take off my chemise for me?"

As she turned to face him, Miles gladly agreed. He'd have agreed to anything she wanted. "Only if I can do this first."

While she looked at him questioningly, he kissed her.

Afterward, she touched her mouth. She smiled at him. "It still works, just like before. I still feel like dancing."

"Ah. You think you've won, then?"

"With you?" Her smile broadened. "Always."

She did want him. Just him. Just the way he wanted her.

Suddenly overcome by a torrent of feeling, Miles couldn't summon a reply to that. All he could do was kiss Rosamond again. All he could do was fill his hands with her hair, luxuriate in its uninhibited disarray, kiss her again and again and again.

Gently, he stroked her cheek. "Tell me if you want me to stop. If there's anything I'm doing that you don't like—"

"If I ever come across such a rare event, I'll tell you."

"I only want to please you, Rose. If I hurt you—"

"You won't." With equal gentleness, she touched his face. She gazed into his eyes. "I wouldn't be here otherwise. Do you think I haven't thought of this? I have. Over and over again."

Humbled by her trust in him, Miles smiled. Warmth swirled between them, heady and full. "Are you sure you're ready?"

"Are you sure you know what you're doing? Because a lady might wonder, given all this prevaricating, whether a man —"

"I do know what I'm doing." To prove it, Miles kissed her again. Stirringly and erotically, he lost himself in Rose's mouth, in her scent, in her heat and her generosity and her spellbinding courageousness. He lifted his hands to her breasts and stroked her there; he drank in the delighted moans that escaped Rosamond when he did. He kissed her again and again.

"I may have underestimated you," she murmured a long while later, wriggling atop his bunched-up, mostly forgotten coverlet.

"'May have'?" Miles offered her a wicked arch of his brow. With concentration and caring, he lowered his mouth to her neck. He gave her a tiny, gentle nip, then kissed his way to her breasts. He could scarcely believe how remarkable she felt. How long he'd waited and how good this was. "You have underestimated me. You've seriously underestimated me. You'll see."

Typically, Rosamond would not admit to being wrong. "Maybe."

Her breathless, aroused tone said more than her words did, though, and Miles savored that, too. With his heart and his mind, with every bit of his lost, forlorn soul, he loved Rosamond. He stroked every part of her, from her toes to her head. He lavished praise on her perfectly shaped toes, on her lithesome knees, on her soft belly and her pleasing thighs. He lulled her with words and seduced her with kisses, and by the time Rosamond was sprawled on his mattress beneath his seeking mouth and searching hands, boneless with delight and thrumming with anticipation at the same time, Miles knew he had done well.

It was time for more. Slowly, he slid Rosamond's chemise higher. It lifted as if by magic, first revealing more of her thighs, then showing him her dewy femininity, then coming off all the way to divulge her creamy pale skin and pink-tipped breasts. Fighting for breath, Miles gazed at her in wonder.

"I've never known anyone more beautiful, Rose."

Dreamily, she smiled. "I could say the same to you."

But that was preposterous, and Miles knew it. "I'm just a man," he disagreed roughly. "Just like any other man."

Rosamond shook her head, her hair flowing against his pillow in a way he'd envisaged countless times. "You're unlike all men. Because you're you. Because you make me feel…"

"Safe? Beloved?" He grinned rakishly. "Satisfied?"

"At home," Rosamond told him. "That's why I need you. Because you make me feel more like myself than I do on my own."

Unaccountably moved, Miles closed his eyes. When he opened them, Rosamond was studying him with a dangerously curious look.

"Can I see you?" She gestured tentatively toward his britches. "You know…before we go any further?"

He knew what she meant, but not why she'd asked.

His confusion must have shown, because Rosamond added, "I'd like to touch you, too." She swallowed. "If that's all right."

She wanted reassurance, Miles realized. He could no more deny her that than he could stop wanting her. Or loving her.

Wordlessly, he stood. To make things easier, he tugged off his shirt first. He tossed it to the rug, then brought his hands to the waistband of his britches. He unfastened the top button.

Rosamond's rapt expression stopped him.

"You are beautiful," she declared in a self-certain tone. "I knew I was right! Look at your arms! And your chest. And your stomach! You're strong and fit." She scrutinized him, shaking her head. "I can only imagine how the rest of you might look."

Her gaze shifted to the front of his britches. Her eyes grew wide, undoubtedly as her overzealous imagination took over.

"Don't get carried away." Hastily, wanting to reassure her, Miles unbuttoned his fly. "I'm not so fearsome as all that."

He wrenched off his britches and drawers, leaving himself wholly exposed to her. He stood in the combined unforgiving glow of the lamplight and the daylight, standing tall and naked.

Rosamond appeared...fascinated by him. Also, a bit alarmed.

"You are fearsome," she declared with a shake of her head. "I know what's meant to happen, Miles. Given the size of you—"

"I'll make sure you don't mind."

"I'm not convinced you can. Just look!"

Her wave indicated that most manly part of him... which chose that moment to swell to even more impressive proportions.

"Maybe you should stop looking," Miles suggested.

"You're right. I should just feel. Just like before."

Uh... At the notion of Rosamond deliberately feeling him, Miles grew weak-kneed again. But since he'd already agreed…

"Go ahead." Attentively, he watched her. "I want you to."

Rosamond sat up. Cautiously, she reached out. Her hand hovered an inch or two away from him. She gazed up at him.

She hesitated. "Will I hurt you?"

"Only if you keep making me wait."

"Oh." Rosamond drew in a breath. "All right."

At the sight of her markedly working up her courage, Miles had to stifle a fond grin. She was so intrepid. He loved that.

"Are you ready?" she asked, her hand a fraction nearer.

His answer was a heartfelt groan. "Rosamond…"

"Ah." She sounded enlightened. But her gaze didn't lift from him. She appeared to be visually estimating his length and girth and firmness. "Now I understand why you kept asking me."

"And I understand why you got so impatient."

"We should have had this conversation earlier."

"Rose…"

Her impish gaze lifted, briefly, to his. She inhaled.

She stroked him from base to tip. He bit back a moan.

"Oh!" Delight sounded in her voice. "You're soft! But hard, too." Then, puzzlement. "Smooth and hard." Rosamond seized him fully. She squeezed, then stroked again. "Quite hard. Very—"

He was going to die. Miles knew it.

"—very hard," she concluded. "I feel relieved, Miles. I was a little worried about…well, you know. But now I feel fine."

"You," he promised, "are about to feel better than fine."

"More kissing?" Her face brightened. "I love kissing you."

"More kissing." Miles nodded. "All-over kissing."

She appeared confounded. "We've already had all-over kissing." A rosy blush appeared on her cheeks. "It was nice."

"It's been too long since you've experienced it," he countered, "now that we've had all this friendly conversation."

"I definitely don't think I could forget any of this."

"No, I'm sure it's possible." With sham regret, Miles shook his head. "We'd better start over again."

Carefully, he settled over Rosamond, supporting himself on his elbows and knees. He gave her a minute to adjust to the remarkable feeling of their bodies being so close together.

Deeply, he kissed her. "I need you so much, Rose."

"I need you! Oh, Miles!" Rosamond clutched his head, holding him to her. "I just feel so…I can't describe it."

"Why don't you try?" Miles suggested. Deliberately and slowly, he made his way down her body, stroking and kissing and awakening every good feeling Rosamond could possibly have.

"I can't try! I can't think while you're doing that."

He arrived at the joining of her thighs. He kissed her there, too—very softly, very sweetly and very erotically.

Rosamond gasped, tensing. "Miles!"

"It's all right," he murmured. "Just feel."

She sounded wobbly. "I'm feeling too much! It's so—"

A low moan broke from her, redoubling Miles's desire.

"This is how I'm going to make sure you enjoy yourself," Miles explained. Intimately, he glided his fingers over her. He loved the way Rosamond arched her back as he touched her…loved the way she drew him nearer to her. "Just feel. Trust me."

"I do trust you. But I just—" Rosamond broke off, tossing her head. Her gaze met his, filled with mingled passion and discovery. "I just never imagined such a feeling."

"I did. For you. I wanted to give it to you."

Miles lowered his mouth to her again, losing himself in that most intimate kiss, coaxing her to new heights of ecstasy.

Whatever else happened, he would give Rosamond this. He would give her the knowledge that lovemaking was beautiful. That it was necessary. That it could bond two people in a way that nothing else could—not promises, not words, not a ring.

Although he wanted to give her those things, too. He did.

"If you'll let me, Rose, I'll give you everything."

Even as he made that promise, Rosamond came undone beneath him. He'd scarcely formed the words before she clutched him to her…before she cried out with desire and pleasure and surprise.

Not long after that, Miles did give Rosamond everything—everything he had and all he was, long into the afternoon and then beyond it. He didn't know what time it was. He didn't care.

From here on, he knew, everything would be different.

Chapter Thirteen

Everything was different now, Rosamond realized as she strode through town, feeling free and strong and complete. Now that she and Miles were together—really together—the sun felt warmer and the breeze felt fresher. The trees looked greener and the birds sounded chirpier. Even the dusty streets of Morrow Creek, chock-full of midday traffic, seemed more vivid somehow.

Miles loved her. Truly and completely. He loved her!

He had loved her, too, Rosamond remembered as she turned to give her friend Savannah Corwin a final good-bye wave. Miles had shown her so much during that magical afternoon they'd shared. Even now, days later, Rosamond couldn't help blushing.

"You seem…different," Savannah had observed during their teatime meeting at the Lorndorff Hotel. "Did something happen?"

Several things had happened, but Rosamond hadn't known where to begin explaining—not even to Savannah, one of her most worldly friends. She liked Savannah. She liked her independence and her verve, her friendliness and her ability to rise above her very challenging and colorful past. Even though Savannah had married her erstwhile mail-order groom, Adam Corwin, she'd still stayed on in her demanding job as a telegraph operator.

"You didn't bring your security man Judah this time," Savannah had pushed. "Are you feeling...better these days?"

Rosamond had only smiled. "Yes. Much better. I didn't bring Judah because I didn't need to." *Also, because he really is smitten with me.* "In fact, I might have to let him go soon."

She couldn't very well let Judah waste his time pining away for her. She was devoted to Miles now. Besides, Rosamond truly didn't require her security men anymore, and Judah was too kindhearted to be strung along with charity. He deserved more.

She knew he could accomplish more, once she let him go.

With that sobering thought in mind, Rosamond carried on through town. She passed the milliner and the dressmaker, the blacksmith's shop and the schoolhouse. She ducked into the butcher's for a bone for Riley—just to prove she could without shaking and sweating and wanting to run—and then headed home.

The only thing that could have made her day better was seeing Miles, Rosamond decided as she walked onward. But they needed some time apart. She had business to deal with; Miles had his job at the livery stable. Taciturn Owen Cooper was understanding, but he was no pushover. He'd hired Miles to do a job. He'd made it plain he expected that job to be completed.

"You'll need to work hard if you want to buy more crackers," Rosamond had joked with Miles, dallying at his quarters after their last rendezvous. "You're almost finished with your initial twenty pounds, and I hear Mr. Hofer just got in a new barrel."

Miles had only laughed in that carefree way she loved, then pulled her into his arms. "Well, loving you is hungry work."

"Maybe you should buy yourself the entire barrel, then," Rosamond had advised him merrily. "Because I expect a whole lot more loving where that came from."

Even now, as she rounded the corner and headed down her quiet street, Rosamond had to shake her head at her own brashness. She'd always been bold—at least until Arvid Bouchard had stolen some of the daring from her—but she'd never before tiptoed along the cusp of respectability the way she'd been doing with Miles lately. If she hadn't been nigh convinced that he was on the verge of proposing marriage to her…

Well, she wouldn't have allowed things to progress as far as they had, that's all. Plain and simple.

But she trusted Miles. She trusted Miles to offer marriage—to make both their futures more secure. In fact, Rosamond believed that Miles would propose to her that very evening. He'd tried not to give away his plans, but she knew him too well not to have recognized the telltale gleam in his eyes.

"Tonight," he'd promised, "we'll do something special."

"Give the puppy two bones? Teach her to fetch?"

A smile. "Even more special than that."

"Well, I plumb can't imagine what that might be," Rosamond had pretended, feeling new gladness uncurl inside her. "With all this anticipation you're building, it had better be good."

"Oh, it will be good. I promise."

"Just tell me now," she'd cajoled, but Miles had refused. He'd never been a man to rush things, as evidenced by the very long time he'd waited to finally hint at his romantic feelings for her, all the way from Boston till now. He still wasn't.

But that didn't mean Rosamond wasn't anticipating the big event, all the same. She wondered if Miles's marriage proposal would take place in her parlor, the way all her mutual society members' proposals did. She wondered if she'd scream with joy or simply smile, if Miles would appear shy but pleased, like Mr. Robertson, or exuberant and thrilled like Gus Winston.

When Miss Abigail had accepted Gus's proposal, Rosamond recalled, he'd actually yodeled out a high-spirited *"Yee-haw!"*

Her neighbors insisted the sound still echoed nearby.

Remembering it now as she approached her gated household, Rosamond couldn't help smiling. She couldn't quite envision Miles screeching that way, like one of Everett Bannon's ranch hands gone wild at Murphy's saloon on a payday. All the same...

All the same...Rosamond was ninety-nine percent certain that was Arvid Bouchard standing at her gate, arguing with Judah.

Miles was sitting on a hand-braided rug on the floor of Daisy Cooper's front room, in the middle of a circle of youngsters, when Seth Durant came in. Broad-shouldered and awkward amid the women and children and babies who'd all joined in for Mrs. Cooper's daily get-together, Seth pushed forward.

"Callaway, you're going to want to come with me."

Miles couldn't explain the suddenly terse quality to Rosamond's security man's voice, but he didn't try very hard.

"Mr. Durant, you can probably see I'm busy." Smiling at the children, Miles turned back to little Tommy

Scott's shoe. With a flourish, he finished demonstrating how to tie its laces. He nodded. "…and that, you see, is how it's properly done."

As though he'd performed magic, they all applauded.

Miles gave a modest wave. That only increased the children's clamoring to have the next turn at learning how to tie a shoe. He could learn to like this, Miles decided with a flush of contentment. He wanted a home. A family. A wife and children of his own. Now that he and Rosamond were together—really together—Miles had a shot at seeing all his dreams come true. Especially if his plans for tonight, with Rose, went well.

Seth tapped his shoulder. "I'm going to have to insist."

"And I'm going to have to decline."

"It's important."

"Is it about Mrs. Dancy?"

Seth scowled at his own hastily snatched-off hat. "No."

"Then it's not important." Miles looked at Tommy. "Tommy, why don't you try it for yourself this time. Just make a bow—"

"It's about the strangers who just got off the train."

Miles went still. The only strangers who would cause Seth any shred of alarm were the roughnecks Arvid Bouchard employed.

Before Miles could respond to that, Mrs. Cooper did.

"If you're fixing to have a disagreement, gentlemen," Daisy interrupted tartly, "I'm going to have to insist you leave."

Quietly, Lucinda Larkin stood from her chair at the edge of the circle. With the baby held, blanket-wrapped, in her arms, she gestured for Tobe to follow her. They slipped outside.

Seth watched them leave, his gaze inscrutable.

Miles should have followed her, he knew. Lucinda

Larkin was the sole reason he'd come upstairs today and allowed himself to be ambushed into entertaining the children. He'd glimpsed her arriving for Daisy Cooper's get-together. He'd finagled himself an impromptu invitation so he could watch her with the baby.

All he'd learned was that Lucinda Larkin was as capable at comforting a fussy baby as she was at playing a fiddle.

He did wonder, though…if that was Rosamond and Arvid's secret baby, why was Mrs. Larkin caring for it herself?

But on the other hand, what better way was there to throw off attention from the child's real mother? Rosamond certainly had plenty of free time between her mutual society duties and seeing Miles. It was possible that she'd been sneaking away to the Lorndorff to pay regular visits to Mrs. Larkin and her baby, just the way a doting mother would have wanted to do.

Because it hadn't taken Miles long to learn that that's where Lucinda was hiding out—at the Lorndorff Hotel. Miles already knew that Rosamond held regular meetings at the hotel. Judah, all gregarious and unwitting, had provided that information to him that very morning. Judah hadn't disclosed whom Rosamond usually met with, but Miles knew—

He knew that right now, he had to think about those men.

"Let's discuss this outside, Durant." Miles rose. He angled his head toward the door, silently suggesting that Seth precede him through it. Miles fetched his hat. He waved it toward Mrs. Cooper and the women and children in a polite farewell. "Thank you kindly for the refreshments and the company, ma'am. Ladies." Miles gave an elaborate bow. "Youngsters…behave yourselves."

Amid a chorus of childish promises to be good—along with several high-pitched feminine goodbyes—Miles took his leave.

Once downstairs in the livery stable, safely amid the hay and the horses and the smell of liniments and leather, Miles turned to Seth. His good-hearted demeanor faded. "What men?"

"I—I don't know." Doubtless surprised by Miles's sudden change of mood, Seth stammered. "I s-saw them at the station. They weren't from around here. They didn't look up to no good." His gaze turned crafty. "I reckoned they'd get your attention, though, being that you're not from around here, either…and you've got some secrets you're wanting to keep, too."

This wasn't an emergency. It was a dead end, Miles realized. Seth couldn't possibly know his secrets. He was fishing, hoping to lure in Miles with the threat of exposure.

Miles wasn't biting. But he was wondering what was so all-fired important that Durant had interrupted him just now.

"What were you doing at the station?" he demanded.

"Waiting for somebody." Seth clutched his hat, turning its brim round and round in his hands. "He didn't come like he was supposed to, though. He didn't meet me. It got me thinking."

"Thinking what?"

"That maybe I need a new source of income, that's what."

Seth's belligerent tone put Miles on guard. "The way I see it, Mrs. Dancy pays you too much already for the lackadaisical work you do. Who in their right mind would pay you more?"

"You. Leastwise, that's what I'm thinking."

Miles didn't understand. "What would I pay you for?" He gestured at himself, indicating his size and strength. "Maybe you haven't noticed, son, but I'm a sight bigger and stronger and more experienced than you. So if you don't start getting real plain, real soon, we are going to have a disagreement."

Seth gulped. But he held firm. "I couldn't help noticing," he said nervously, "that you have an interest in Mrs. Larkin."

Miles frowned. He didn't like thinking he'd been that obvious. But to someone who'd been paying attention… maybe he had. Maybe he'd let himself get too distracted loving Rosamond.

"I couldn't help noticing you're in deep to a thirteen-year-old," Miles pointed out acerbically. "I guess we both have our complications when it comes to the Larkin family. How much do you owe Tobe now?"

"Sixty dollars. But that's nothing compared to what I got from that kid." Seth shifted his gaze to the stable's wide doorway, where Owen Cooper was helping a customer. "He likes to talk, Tobe does. What he told me might interest you, I think."

Of course. Miles couldn't believe he hadn't thought up that angle for himself. Tobe would know if his mother had had a baby. Tobe would also know if his mother was just watching Rosamond's child, keeping the baby secret from nosy neighbors…and from the prying eyes of a man who'd come calling from Rosamond's past.

"Look, if you think you can hold out on me, you're wrong," Seth burst out, shifting on his massive feet. He darted another tense glance toward the stable's entryway. "I spent my damn nest egg, tossing dice with that boy while listening to him talk. I want to be paid! I've got information you want."

If that was true, Miles could wait a few minutes longer for it. "Who were you waiting for at the train depot?"

Frustrated, Seth swiveled his attention back to Miles. "You don't know him. Judah was supposed to help him, as a favor to his brother, Cade. But he didn't want the job. He was afraid of crossing Mrs. Dancy by spying on one of her friends, so I—"

Miles lowered his voice. "Who? I'm not asking again."

"His name's Blackhouse. Simon Blackhouse." Seth looked beleaguered. "He wanted somebody to watch over Mrs. Larkin. I don't know why. All I know is, Blackhouse didn't turn up when he said he would. He was supposed to come today. He was supposed to pay me. Today. But there aren't any more trains coming in from California." Seth paced. "The bastard stiffed me!"

Frowning at him, Miles tried to make sense of it all. He'd heard of a certain Blackhouse family. Back in Boston, at the Bouchards', conversation had swirled about the Blackhouses…about how ruthless, how conniving, how impossibly wealthy—and thus welcome into polite society—they all were. Miles couldn't think why someone like that would be interested in kindly Mrs. Larkin.

"These men you saw at the station," Miles pressed. "What did they look like?"

Seth seemed taken aback. "Big. Dangerous. Rich. They all had on fancy suits. They got out of a private railcar. That's why, at first, I thought they were with Blackhouse." He shook his head at Miles. "If you want to know more, you can pay me."

Miles compressed his mouth. He shook his head at Seth. "You've put Mrs. Dancy in danger. While you were busy trying to get money from me, you left her alone."

Rather than dole out the greenbacks the man expected, Miles turned on his heel. He headed for the stable's exit.

"Hey!" Behind him, Seth blustered. "Hang on a damn minute!"

But Miles couldn't. He stopped in the double doorway where Owen Cooper stood with one hand full of a black mare's reins.

"I'm sorry," Miles said. "I've got to leave for a while."

Cooper eyed him. "It's the middle of a workday."

"It's urgent. If I don't come back, sell all my things. Keep what you need. Give the rest of the money to Mrs. Dancy."

"Ah." Owen Cooper nodded knowingly. "Woman troubles?"

Miles couldn't imagine how the man could possibly know that. Owen Cooper seemed nothing if not blissfully wed to Daisy.

"Something like that," Miles said. Then he turned and left, hoping he still had time before everything went wrong.

Fixedly, Rosamond stared at the men standing near her gate. Her heart started hammering. Her breath caught up short.

This could not be happening, she reminded herself.

Arvid Bouchard was in Boston. Savannah Corwin, she knew, had received a telegram from Bouchard more than two weeks ago. She'd told Rosamond that much today, at the hotel. Rosamond had asked her friend to be alert to any communications from Arvid, and Savannah had dutifully reported that one. She'd been curiously indistinct on the details of the telegram, but the most crucial fact remained. On the day of Rosamond's panicky attack in town, the man she feared had been in the state.

He'd been much too far away to hurt her again.

On the other hand, two weeks was enough time to

cross the country by rail—especially if you were a man with influence.

If you were a man with influence, you could pay someone to send a telegram westward with your name on it, too…couldn't you?

Gulping back a fresh wave of terror, Rosamond watched. Twenty or thirty yards away, Bouchard shook his fist at Judah.

Judah said something fierce that she couldn't understand. His intimation was plain, though. He wasn't backing down.

Thank heaven for her protectors. When the chips were down, Judah wasn't afraid. He wasn't even intimidated. He was bigger and tougher than heavyset Arvid Bouchard, even if Judah did come up short in pure meanness. Rosamond, on the other hand…

All she wanted to do was flee.

She could do it, too, she realized as she clutched her hands in fists, frozen in place. She could just run away. She could avoid Arvid Bouchard forever. She could let Judah and Dylan and Seth handle him. She could be free. No one would ever know that she'd come this way. She could simply walk away.

The idea held merit. She was afraid of Arvid Bouchard.

She was afraid of confronting him. Afraid, even, of being close enough for him to grab her and hurt her. It didn't matter that she knew Judah would move mountains to protect her.

Her fear was unreasoning and inescapable.

That's how Rosamond knew she had to face it down.

Hauling in a huge breath, she fixed Arvid Bouchard with her sturdiest gaze. She made her feet move, going straight toward him. She knew, all the while, that she was crazy to do so.

What if Bouchard hurt her? Hit her? Ruined her?

He could do it. He'd always held unfair power over her. That's why she'd never challenged him before. It would have been useless to try. Arvid and Genevieve Bouchard had controlled everything in Rosamond's life—her livelihood, her living arrangements, her friends and her future.

But now, Rosamond reminded herself, she'd forged a new life. She'd become strong and resilient. Thanks to everything she'd gone through, she was braver than ever.

Then, too, there were things she knew now—things that had become clear to Rosamond only after she'd fled Boston…

"I'm telling you, Mrs. Dancy is not at home," Judah was saying as she approached. He caught sight of her. His eyes narrowed. He signaled for her to escape. "You'd better leave."

"I'm not leaving until I see her," Bouchard insisted, adding a vile epithet for Judah. He had the arrogant bearing of a man who expected to get what he wanted because he always had. "She's got something of mine. I came a long way to get it."

The sound of his voice made her feel ill. Rosamond kept going. Gravel crunched under her shoes. The sun shone down.

It shone down just the way it had on the day Bouchard had violated her. The sun didn't warm her, but it did remind her.

Judah crossed his arms, big and menacing. "I think I just heard you call Mrs. Dancy a thief. You'd better apologize."

"Apologize? To that whore?" A bitter laugh. "I'd sooner—"

In an instant, Judah had Bouchard by the throat.

Rosamond wanted to let her security man wring Arvid's neck like a dog with a ragdoll. She was ashamed of the impulse.

"Let him go, Judah. I'll handle this."

Judah's gaze shifted to meet hers. "Go inside, ma'am."

"I'll stay right here." Deliberately, Rosamond moved her gaze to her former employer—to her attacker. "I'm done hiding."

Bouchard seemed incongruously delighted. "Rosie!"

Judah gave him a rough shake. He sputtered into silence.

"I mean it, Judah," Rosamond urged. "Let him go."

Reluctantly, her security man eased his grip. Freed, Arvid stumbled backward a pace, both hands at his neck. He glared.

"I'll be the one to tell him." Rosamond stepped nearer. Her pulse beat hectically in her neck. Her face heated. It felt as if she were walking on water, the whole world unreal and dull.

"Tell me what?" Bouchard sneered, looking her up and down with familiar disdain. "Tell me where my bastard baby is?"

"Tell you to leave." Calmly, Rosamond drew in another breath. She looked down the street, then at him. "Go away, Mr. Bouchard. I want you to leave me alone and never come back."

He laughed, plainly disbelieving. He shifted his attention to Judah, ready to share that disbelief with him. Whatever Bouchard saw in Judah's face made his affability die quickly.

He was afraid of Judah. Now that the crisis she'd feared had arrived, her protector had come through for her.

Nonetheless, Rosamond had to do this on her own. She had to make Bouchard leave on her own.

"You can't tell me what to do." Glancing around uncertainly, Arvid shifted. "You're a housemaid."

"I *was* a housemaid," Rosamond agreed, feeling her courage grow with every moment she held her ground. Bouchard was just a man, she saw. Just a pathetic, bullying man. Stripped of his Boston influence, he had no hold over her or anyone else here. And he'd cost her too much happiness already. "I was a housemaid who knew a great deal about Mrs. Bouchard and her fortune."

Arvid blanched. "You can't know about that."

"Can't I?" Rosamond raised her eyebrow. She'd been too afraid—too helpless and too stuck—to use this knowledge before now. Today, she had no qualms about speaking out. "Can't I know that your wife holds the purse strings over you? I guess you'll find out if that's true, once my telegram reaches Genevieve."

"You can't call her that! She's your mistress!"

"She's my secondary plan." Rosamond crossed her arms. Her trembling had gone. "It's my belief that a woman should always have one. Your wife is mine." While Judah and Arvid boggled at their encounter, Rosamond continued. "What do you think Genevieve would say if she knew you were here, following me?"

Bouchard gulped. "I'm not following you," he blustered.

"It looks as if you're a lovesick fool. Over a housemaid." Rosamond gave a headshake. "Just the way Genevieve feared."

"No. I'm merely making a stop during my business travels."

"Is that what you told her? That you were called to travel westward on business?" Rosamond gave an unpleasant laugh. "Your wife was coldhearted enough to sell me to an evil man. Do you truly believe that she's deceived by you? That she'll be at all forgiving when she knows the truth?"

Arvid changed tactics. "I only want what's mine. The baby—"

"There is no baby."

"But I—" His shifty gaze moved to Judah. "But you—"

"There is no baby. I know Genevieve believed there was going to be one. That's why she was so desperate to make me leave." Rosamond wasn't quite credulous enough to feel sorry for the woman. All the same, she tried to sound contrite. "Poor Mrs. Bouchard. Do you think she's concerned about babies because she's never been able to have one of her own?"

Bouchard gawked. He frowned. He took a step back.

Clearly, he hadn't been prepared for this—for the extent of knowledge that the women and men in service sometimes gleaned about their employers. For the possibility of being stood up to.

He hadn't been prepared for her.

The realization gave Rosamond a new burst of strength.

"I know you'd both like an heir," she went on, "but you won't be finagling one from me." She gave Bouchard an icy look. "Maybe the problem isn't with Genevieve, the way you've browbeaten her into believing. Maybe the problem is with you."

Bouchard held up his hands. Fearfully, he looked at Judah.

"Maybe the problem is your inability to father a child," Rosamond pushed on starkly, just the way she'd imagined doing so many times. The reality of it surpassed her most rancorous expectations. She wasn't proud of that, either.

But she was unafraid. "I think Mrs. Bouchard would like to know about that."

"You can't." Arvid shook his head. "You wouldn't."

"I've already written the telegram."

"I won't let you send it!"

Judah stepped up. Ominously. "Now, that's a threat. I heard it plain as day." He glared. "You'll want to shut your mouth."

"It's all right, Judah." Rosamond tugged his arm, urging him to back away. "I'm not afraid." She looked directly at Bouchard. "There's nothing he can do to me. Nothing at all."

Bouchard darted his gaze sideways. He drew himself up.

He still seemed pitiful. He was caught. He knew it.

"Please don't tell Mrs. Bouchard I came here," he pleaded. "Don't tell her about me. Don't tell her there's no baby! If she thinks I can't father a child, she'll cut off my money."

Rosamond angled her head, listening carefully to him. "I never in my life thought I'd hear you beg me for something."

"I am begging! I am! I'll give you anything you want."

"I'd have thought the sound would be sweeter." She still felt sick. But now she felt…liberated, too. "It's not."

"That's because you're a good person," Judah put in loyally. He aimed a threatening look at Bouchard. "Isn't she?"

"Yes!" her former employer yelped, perspiring. "Please don't ruin me. I swear I'll give you anything you ask for. A reference, a new position, money of your own. Just name it."

"I don't want anything from you," Rosamond said coldly.

Arvid appeared visibly relieved.

"Except an apology," she went on. "An apology for every time you hurt me. Every time you demeaned me. Every time you made me feel I was less than human because you were stronger."

Arvid Bouchard opened his mouth, obviously distraught.

"He wasn't stronger," a man said from nearby. "Not ever."

Rosamond looked. Miles. He came striding from the street beyond, tall and terrifying, obviously having heard everything.

"You were always stronger, Rosamond," he said. "Always."

Miles reached for her hand. Rosamond couldn't believe he dared. Not now. Not after this. She held herself apart from him.

"I'm sorry!" Bouchard cried, his apology bursting forth with weaselly insistence. "I'm sorry, Rosamond. I'm sorry."

He backed away, aiming a skittish glance at…unbelievably, she saw, at her. Not at Miles, the way she'd expected. Not at Judah. Arvid Bouchard, her longtime tormentor, was afraid of his former housemaid. Arvid Bouchard was afraid of her.

"I'm sorry!" Bouchard cried one more time. "You'll never see me again. Just don't send that telegram!"

Rosamond hesitated, then gave a terse nod. He hurried away.

Standing between Judah and Miles, Rosamond watched him go. She knew, dimly, that seeing Arvid Bouchard run away from her should have been one of the most victorious moments of her life.

Instead, Rosamond learned, it was merely…final. And

it was sad. Because even though she could now make Mr. Bouchard cower with a well-placed threat to his treasured bank account, she could never get back everything he'd stolen from her.

Beginning and ending, she knew as she stood there feeling alone and unwantedly wise, with her trust in Miles. That was gone forever now, and she didn't know how she could regain it.

Grimly, Miles watched Arvid Bouchard hightail it down the street outside Rosamond's house. Bouchard cast a swift glance over his shoulder. He glimpsed Miles, Judah and—most important—Rosamond. He broke into an undignified trot, suit coat flapping in the breeze, then vanished around the corner.

Aptly impressed, Miles turned to Rosamond. "You did it. You faced him. And you're all right. I'm so proud of you, Rose."

Her profile looked stony as she watched Bouchard go. It remained flinty as she turned to look at Miles.

"I want you to leave, too," she said.

He was sure he couldn't have heard her correctly.

"Leave? Why?" Miles looked at Judah for confirmation, but the big man didn't meet his gaze. "I got here as fast as I could," Miles objected. "As soon as I realized Bouchard was—"

He broke off, belatedly remembering that there should have been reinforcements here with Bouchard. According to Seth, he'd brought along several of his thugs. Where were they?

That problem could wait, Miles decided.

Right now, the important thing was Rose's triumph.

"You were magnificent." Meaning it, Miles stepped

nearer to her. "The way you faced down Bouchard…it was remarkable."

"I'm not proud of it. It was necessary." Finally, Rosamond met his gaze. Her eyes were shiny with unshed tears. "So is this."

"So is what?" Damnation, but she was upset. Too upset, he reckoned, to make sense of just then. "I came to help you."

"I don't need your help. I don't need you."

"What?" He had to be having some sort of awful nightmare. Had he fallen on the way to save Rosamond? Had he gotten bashed in the head again? Drugged, like before? "Yes, you do. You do."

"No, I don't." With her voice shaking, Rosamond drew in a breath. She gave him a devastating look. "Don't you think I know how Arvid Bouchard found me? Don't you think I know it must have been you who led him here? You who betrayed me?"

Oh, no. "No, Rose. Wait. You don't understand."

She shook her head. "I wish I didn't."

"I never told Bouchard anything!" Miles protested. "I was supposed to tell him. I promised to tell him, but I—"

"With you, I guess promises come cheap."

"—I didn't. I swear, I didn't. I tried to make him stay away!" Desperately, Miles reached for her hand. She snatched it away before he could touch her—before he could make her understand. "Yes, I should have told you how I got here. I should have told you how I got that money. I should have told you everything," Miles admitted, full of anguish and the need to explain—no matter how tardy his explanation might be. "But things were going so well between us! I thought—"

"They were going well. I thought so, too." She lifted

her head. One of those tears trailed down her cheek, doing its utmost to break his heart. "Now...they're over."

"Over? No." With new urgency, Miles tried to clarify things. He told her about the breakthrough he'd had when Genevieve Bouchard had boasted with her friends about her devious agreement with Elijah Dancy—about the desperation he'd felt by the time Arvid had offered to finance Miles's eventual search for Rosamond. "There was no other way to find you!" he insisted. "Don't you see? I had to do it. I had to find you."

She had to see the love that had driven him there. She had to. Miles clenched his hands, watching her, praying she would.

"I understand." Rosamond met his gaze unflinchingly. Directly. Sympathetically enough to give him foolhardy hope. Then she crushed that hope forever. "I understand that you wanted to find me," Rosamond agreed. "I only wish you hadn't."

Her words were a knife to his heart. "That's not true."

"If it wasn't, I wouldn't say it. Unlike you, I only say what I mean." She lifted her skirts. She gave him a ladylike curtsy. "Goodbye, Mr. Callaway. Please don't bother me again."

Surprising him one last, cruel time, Rosamond turned away. She went through the gate with Judah hovering protectively at her elbow. Back straight, she trod up the walk. She went inside her flower-bedecked stronghold. She didn't once look back.

That was because Rosamond McGrath Dancy was strong, Miles realized then. He'd been wrong before, when he'd told himself he was stronger. She was the stronger of the two of them. Rosamond was strong enough and brave enough to accept nothing less than total respect and compliance from the men who'd hurt her.

Both of them.

Heartsick and broken, Miles turned away, too.

He'd tried and he'd failed. From here on, there was nothing left for him. Not a new beginning. Not a second chance. Nothing.

Nothing, that is…except Bouchard's men.

They were waiting for Miles as he left the busy street and entered the livery stable, quiet now at the end of business.

"We're here to collect Mr. Bouchard's money," one said.

Miles raised his arms in defeat. "I don't have it."

"He won't be happy to hear that."

Aggressively, they surrounded him. Miles didn't care.

"I spent it all on love," he told them. "On making sure love kept going."

He had, too. Just two days ago. He was glad of it.

One of Bouchard's thugs hesitated. He swore, then aimed a disgruntled look at their ringleader. "We can't hit him. He's backward. Bouchard didn't tell us he wasn't right in the head."

A grunt. "Bouchard wouldn't have cared."

They all came closer. Two of them held knives.

"Give us the damn money," the biggest of the knife-men said. "All of it. Now."

Miles shook his head. Crazy with despair, he smiled.

"I guess you'll just have to beat it out of me," he told them in a low voice. "Go ahead and try. I dare you."

Chapter Fourteen

Sitting in her parlor, surrounded by her bookshelves and her fine furnishings and the ordinarily useful accoutrements of her life as the proprietress of Morrow Creek's most successful marriage bureau, Rosamond could do nothing except feel glum.

These days, she could find love for anyone she might meet, Rosamond knew. She could pair up grizzled miners and warmhearted widows, stoical lumbermen and fresh-faced suffragettes, brawny wheelwrights and prickly spinsters. She could host soirees and schedule literary meetings. She could recognize that the only thing that truly bound together anyone in the world was true and lasting love…and still be incapable of finding it for herself.

Ironically, with Miles gone, none of her usual activities seemed to matter—especially not the ones that involved romance. Rosamond didn't have the heart to feel bitter or angry. All she felt was sad. All she knew was an overriding determination to turn away from the world— to make sure that nothing touched her.

She was back in her sanctuary, with all its protections— and its loneliness—still safely intact. Just the way she'd left it.

As though sensing her gloomy mood, Riley whined. The puppy wriggled in her arms, wanting to get free. Rosamond had carried her here to the parlor, hoping for comfort. It hadn't worked.

Even her devoted pet wanted to get away from her.

Sighing, she set down the puppy. It shook its little furry body, then trotted toward the doorway. It skidded to a stop.

It spotted Bonita Yates coming in and scampered to be held.

Improbably, Rosamond knew, Riley loved Bonita the best of everyone in the household. It was as if the puppy felt irredeemably drawn to the one person who was least likely to cuddle and nurture her. Even now, tail wagging with canine eagerness, Riley yipped for Bonita's attention.

Bonita glanced downward. "Humph. The last thing I need is an overexcited puppy. Can't she tell I don't have time for this?"

Rosamond suppressed her first smile of the week. "Evidently not. Riley leaped straight from my arms to get to yours."

Her friend's curmudgeonly gaze shifted to Rosamond, filled with suspicion. "Have you sewn meat scraps into my dress hem?"

"Not me. I can't be bothered to lift a needle."

"I can't figure out why this creature likes pestering me."

Rosamond could only lift one shoulder in a shrug. "What can I say? Some of us just can't learn to leave well enough alone."

"Some of us can't learn that being bright-eyed and bushy-tailed only leads to trouble." All the same, Bonita scooped up Riley in her arms. As she looked at the joy-filled puppy, a reluctant smile quirked her lips. "Sometimes it takes a while for the trouble to kick in," she alleged, "but it always shows up."

Rosamond agreed. "How do you think I feel? My own puppy isn't loyal enough to stay by my side in my hour of need."

"Aw." Bonita gave her a sympathetic look. "Still feeling poorly?" She nodded at Rosamond's nearby account book, abandoned on the table. "Did you get some work done at least?"

Rosamond shook her head. "I don't have the heart."

What was the point anyway? Nothing she did would ever amount to anything, Rosamond knew. Not in the state she was in.

Worst of all, it was all because she missed Miles.

Stupidly and irredeemably, she missed the man who'd betrayed her. Wasn't that worse, when she thought about it, than being hurt in the first place? For this regretful feeling—for being tied up in knots now—Rosamond had only herself to blame.

She was the one who'd naively trusted Miles in the first place. She, of all people, should have known better.

She didn't know how she could forgive herself for giving in.

"It might make you feel better to work." Bonita sat on a nearby chair, absentmindedly petting Riley. "Why don't you try?"

"You seem awfully eager to watch me tally accounts and moan over not having enough income." Rosamond frowned. "What's going on?"

"I'm worried about you, that's all. Ever since…that day, you've been like a ghost. You haven't spoken much, you haven't eaten, and I know you haven't slept. You're up pacing half the night like a brigadier general." Bonita

shook her head. "My bedroom is right next to yours, remember? We set it up that way when we first came here,
so we could enjoy our midnight chats."

They had. Reminded of that, Rosamond gave a faint
smile.

"That was nice, wasn't it? You were so kind to me,
right from the beginning." Newly struck by that, Rosamond glanced at her friend. "Why was that anyway?
You're the most cynical person I know, Bonita. Why
didn't you suspect me of something?"

Maybe, she thought, she should take distrustfulness
lessons from Bonita. Then she could be protected from
heartache in the future. She'd never have to feel this kind
of regret again.

"Pshaw." Bonita waved. Briefly, she curled up to nuz-
zle Riley on her lap. "Nobody could suspect you of anything except audacity, Rosamond. You've got enough of
that to spare."

"That's not really an answer. Back then, when Elijah was still alive to lie, steal and cheat, you didn't even
know me."

A faraway glance. "I knew enough. I knew that you
looked at a fallen woman like me and you didn't flinch
once. Unlike other people, you saw me as a person first
and a working girl last."

Rosamond didn't understand. "You are a person first."
You're a person who secretly likes puppies. "You're my
friend."

"Well, I was grateful to you for that, that's all."
Gruffly, Bonita cleared her throat. "Anyway, I was hoping you would get over that man of yours a lot faster
than this—"

"I don't want to talk about him."

"—but since it's obvious you're just going to pine away

for him until you're scrawny as a stick, pale as a coal miner's rump and exhausted enough to nap on a railway track—"

"Bonita!"

"I guess I'm just going to have to come clean."

"Come clean?" Rosamond didn't like the sound of that.

Her friend nodded. "I'm going to have to tell you what I did. So you can quit taking it all out on Miles Callaway."

By the time Miles was able to sit himself upright, slowly and creakily in a ladderback chair in his quarters downstairs at Owen Cooper's livery stable, he'd have thought he'd have a new perspective on things. But the fact was, he didn't.

He didn't have anything new except bumps and bruises. He didn't have a second chance. He didn't have a valise full of money. He didn't have Rosamond to make his days complete.

What he did have, improbably, was Dylan Coyle for a nursemaid. Even now, Rosamond's hard-nosed protector hunted around in Miles's kitchen cabinets, looking for something.

Coyle uttered a curse word. "Don't you have anything except crackers in here, Callaway? All I see are piles of hardtack."

"I like crackers." With dignity, Miles rested his head on the chair. Damnation, but settling in that chair had tired him out. He felt approximately as tough as Rosamond's puppy.

"I like crackers, too, but there ought to be limits." Coyle turned, hands near his gun belt. Upon glimpsing Miles, he issued a new and formidable frown. "You're supposed to be in bed."

"I didn't ask for a damn nursemaid." *If I had, I would*

have asked for Rosamond. Hellfire. He missed her the way he missed unlabored breathing and able walking. Miles clutched his bandaged broken ribs. "You can leave whenever you want."

"That isn't what you said the other day."

The other day. In the livery stable. When Bouchard's men had surrounded Miles. When they'd threatened him. When they'd readied their knives and their fists. When they'd knocked him to his knees with their first few blows, because Miles hadn't cared about defending himself. When they'd gone on pounding away brutally at a defenseless man on the ground. When their ringleader had reared back, his heavy boot blocking the light from the nearest open doorway, and aimed it menacingly at Miles's head.

When Dylan Coyle had stepped from the shadows and improbably put a stop to it all with that unexpected gun of his.

Bouchard's roughnecks hadn't been able to skedaddle fast enough. One of the knifemen had even left his weapon. Miles had watched, foggy with pain, as Coyle had pocketed that knife.

It was almost as if he'd wanted an inexplicable souvenir.

"Yeah." Miles winced as he tried to get comfortable. His damaged insides made that tricky. Despite the pain, he managed a sarcastic grin. "It turns out, coldhearted thugs get pretty excited about being dared to issue a beating."

A grunt. "That wasn't smart." Coyle kept rummaging around.

"I didn't have what they wanted." *Now I don't have anything. Not even money.* "Besides, it didn't matter anyway."

"It did matter. A pinch." Unceremoniously, Coyle clat-

tered a bowl of cold tinned beans onto the table beside
Miles. He glared at him, all but challenging him to eat
them. Surprisingly, he grinned. "That dare of yours is
what made me want to help you."

Miles disagreed. He shook his head. "You helped me
because Rosamond made you do it. She sent you to protect me."

He felt awash with love for her at the very thought.

He was a certifiable fool. No doubt about it.

Coyle tilted his head curiously. "Is that what you
think?"

"That's the only explanation." Miles ignored the
beans. He didn't care about getting better or stronger.
He might never care about anything again, the way he
was feeling these days. If not for Coyle—and for the later
arrival of Owen Cooper—Miles might have bled to death
beside that big black mare's stall and not given a damn.
"I've had a lot of time to think about it."

"Not enough time, apparently." Coyle gestured. "Eat."

Miles refused, still bothered by what Dylan had said.

"You were there when those knucks jumped me because Rosamond made you do it," Miles insisted. "That's
why you helped me." *Back when Rosamond still cared if
I was alive or dead.*

"I was there because Mrs. Dancy hired me to follow
you. I happened to follow you to the stable, just like I
was paid to do. I was supposed to find out who you might
be working with. And why." Looking exasperated and
tough—despite that startling revelation—Coyle jammed
a spoon into Miles's grasp. He waited impatiently for
Miles to start shoveling in beans. "Did you really think
Rosamond needed a former Pinkerton man to watch her
back door?"

Halfway toward digging into the beans—if that's what

would make Dylan shut up—Miles went still. He had to admit…

"You have a point there." Then, "Rosamond didn't trust me?"

Coyle actually laughed. "You're offended? That takes a lot of nerve, considering what Mrs. Dancy suspected you were up to."

"I wasn't up to anything," Miles said mulishly. Except falling harder, faster and ever more foolishly for Rose.

"You got all that money from someplace," Coyle insisted with typical nonchalance. "It didn't fall from the sky."

"That money was a means to an end. I didn't 'earn' it, not the way Bouchard wanted me to. I never intended to do that. Not to Rose." Miles felt too tired and too broken to go into this. "The money's gone now anyway. That's what I told Bouchard's men, and it's what I'm telling you. If you don't believe me—"

"I don't believe in much of anything. Except keeping my word." Coyle strode across Miles's clothing-strewn quarters. He stopped to examine the bandages and medicine and laudanum Doc Finney had left after his visit, seeming oddly adept with those items. With a new wave of apparent frustration, Coyle put down a bandage. "At least I had the integrity to do underhand work for somebody who deserved it."

For Rose. Miles understood…and couldn't really blame her. He would have been justifiably suspicious of himself, too. He hadn't been working for Bouchard, but he had taken that money from him. Rosamond had been correct to suspect him.

He couldn't really be surprised she'd hired Dylan to find out more about Miles's dealings. Rosamond might be kind, loving and capable of making him giddy when they were together beneath a coverlet, but she was hardly a helpless innocent.

She was resilient. She was capable. She was smart.

She was also justifiably infuriated and hurt by him. Not that Miles didn't have a few legitimate complaints of his own. He did. Rosamond hadn't exactly been a model of trustworthiness herself. Since the day he'd arrived in Morrow Creek, Rosamond had had him drugged, searched and knocked out. She'd misled him and beguiled him. Worst of all, she'd made him believe that she loved him back.

Rosamond was hardly blameless in all this, Miles reminded himself harshly. She had to have known how he felt.

Even though he hadn't distinctly explained his feelings for her, she had to have known about them. His unrequited love for Rosamond was plastered all over him, like bandages and ointment.

Another grunt from Coyle broke Miles's reverie. He glanced up, spoon still in hand, to see the security man frowning.

If Coyle was trying to prod him into confessing…

"I never spied for Bouchard," Miles felt compelled to clarify. "I never intended to. I needed money, that's all. Money to find Rosamond." Something awful occurred to him. "Did you tell her I was working for him?" Coyle must have done, given everything that had happened. "You miserable—"

"I didn't tell her anything. She's got eyes of her own. As soon as that citified bastard showed up, she could see—"

"I'm not the one who brought him here!" Miles said. "I tried to throw him off the trail. He must have had me followed."

"A beginner like you?" A slight grin quirked the security man's mouth. "Hell, you probably couldn't help being followed."

While delivering that offhanded insult, Coyle didn't so much as look up at him. He was busy checking his guns. That was a habit of his, Miles had observed over the past days.

"Go on." Miles gave a grumpy wave, still upset to know that Rose hadn't really trusted him. "Beat a man when he's down."

"I'm not the one keeping you down. You're doing a mighty fine job of that all on your own." Dylan's tone remained light. "All I can say is, women like Mrs. Dancy don't come around every day. If I ever had a chance with her—"

"I'll break your legs if you try anything."

Coyle flashed a grin. "Then you do still care about her?"

Disgruntled at the man's shrewd tone, Miles looked away. He did care. But he didn't want to. What was the point in caring when there was nothing he could do about it?

He'd already tried everything. He'd loved her. He'd lost.

"Not ready to admit it? Fine. Your loss." Coyle tucked away his gun with a practiced whirl of his fingers. He didn't seem to notice Miles's attentiveness to that inimitable gesture. "All I'm saying is, if I had a chance with a good woman like Mrs. Dancy, I'd crawl on my hands and knees to claim it."

"I would have to crawl on my hands and knees," Miles joked, wanting this uncomfortable conversation over with. "My legs don't work right on account of all the kicking I took."

Coyle wasn't amused. "You don't know what you're throwing away." His jaw tightened. "It's a rare thing, having a woman who knows you clean through. A woman who loves you, all the same."

New insight struck Miles. "A woman like you had... once?"

For the first time, Dylan stood on the defensive. Despite his gun belt and his tough stance, he seemed almost vulnerable.

If Miles hadn't seen it with his own eyes, he wouldn't have believed it could happen. Dylan Coyle...made defenseless by love?

Or by the loss of it, Miles considered, and felt new commiseration for the man's struggles. After all, Coyle had lingered there with him for days, caring for an injured not-quite-friend he barely knew. He was a good man. Or he was trying to be. Either way, he kept too much to himself to tell.

Coyle muttered a swearword. His aura of vulnerability vanished, tucked away behind a frown and another hard look.

"If I'd known you were going to footle around like a damn idiot," he said sternly, "I would have let you get kicked to death."

Miles didn't believe it. "I'm glad you didn't. Thank you."

"Thank me by not being a nitwit. Go see Mrs. Dancy. Make things right with her. Do it before it's too late."

"That's impossible." Miles regarded him closely. "But maybe you ought to take your own advice. That's what I'm thinking."

He didn't know much about Coyle's past.

An instant later, he realized he wasn't going to, either.

"Maybe you ought to mind your own damn business."

All at once, Miles wasn't sure if Dylan Coyle was pretending to have had a grand, long-lost love or if he really had found someone to give his heart to…and then had it stomped to pieces while he watched. Studying the man's enigmatic expression now, Miles reckoned it could have been either one.

"It doesn't matter," Miles maintained. "Rosamond won't have me. I tried to explain over and over. She wouldn't listen."

"Then you're doing it wrong."

"If I weren't wrecked and broken, I'd punch you for that."

"So…you're giving up," Coyle said. "You're done, then."

"You make it sound unreasonable. It damn well isn't."

He had his pride, Miles knew. He had his reputation.

No Callaway man had ever tried to woo a woman and failed. Miles had learned that legend from his father. He believed it.

Casting a final warning glance at Miles's beans, Coyle put on his hat. He tugged it down low, then nodded. "I've got things to do. Don't stay out of bed too long. Don't forget to eat."

"Yes, ma'am."

That feisty rejoinder earned Miles a glare that would have flattened a lesser man—a lesser man who cared about living, at least. Miles didn't care about much of anything just then.

"Eat a damn spoonful of beans, or I'm not coming back," Coyle told him. "Until now, you've been too hurt to complain about helping. I felt obliged for Mrs. Dancy's sake, too. It's what she would have wanted. But I'm not in the business of giving out charity." His face grew flinty.

"I won't put myself out—not for a man who won't even watch out for himself."

"Then I guess you'll be finding a new way to spend your afternoons," Miles retorted, "because I intend to wallow here in misery." So far, not even Daisy Cooper's commiserating molasses cookies had helped drag Miles from the slump he was in.

Then he realized the rest of what Coyle had just said.

"Why did you feel obliged for Rosamond's sake? Why would you think it's what she would have wanted?" Miles wanted to know. "I already told you, she doesn't care about me."

Coyle gave him a perceptive look. "You don't think so?"

"You do think so?" Idiotically, a spark of hope ignited Miles's battered-up spirit. "You think she still cares?"

"I think," Coyle said, "you've got thinking to do."

Then he set his boots in motion, crossing Miles's newly messy quarters and leaving him behind to wonder and heal and eat and fret and—damn it all—to start in hoping, all over again.

"What do you mean, what you did?" Rosamond gave Bonita a cautious look, surprised by her outburst. "The only things I'm 'taking out' on Mr. Callaway are the things he's responsible for." Like breaking my heart. And destroying my faith.

He was definitely responsible for those things.

"Well…" Bonita shifted her gaze to the unlit fireplace. Inscrutably, she went on stroking Riley. The puppy all but purred with contentment in her arms. "First off, there's the matter of that telegram. I guess I ought to get that off my chest right away. You'll be wanting to know, I suppose."

"Telegram?" Perplexed, Rosamond considered what that might mean. "You mean the telegram I threatened Mr. Bouchard with?"

Bonita knew all about the confrontation she'd had with her former employer at the front gate, of course. All the women in her household did. Thanks to Rosamond's system of secret signals, Judah had managed to alert Bonita to clear everyone from the premises—a safeguard lest Arvid Bouchard become even meaner and more vengeful than Rosamond had feared he would.

After they'd all returned, Rosamond had had no choice but to explain a few things about her past. With all of her secrets out in the open, she and her "ladies" were now closer than ever.

Even if none of them quite blamed Miles as much as they ought to have done, as her longtime friends, for this mess.

In fact, some of them had even had the gall to stand up for him. That wasn't counting the caterwauling the children had done when Rosamond had told them Miles would not be coming back. She sometimes doubted little Seamus O'Malley would ever forgive her.

"That's the one." Bonita nodded. "The telegram that's going to give that bastard his rightful comeuppance. That one."

At her friend's merciless tone, Rosamond shook her head. "I didn't send it, Bonita. It would have ruined him! Bouchard left, just like I wanted. It was only a threat. That's all."

"It was your secondary plan, and it was a good one."

"Yes, but I didn't send it! I only arranged for Savannah Corwin to send it from her station if I asked her to." That was one of the things they'd discussed over tea at the Lorndorff the other day. Now, Rosamond tried to soothe Bonita. "I know you'd like to see Mr. Bouchard punished for what he did." Truthfully, there was a part of Rosamond that would have liked that, too. "But no matter what I do to him, I can't undo the past. All I can do is go forward. So I didn't send that telegram."

For a moment, the only sound was the clock ticking. Then, "You didn't send it. That don't mean I didn't."

Rosamond stared at her. Bonita went on petting Riley.

"Like I said, I knew about your secondary plan. I knew about Bouchard, too—enough to know that he deserves what he got. And I'm acquainted with Mrs. Corwin, remember?" Bonita went on, sounding defensive and a little pugnacious. "We have more than a few things in common. She didn't mind helping me."

Rosamond couldn't believe it. "You sent that telegram?"

Arvid Bouchard was going to get his just retribution.

Rosamond forced her attention from that startling news.

"I was on my way to Mrs. Corwin's adjunct station just as soon as I saw Bouchard try to take down Judah." Bonita smiled fondly at the memory. "That boy did prove himself, didn't he?"

"He did." For that, Rosamond was glad. But she still didn't understand. "You and Savannah were working together?"

"Together to watch over you." Bonita gave her a warm look. "When I found out for sure that Mr. Callaway had gotten a telegram from Bouchard, I wanted to tell you straightaway. But Mrs. Corwin disagreed. She made me wait. She said there was probably another reason Callaway was here—something we didn't know about." Bonita shook her head. "She's a mite more trusting than I am. She's a real romantic, that one. Probably because of that husband of hers. The way they met—it was darn unlikely."

Rosamond couldn't consider Savannah and Adam's courtship just then. She was too busy remembering Savannah's uncharacteristic lack of detail about the telegram she'd relayed to Morrow Creek from Mr. Bouchard. At the time, Rosamond had been too relieved to know she hadn't seen Arvid in Morrow Creek to pursue the matter any further. But now, she understood.

"Mrs. Corwin thought that, whatever Callaway was up to, he must have had a good reason for it—a reason he'd tell you, sooner or later." Bonita looked unconvinced. "She thought you probably knew him better than all of us did, and if you were ready to trust him, we could do the same." A pause, followed by a frown. "All we ever wanted was for you to be happy."

Unaccountably touched by Bonita's concern for her, Rosamond looked toward the fireplace. She hadn't trusted Miles. Not at first. At first, she'd hired Dylan Coyle to watch him, certain that Miles was in Morrow Creek on behalf of the Bouchards.

But after Dylan had been unable to turn up any evidence of wrongdoing on Miles's part—and after time had worn on and Rosamond had gotten closer to Miles—Rosamond hadn't cared. All she'd wanted was to be with him. Then. And now.

No matter how foolish that might have been.

"I can't believe I didn't see what was going on." Rosamond shook her head. "I've been more distracted than I realized."

"I suppose that's a fact," Bonita told her sympathetically, cutting off the self-pity Rosamond had been prepared to indulge herself in. "For instance, you haven't even guessed why I've been so keen to have you do some account work today."

Come to think of it… "That was unexpected."

Frowning, Rosamond glanced at her account book.

"So is the big bunch of money you're going to find in there." Bonita nodded at it. "Go ahead. Take a look."

Confused, Rosamond did. She picked up her familiar, worn, leather-bound account book. As she did, she accidentally turned the whole caboodle upside down. Greenbacks fluttered from the pages. They fell to the floor like overeager autumn leaves.

"What is all this?" Astonished, Rosamond transferred her gaze from the money to Bonita. "You knew about this?"

"I did all that." Her friend looked unusually pleased. "You don't know how long it took me to arrange each bill between the pages like that. I wanted it to be a big surprise for you."

"But I—" Still stunned, Rosamond picked up a note. "I've never seen so much money in all my life! At least I haven't—"

Since I saw all that money in Miles's valise.

Rosamond finally understood. "This is from Miles."

Aside from Bonita, Miles was the only one who knew about Rosamond's money troubles at the mutual society.

"It's from an anonymous donor," Bonita maintained primly.

"Do you think I was born yesterday? I know Miles took money from Mr. Bouchard. He took it to find me. He said so!"

"This money is earmarked for the maintenance and upkeep of the Morrow Creek Mutual Society." Bonita appeared to be trying not to grin as she petted Riley. "That's all I know."

"I don't want money that came from Arvid Bouchard!"

"I reckon that's what the anonymous donor thought, too. That's why the anonymous donor wanted to get rid of it, maybe."

"Your 'donor' is Miles." Rosamond wasn't fooled. "What I don't understand is why you took it. You don't even like him."

"That would give me a problem with taking his money from him…how, exactly?" Bonita did smile. "You know…hypothetically."

"I still don't want Bouchard's money. It's tainted."

"It's for love. It's for making sure love keeps going." Bonita gave her a straight look. "That's what the donor said."

Exasperated, Rosamond threw up her hands. "Just tell me it was Miles! You clearly think his giving us that money was a good thing. Do you want me to forgive him or not?"

"I do." Bonita hesitated. "But I'm not sure you ever will, given the state you're in." A frown. "Also…there's more."

"There can't possibly be more."

"There is." Scooting to the edge of her chair, Bonita set down Riley. She gave the puppy a little push to persuade it to scamper away. Then she looked at Rosamond. "I hired Dylan."

Rosamond frowned. "I hired Dylan."

"I hired him, too. To find out about your past," Bonita confessed. "Then, after I knew everything I needed to, I wired that Bouchard character and brought him here to Morrow Creek."

Gobsmacked, Rosamond froze. "What?"

"I thought that if you saw Bouchard, you'd blame Miles. I thought that you'd quit being with him." Bonita shifted again. She cast Rosamond an anxious look. "I wanted things to go back to the way they were! I knew if you married Callaway, everything would change around here. The mutual society would close. You would move on…" Bonita drew in a breath. "I'd be alone."

"Oh, Bonita. I would never leave you alone." Rosamond felt full of confusion…but commiseration, too. "For you to bring Arvid Bouchard here, though…that was an awful thing to do."

"I know. I'm so sorry." Bonita nearly burst into tears. "I never meant to hurt you. Can you ever forgive me?"

At her friend's outright regret, Rosamond had only one choice to make. "Of course I can, Bonita. Yes. I forgive you."

Her friend whimpered. "Truly? You can?" A sniff. "You do?"

Touched, Rosamond nodded. "Of course! You didn't mean it. You were acting out of desperation and confusion and some misguided notions. You should have talked to me first, that's all, so we could sort it out. But I can't hold what you did against you." She shook her head. "After all, if Arvid Bouchard hadn't come here, I never would have had the satisfaction of confronting him. I never would have broken free at all."

"Yes." Another mighty sniffle. "That's what I thought."

"Don't cry, Bonita! It's going to be all right."

"Yes, it is." Suddenly, Bonita raised her head. Incredibly, she was dry-eyed. Chipper, even. "Because I didn't hire Dylan. I didn't contact Bouchard. I didn't bring him here."

"What?" Rosamond felt bewildered. "You just said you did."

"I fibbed. I'm afraid it's true, may the Lord bless my

soul. You'll have to forgive me for that, but I had to know how you felt about things." Bonita looked savvier than Rosamond had ever seen her. "I had to make you see the truth."

"What truth? That my best friend is a lunatic?" Rosamond pondered everything. "Did you truly send that telegram?"

"Yes. That I did, I can promise you." Bonita smiled, then went on. "And the truth is that you were ready to forgive me immediately. You didn't even have to think twice, did you?"

Rosamond felt too hungry, too uncommunicative, too sleepy and too out-and-out flustered for all this confusion. "So?"

"So you might want to think about who you're really mad at," Bonita said. "Is it me? Is it Callaway? Or is it yourself?"

"Honestly?" Flustered by Bonita's abrupt "confession" and subsequent staggering turnaround, Rosamond couldn't think straight. "I don't know anymore."

"Because it seems to me that you're more mad at yourself for trusting Mr. Callaway than you are at him for accidentally 'betraying' you. It seems to me you know full well that man never meant for Bouchard to follow him here."

Rosamond pressed her lips together, suddenly not interested in continuing this line of thought. "You don't know that."

"No, I reckon I don't." Bonita stood. She studied the scattered money and Rosamond's baffled face. "But you do. You know what the truth really is. You know if it's Callaway or yourself you're trying to punish by hiding away in here. So I think I'll just leave you alone to ponder that idea a while."

Then, sashaying out, that's exactly what Bonita did...
leaving Rosamond with no excuses—and nothing but a
big pile of cold hard truths—for company.

Chapter Fifteen

Miles Callaway was a man who believed in second chances.

He had to be. By the time he made it from the livery stable to the unobtrusive street where Rosamond Mc-Grath Dancy's house was situated, Miles didn't have much choice except to hope for a second chance. To have faith that she would forgive him. Because he wasn't entirely sure he could make it back to the stable again. Not while hobbling along on his temporarily rickety, no-good, kicked-up legs. Not while squinting through his one good eye and keeping the other puffy, bruised eye closed tight.

Thanks to Arvid Bouchard's men, Miles was a broken-up man.

But thanks to Rosamond, he was a hopeful one, too.

No other woman could have inspired Miles to make that trip. It had been arduous and painful. It had joggled his broken ribs and his sense of pride alike. Townspeople had stared as he'd made his way through the streets; people he'd come to know and like as friends and neighbors joked with him that he belonged at home with old Doc Finney by his side to make him whole again.

But Miles knew that only one person could make him whole.

Rosamond.

He'd thought of little except her since...well, since as long as he could remember. But especially since he'd awakened in his lonesome bed with a sore head and bashed-in ribs and assorted bumps and bruises. He'd thought of how enchanting Rosamond had been. How challenging. How brave to have loved him at all.

He didn't have much to give her, Miles knew. Only a fierce heart and a sense of hope and a pair of sheltering arms. But if Rosamond still wanted any of those things—and he dearly hoped she did—then Miles wanted desperately to give them to her.

He wanted that so much that he didn't even care, as he careened down her street and spied two of Rosamond's security men at her gate, if he got beaten to hell and back again.

It was entirely likely that she'd left orders with Judah and Seth and even Dylan Coyle to wallop Miles on sight, he knew. Rosamond didn't fiddle around with half measures. Not once she'd made up her mind. So it was with a thimbleful of trepidation and an ocean full of heroism that Miles ignored his various banged-up limbs, midsection and head, then swaggered up to the gate.

He was going to see Rosamond or die trying.

He was going to see her through only one good eye, granted. But by God, Miles swore as he girded his courage, he was going to make sure that Rosamond knew exactly how he felt this time.

If he had to, he'd shout it to her between thumpings from her young, dumb, brawny protectors. That's how all-fired certain Miles was that he needed to make things right with Rosamond.

Feeling ready, he jutted his chin. His stuck out his chest.

He winced, because sticking out his chest hurt like the devil. But then Miles gritted his teeth and did it again. Because he was fearless. He was fearless in the face of needing love. Needing to give love. Rosamond deserved that…and more.

"I need to see Mrs. Dancy," Miles said firmly.

In unison, Seth and Judah turned their backs to him. With a marked degree of casualness, they started up a conversation about Griffin Turner and the outrageous lady architect he'd had brought in from the States to work on designing his new hotel.

"You don't have to tell her I'm here," Miles said more loudly, baffled by their behavior. "I'll go straight in."

Neither man acknowledged him. Had they been deafened?

No. They were talking to one another, so that wasn't it.

"If Mrs. Dancy isn't at home," Miles shouted. "I'll wait."

Still no word from Judah or Seth. But the former leaned an inch or two sideways. Nonchalantly, Judah kicked open the gate. It swung into the yard with an unwelcoming creak. Wide open.

Miles frowned in bewilderment. He didn't know what was wrong with these two. But he did know that he had a limited amount of strength for standing at his disposal. His insides ached like the dickens. He was starting to get that familiar light-headed feeling that told him he'd overexerted himself.

Determinedly, Miles stepped through the gate. He half expected Judah and Seth to wake up, realize there was an intruder in their midst and start delivering sockdolagers.

In his current state, Miles wouldn't be able to fight

back. He wasn't a man who ordinarily backed down, but even the best man had his limits. For now, Miles was temporarily a pacifist.

Oddly enough, it didn't come to that. Because even as Miles looked around to make sure he'd actually landed on the inside portion of the fenced yard—and hadn't accidentally hallucinated it on account of the pain—he saw someone hurrying to him.

"I knew it!" a woman cried out. "You're here!"

Miles blinked. Blinking hurt, too, he discovered. "Rose?"

"No, Mr. Callaway. It's Miss Yates." She took his arm, all but exuding warmth and charm. "Just let me help you, all right?"

Her voice was as sweet as honey, her smile as enchanting as an angel's. Vaguely, Miles realized that Bonita Yates could be a captivating woman. She'd just never tried to be one with him.

"I need to see Mrs. Dancy," he said urgently. "Right now."

Instead, Miles found himself bustled inside the cool interior of Rosamond's household. Today, there were no dance lessons. There were no literary meetings or social events.

There was only Rose, nearby somewhere, needing him.

"I've got to talk to Rose." Miles said it more directly, feeling a little of his vigor return as he realized how close Rosamond was. "You've got to take me to her! It's important."

"I know it is." Miss Yates shushed him gently. Her skirts swished as she led him by the arm down the hall. "There, there."

"This is the wrong way," Miles protested. "I need to go to Rosamond's parlor! That's where she always is."

"Yes, yes. Soon enough, you will. Well, maybe you will." Miss Yates stopped in front of a closed door. She faced him, looking authoritative and determined. "First, there are some people here who would like a word with you. I don't think they're in any mood to take no for an answer, either."

Miles wasn't in an especially benevolent mood himself. Not now that he was being delayed from seeing Rosamond. But since he didn't have the strength to spare for arguing—since he needed that strength to convince Rosamond to let him love her and take care of her and make sure she was happy forever—he nodded.

"Very good." With a mysterious smile and a showy flourish, Miss Yates opened the door. "Go right on in, please."

Miles glanced in. He gave an inward groan.

He'd thought he'd tackled every barrier.

In that moment, Miles learned, he decidedly hadn't.

The trouble with having a personal catchphrase, Rosamond had learned over the past few days, was that pretty soon, folks started expecting you to live up to it. They started chiming in saying it to you, irksomely, when they passed you in the hallway or sold you a newspaper or brought you your milk delivery. They started behaving as if you were capable of doing it.

When your personal catchphrase ran along the lines of, *I'll master this eventually. I will,* that tended to be problematic.

Especially when you were trying to avoid trying at all.

Because that's what she'd been doing, Rosamond realized as she stared out her parlor window while letting her coffee grow cold. She'd been trying to avoid trying to do anything—anything that had to do with not being safe, not being sure, or not being in charge of the outcome. Rosamond liked being in charge.

When it came to love—to Miles—she couldn't be in charge.

Not really. That didn't mean Miles was in charge, either, she reckoned as she glanced at her abandoned coffee cup. He wasn't. Love made fools and bumblers of everyone. Even Miles.

The lucky fools and bumblers—the ones who went on to live happy lives together—well, they just welcomed the risk, that's all.

Heaving a sigh, Rosamond stood. She paced. She thought.

She thought about Miles...and how best she could approach him. She needed a grand gesture. She needed to prove to Miles, beyond a doubt, that she'd made a mistake. She shouldn't have blamed him for bringing Arvid Bouchard to town. Miles hadn't meant to do that. And she shouldn't have made Miles leave, either, trudging away in the path of Arvid's cowardly footsteps.

Those two men could not have been more different, Rosamond reminded herself assuredly. Why she'd let herself forget that, even for an instant, she couldn't imagine. She could only blame fear and impulse and desperation for it. She'd made a mistake.

Just like Miles, she was fallible. She was human.

She was vulnerable and she was afraid. Sometimes. Sometimes she was brave and silly and ambitious, too. But that was part of what it meant to be human, wasn't it? Taking chances. Reaching out. Trying to find love even when it appeared faraway.

I'll master this eventually. I will.

Rosamond remembered that stubborn catchphrase of hers and realized that as much as it had helped bolster her at times, it had also held her back. Because sometimes, her motto was just a way to keep claiming she was trying…even when she was standing still. Sometimes it was just a way to feel better about things, even as she locked herself away behind self-made brambles and barriers…and then wondered why she felt so lonely all the time.

She couldn't wait to devise the perfect approach. That was simply more stalling. She had to go see Miles now. Now.

Determinedly, Rosamond headed for her parlor door.

At the same moment, Dylan Coyle came through it. Hat in hand, he nodded. "Afternoon, ma'am. Do you have a minute?"

Brought up short, Rosamond frowned. "Not really. I'm—"

"Good. Because we need to talk." Behaving as though she hadn't just brushed off his request, Dylan carried on speaking. "The thing is, ma'am, I'm quitting. I'm leaving Morrow Creek."

"Oh. I'm sorry to hear that." Rosamond inhaled, dredging up a smile for him. "You're a good man. You were very helpful."

A mysterious smile quirked his mouth. "Not as helpful as I might have been, but I gave it full effort. Just like always."

"Yes, I imagine you did." With a businesslike air, Rosamond nodded. She didn't want to lose Dylan, but she couldn't very well keep him employed. Not anymore. She held out her hand. "Thank you kindly for looking out for me. I appreciate it."

Sobering, Dylan grasped her hand. "It was my pleasure." His grip was callused. Steady. The significance of their handshake was not lost on him, she saw. "Good luck to you, ma'am."

Dylan put on his hat. He ambled out, boots ringing.

Good. Rosamond inhaled. Now she could go see Miles.

She made it all the way to the doorway again before Seth appeared. He unwittingly blocked her exit with his huge body.

"Mrs. Dancy?" He tipped his hat. "I'm awfully sorry to bother you like this. It's just that—"

"I don't have time to talk, Seth. I have to leave."

Her security man didn't appear to understand. He didn't so much as budge. "I have to quit working for you, Mrs. Dancy. It's been a real pleasure and all. I can promise you that."

Oh dear. Two of her security men were leaving?

It was a good thing Rosamond had decided to rejoin the world again. Starting with Miles. Starting with going to Miles. Because there wouldn't be anyone around to guard her haven.

"But the fact is, I have another job on offer, and I'd sorely like to take it. Jack Murphy's faro dealer is leaving Morrow Creek, and I aim to grab his spot at the table."

"You're going to gamble professionally?"

"I already done it like an amateur." Good-naturedly, Seth grinned. "But I learned a few things. I think I'm ready."

"Well, I can't stop you. Nor would I try to, if this is what you truly want." Rosamond offered a handshake, feeling perplexed by the suddenness of his decision. "Good luck."

Solemnly, they shook hands. "Good luck to you," he said.

After a bit more chitchat, Seth meandered out, leaving Rosamond scrabbling to collect her things, fetch a parasol, head for the door...

As she stepped outside her front door, Judah rushed over.

At his worried expression, Rosamond lost the last thread of her patience. Didn't they know what was at stake here?

For all she knew, Miles was leaving town.

"Oh, for Pete's sake, Judah. Are you quitting, too?"

Her security man gave her a funny look. "No, ma'am. I'm not leaving till you make me go." His spoony-eyed glance reminded her that might not be a bad idea. "I came to tell you that Mrs. Larkin has a visitor—and he's an awfully insistent one, too."

Miles had never been accused of a crime. Not even a minor one. He'd never stood on trial or been forced to defend his good name.

That day, in the inner sanctum of the Morrow Creek Mutual Society, Miles felt he had to do all those things. Expertly.

"Exactly how do you intend to make a living, Mr. Callaway?" Katie Scott intoned. Surrounded by the other ladies, she consulted a sheet of paper in front of her. She frowned up at him. "I understand you're a stableman by trade. Is that right?"

"You know darn well it's right. I gave you and Tommy riding lessons down at Cooper's stable last week." Miles swept all the assembled women with an impatient look. He'd been here for several minutes, being interrogated. "Now, you're all just wasting my time. Am I admitted to this marriage bureau or not?"

"Mutual society," Libby Jorgensen corrected, adjusting her spectacles. "And we'll make our decision in our own time."

"We have to decide if you're man enough," Maureen O'Malley told him. Her lingering gaze suggested she was making her decision based on the fit of his shirt. Or his britches. Or both. "This decision can't be rushed. Turn around, please."

Miles protested. "What for? I'm hardworking, honest and capable of reading a book. I have a good job, and I haven't touched a drop of liquor for more than three weeks. What else—"

"Just turn around, please," suggested Miss Scott.

Maybe it was better to cooperate. Then he could get to see Rosamond more quickly. Obligingly, Miles turned. He stood.

A collective sigh fluttered through the room.

Miles heard it. "I'd like to know what my backside has to do with my capacity for membership in this society. Because—"

"It has nothing to do with that." There was tart humor in Bonita Yates's tone. "We all just want to look. Ladies?"

"We approve," they chorused to Miles's vexation.

Fed up, he turned around. "Now I'm going to see Rose."

They looked alarmed. Chairs scraped across the floor. Women came hurrying toward him, muttering amongst themselves.

Miles couldn't listen to their nattering. He had important things to do. He had to find Rosamond. He had to tell her—

"You haven't found out about the baby yet." Lucinda Larkin's voice rang above all the others. "Aren't you curious?"

Caught, Miles paused. He glanced at Mrs. Larkin, taking in her defiant demeanor—and the baby in her arms. Tobe stood nearby her, doing his utmost to sport a poker face that would hide whatever secrets his mother—and Rosamond—wanted under wraps.

"I love Rosamond," Miles told them all, giving up his quest to learn the baby's origins for good. "I'll love her baby, too, if it comes to that. Now, if you'll all excuse me, I'm leaving."

He charged for the door—at least as ably as his battered body would allow him to. It felt more like a limp. It felt...

It felt as if half a dozen fallen angels were holding him by the arms, carrying him forward, bringing him to Rosamond.

The ladies of the mutual society were fully on his side. They bustled Miles in their midst all the way down the hallway.

There, he spied Rosamond with her back to him, speaking with a man at the front door. No, there were two men there, Miles saw. One was indisputably in charge, from his aristocratic face to his expensive suit and fancy shoes. The other was in service, gray and dignified, with an armful of wrapped gifts.

Simon Blackhouse, Miles surmised, remembering what Seth had told him about expecting someone rich, powerful and willing to break every rule to find out what Lucinda Larkin had been up to.

Behind him, Mrs. Larkin came to a halt. Her gaze flew to Blackhouse's face, then dropped tellingly to the baby in her arms.

In a heartbeat, Miles recognized the truth.

The child had been Lucinda's all along. Likely, Rosamond had helped her hide the baby from him. Because, undoubtedly, Lucinda had guessed someone might be keeping watch over her—someone in Simon Blackhouse's employ. She'd simply—mistakenly—surmised that Miles was the man to be wary of…when it had been Seth interrogating Tobe, reporting in to Blackhouse, all along.

He had to admire Rosamond's loyalty to the women of her household. He knew she would have done whatever her friends asked her to, with no limitations or questions asked, purely for the sake of protecting them. Even clobbering a man like him.

He didn't have long to contemplate his onetime sore head or those startling realizations, though. The ladies of the mutual society bowled Miles forward, pushing him into the parlor like a pack of determined and lace-bedecked sheepdogs.

Miles stumbled inside, inadvertently poked and prodded in all his most injured places. If not for the saving glimpse he'd had of Rosamond, he might have resented that rough treatment.

As it was, it was all he could do not to run to her.

"Stay here," Miss Yates ordered. Then she shut the door.

Inwardly, Miles gave a sardonic laugh. If Bonita Yates and her cohorts thought they were keeping Miles from reaching Rosamond now, they'd better think again. Because he was damn well going to get to her. He was going to get to her now.

As he reached the door, a clink sounded.

He tried the knob. Damnation. He was locked in the parlor.

It looked as if Rosamond wasn't the only one who could surprise a man in Morrow Creek. She'd cultivated a whole houseful of meddlesome women who could do the same damn thing.

"…so I insist on seeing Lucinda Larkin."

Rosamond heard the patrician man in front of her

repeat his earlier demand, but only with half an ear. The man who'd arrived—the man whose accompanying valet, Adams, had announced as "Simon Blackhouse, ma'am,"—was tall, handsome and insistent. He had an overall aura of power, a sheen of personal wealth and a pile of gifts. Those were all lovely and intriguing things.

But Rosamond had just glimpsed Miles being bustled past her. She only had eyes for him. He was there. He was there!

"Don't make me sic Adams on you," Blackhouse was saying, looking beleaguered and intent and very unused to being refused anything he wanted. "He's a war veteran. He's fearsome."

Rosamond examined the refined man holding all the gifts in his arms. He gave her a polite smile. She smiled back at him.

"Yes, I'm sure that would be terrifying, Mr. Blackhouse," Rosamond told her visitor impatiently. "But the fact remains that we don't allow unexpected visitors here. So I'm afraid—"

"I'll see him." From behind her, Lucinda stepped forward. With Tobe trailing her and her baby in her arms, she stared at Blackhouse. "If you can confront your past, Rosamond, so can I."

Rosamond didn't understand. "Judah is right there. He can help," she insisted. "If you want Mr. Blackhouse to leave—"

"You've done enough." Gently, Lucinda transferred her baby to Libby's arms. "You have a visitor of your own to see to."

Miles. Rosamond remembered him and lost a bit of her zeal for making sure that Lucinda and her baby— for it was Lucinda's baby, hers and someone Rosamond didn't know—were seen to. Because ultimately, this was Lucinda's decision to make.

"I never thought I'd see you again," Blackhouse was saying, his unfathomable gaze fixed on Lucinda. "You look…well."

Rosamond felt Judah tapping her arm. She looked his way.

"You have a gentleman caller," her security man told her with apt gravity. "He's waiting for you in the parlor."

Rosamond picked up her skirts and all but ran to see him.

When the parlor door finally burst open, Miles had the window raised. He had one poor, abused, nearly uncooperative leg flung over the windowsill. He had both nicked-up hands grasping the ledge. He had a single desperate heart ready for escape.

"Miles!" Rosamond's eyes widened when she saw him. She rushed to the window, her hands aflutter. "What are you doing?"

"Getting out to see you." Miles withdrew. With effort. He couldn't help grimacing as his insides twisted. "By whatever means possible." With both feet grounded, he brushed off his hands. "Good news. Your ladies say I'm in the mutual society."

Rosamond's smile beamed up at him. "They do?"

"Yep." He aimed a disgruntled glance toward the hallway, knowing they were all probably still congregated there in an interfering, overly curious mass of femininity. "They've got a funny way of showing it, though. They were a lot more demanding than you were, too." Miles remembered their final mandate that he turn around and flaunt his backside for them. "In some areas, at least."

That last request had not been one of the more de-

manding areas, though. Rosamond had been quite fond
of his posterior. For whatever reason, she'd declared his
personhood "remarkable."

Just then, Rosamond seemed less than pleased, though.
She'd come close enough to catch sight of his bruised
face and awkward stance. More than likely, both of those
things betrayed his injuries. At least they probably did if
Coyle had tattled about those things already. Judging by
Rosamond's shocked expression, Dylan hadn't. At least
the man had left Miles with some dignity.

If he'd waited, he could have spared himself Rosamond's concerned, pitying look altogether. But he'd refused to wait.

"But what happened to you?" Gently, Rosamond put
her hands to the sides of his face. She turned his head this
way and that, examining his lumps and bumps. "Who
did this to you?"

"Would you believe…Coyle?"

Miles was still peeved at the man for forcing him to
realize what a chowderheaded mistake he'd made with
Rose.

"Dylan? No. Absolutely not."

"Seth? Judah?" Miles grinned, nearly overcome with
joy at being so close to Rosamond again. "Agatha Jorgensen? Tobe?"

"No, no. No." She considered Tobe. "Maybe…"

"It's not important," Miles told her, drinking in the
sight of her. "What matters is that I'm here. You're here."

For an instant, they only stared at each other.

Then, "I'm so sorry, Miles!" Rosamond burst out,
brave and sure. "I never should have behaved so poorly
with you. Drugging you, searching you, having Dylan
knock you unconscious—"

At her mention of Coyle, Miles narrowed his eyes.

"—making you leave me! I don't know what I was thinking. Only that I was scared and alone and desperate to be safe, and I knew that if anybody could threaten me, it was you—"

"I would never hurt you, Rose. Never."

"—because you were the only one who could really see me. The only one who could understand me and know me and tempt me to leave my hiding place at all. Because I didn't want to go—"

"I only wanted to help you, I swear."

"—but I needed to go, and you saw that." Tenderly, she took his hands. "You did help me, Miles. You helped me in a way that no one else ever could have. I'm so grateful for that. For you."

Humbled by her gratitude, Miles squeezed her hands.

Then he realized…this wasn't a declaration of love. This was an apology. Maybe Rosamond didn't love him. Maybe he'd dragged himself all the way across Morrow Creek for nothing.

He'd be damned if he'd allow all that effort to go to waste.

"Mrs. Dancy," he said soberly, "I didn't come here for an apology. As kind and eloquent as yours was, I—"

"I thought I told you to call me Rosamond." She frowned, looking delectably put out. "Please call me Rosamond."

"But this is a formal occasion," Miles protested, wanting to do this correctly. "I have to address you properly." He grinned at her. "My mutual society membership is at stake."

"Yes." Evidently reminded of that, Rosamond gazed at him with shining eyes. "You know why my friends voted you in, don't you?"

"Because I'm the finest man in all the West?"

Her besotted expression agreed. Her headshake did not.

"Because, officially, only mutual society members are allowed to call on the proprietress of the mutual society in her parlor."

"Oh." Miles pretended to be perplexed. "I wasn't aware of that rule. Are you—" He broke off, pointing at her. "You're the enterprising, fascinating, utterly lovable woman who runs this place? You? Because if you are, I have a few complaints."

"You do?" Rosamond arched her brow. "Such as?"

"Such as the objectifying treatment of male members."

"I see. I'll make a note of that."

"And such as the very long distance this place is located away from Owen Cooper's livery stable."

"That's Cooper's fault, not mine. Anything else?"

Her pert, expectant face nearly made Miles swoon on the spot. It wasn't a manly thought, but there it was. He needed her. He didn't care if it made him helpless with longing.

"Yes, there is. I came in here to make a damn proposal," Miles said, "and your busybody ladies locked me in."

"I reckon they wanted to make sure you wouldn't escape," Rosamond told him gaily. "A good man is hard to find."

"Even harder to keep from crawling out the window."

"And what's more—" Abruptly, Rosamond broke off. Her gaze swiveled to his, bright and hopeful. "Did you just say—"

"Proposal? Yes, Mrs. Dancy, I did."

"Miles, honestly. Please call me—"

But he couldn't let her finish. Not now. "Because that's what this is. A proposal. So you'd better get yourself ready."

"I am ready." She crushed his hands in hers, demonstrating her eagerness with an iron grip. "Do it! I'm ready."

Miles wasn't sure. "Are you certain? Because if you would rather be proposed to elsewhere—say, a forest glade or a riverbank or a town square...anyplace at all—I can oblige you."

"No! Here is fine. Here is excellent." Rosamond gazed up at him, trustingly and—he dared to think—lovingly. "Do it. Go ahead. I'm ready!"

Holding back a laugh at her eagerness, Miles waited. He pretended dubiousness. "I'll have to know a few things first."

"Anything."

"Well, first..." Miles gazed at the ceiling in thought. "Do you know that the only thing that hurt more than my broken bones and lumps and bruises over the past few days was missing you?"

Her gaze softened. "Oh, Miles. I missed you, too."

He swallowed around a suspiciously sentimental-feeling lump in his throat, then went on. "Did you know," he continued, still holding her hands, "that the only thing I ever wanted more than finding you was being with you? That I searched for you and dreamed of you, and when I finally, finally found you—"

"I'm sorry I ran away."

"—all I wanted to do was hold you in my arms forever," Miles confessed roughly. "But you were suspicious, and you had a right to be, and I knew I should tell you how I came here and why. But once I looked into your eyes again—"

"It's all right, Miles. I forgive you. I do."

"—I knew I couldn't risk losing you again. So I didn't say anything." Full of contrition, Miles lifted her hand in his. He raised his gaze to meet hers, too. "I'm sorry, Rose. I'm so sorry for Bouchard following me here, for putting you at risk, for putting you through that awful experience. I didn't mean to."

"I already told you I forgive you." Rosamond sniffled, her eyes bright with unshed tears. "We both made mistakes."

"Walking away from you was the worst thing I ever did," Miles told her, his voice broken with emotion. "I didn't care about anything. Not living, not dying, not seeing out of my right eye the way God and Doc Finney intended."

A startled laugh broke from Rosamond. Then, "Wasn't there supposed to be a proposal in here someplace? I distinctly remember hearing something about a proposal."

He cleared his throat. "I'm getting to that."

"Well…" Urgently, she gestured. "Hurry up."

"Don't you want to take this slowly? To savor it?"

"Savor it?" Rosamond shook her head. This time, one of those tears slipped down her cheek—but its downward slide didn't break Miles's heart, because they were together now. "I've been waiting my whole life not to be lonely anymore, Miles. If you make me wait more than about thirty seconds longer, I swear I—"

Miles glanced at the mantel clock. Holding her hand, he fell to one knee. Masterfully, he managed not to groan in pain.

"Rosamond McGrath Dancy," he said, gazing raptly up at her, "I've waited a whole lifetime to make you mine. I need you like I need breath and rain and long slow nights to hold you close. Without you, I feel broken. With you, I feel whole. I love you more than I can say and more than I can prove, but I promise you that I'll move heaven and earth to make you happy. If you agree to be mine, I'll run the risk of dying of joy, but since I'm pretty far gone already, I reckon I'll take that chance."

Beautiful and smiling, Rosamond gazed down at him. Her presence and her patience and her awe-inspiring bravery pulled him through.

"So please, Rose. Please for me and for you, for all the happy days to come and all the crackers we can share," Miles begged, "please say you'll be mine. I love you, Rose. Please, please say you'll do me the honor of marrying me."

Urgently, surprised to find he was shaking, Miles looked up at her. He'd laid his heart out bare. Now all that remained…

…was for Rosamond to surprise him again?

"Yes, Mr. Callaway. I will marry you!" She yanked him to his feet with a mighty and undoubtedly unwise tug. *"Yee-haw!"*

Miles couldn't help laughing. "Did you just say yee-haw?"

She shrugged. "It's what happens in all the best proposals. I have it on excellent authority."

"I see." He beamed at her. "I guess that's good?"

"Nope. Loving you is good," Rosamond disagreed with an impish tilt to her smile. "In Morrow Creek, an occasional yee-haw is simply good manners. It's an important distinction."

"If you say so."

"I say so. Also…" Rosamond stepped nearer. "I say I love you, too, Miles. You saw what was broken in me and you didn't shy away. You saw what I needed, then stood by me while I got it. You pushed me just enough and you argued just enough—"

"I disagree with that," he objected complacently.

"—and you did a mighty fine job of rescuing me for

a man who's been contrary the whole time I've known him."

"That was just part of my brilliant plan, ma'am."

"I'm grateful for it, too." Rosamond gave him a contemplative look. "I'm sorry to tell you, however, that this proposal is not yet complete."

Hellfire. Wondering what else he might have done better, Miles raked his hand through his hair. "It's not?"

"No. Not until I do this." With both hands, Rosamond grabbed his shirtfront. She pulled him nearer. She brought her mouth to his in a kiss so sweet, so heartfelt, so moving...

"Yee-haw!" Miles said when it was finished.

Rosamond gave him a questioning look.

"Just being polite," he explained with a cocky grin.

Then he pulled her into his arms and repeated that kiss—again and again. Because if there was one thing that Miles knew about second chances, it was that they were rare. That meant that they had to be treasured... preferably with another kiss or twenty to prove that a proper amount of reverence was present.

"I'm awestruck by you, Rose." Satisfied, Miles stroked back her hair—all the better to see her beautiful face. "You're the woman I've dreamed of. You're amazing, inside and out. If I could only figure out what I did to deserve you—"

"I think it's better if I keep you on your toes."

"—I would do it again and again, just to bring you joy."

"Aw. Too late." Rosamond lifted to kiss him again. "You already have." She thought about it. "Although there is one thing you can still do for me..."

Looking unexpectedly vulnerable, she whispered her

request in his ear. Miles frowned. "That's all you want? Really?"

Silently, eyes shining, Rosamond nodded.

"All right. I'm just the man for that job." Deliberately, Miles escorted them both right up to the parlor door. Beyond it, shuffling could be heard. Clearly, all the ladies in Rosamond's household were awaiting the outcome of Miles's proposal.

He smiled. "Why, Rosamond!" Miles bellowed at the top of his lungs. "You've made me the happiest man on earth!"

A chorus of excited squeals came from the other side of the parlor door. Then, applause. On Miles's side, though…

Rosamond gazed up at him with evident delight. "Thank you, Miles. You don't know how much that means to me."

"It's nothing but the truth," he said, taking her hand again. In this, as in everything, they were united. "Ready?"

Rosamond nodded. "Ready."

Then Miles opened the door and they walked out into the melee together, ready to grab hold of love with no reservations, no misgivings…and no time to waste.

Epilogue

Filled with love—and a fair quantity of delicious biscuits, courtesy of Libby Jorgensen—Rosamond sat around her dining room table on the night of her first and last marriage proposal, laughing with her new fiancé and her onetime security men and all her friends, hardly able to believe her good fortune.

She wasn't alone anymore. She wasn't afraid, either.

Because of everything that had happened, Rosamond had a real home, a real family and a passel of biscuit-gobbling children to light up her life. She had a respectable and flourishing mutual society to call her own. She had the memory of finally being the one to inspire a bent-knee proposal.

That event had thrilled her beyond compare.

Rosamond leaned toward Miles. "I hope I didn't hurt you earlier when I hauled you to your feet so I could say yes."

"You mean yee-haw?" Miles asked with sham confusion.

She didn't take the bait. What were a few yee-haws between them? "You seem pretty tough, but you've been through a lot."

"Nothing that wasn't worth it," he assured her.

"Still, you're hurt pretty bad." She was sorry for that. Without her there as a lure, Arvid Bouchard and his men would not have come for Miles. "If our local posse hadn't already run the responsible parties out of town, I'd wallop them myself."

While Rosamond had been preoccupied with feeling miserable, several of the Morrow Creek men—Jack Murphy, Daniel McCabe, Marcus Crabtree, Owen Cooper and Adam Corwin among them, along with her own security men—had seen to it that those undesirable elements were forced out of town. Even Sheriff Caffey and Deputy Winston had lent their official authority to the endeavor.

"That's the first decent thing Sheriff Caffey's done in a long while." Dylan Coyle raised his glass. "Here's to miracles."

Hmm. Rosamond watched as he offered that toast. Dylan still hadn't left town, but she had a feeling he would do so soon. Whatever bedeviled Dylan Coyle was not in Morrow Creek. He didn't seem like a man who'd leave business unfinished, either.

"To miracles." Everyone accepted his toast—Miles with extra vigor. He winked at Rosamond, clearly thinking of something other than the unlikely odds of crooked lawmen reforming.

Rosamond was, too. It was a miracle, she thought, that she and Miles had found each other again—across so many miles and through so many difficulties. Now that it was all said and done, she truly believed they'd always been meant to be together.

"All I can say is, it's a good thing that posse came back when it did." Seth cast a jovial glance at Judah. "Otherwise, we might not have gotten the signal about Callaway in time."

Rosamond stopped. "Signal?"

"Yes, ma'am." Judah gave her a mischievous look. "You didn't think you were the only one who could make up secret signals, did you?"

"Actually…" Rosamond frowned. "I did."

"Well, you're not." Appearing mighty pleased with himself, Seth snatched up another biscuit. "Judah and I had a few, too. We shared them around with all the menfolk, just in case."

Remarkably, Dylan Coyle nodded in casual confirmation.

Miles did not. He seemed as mystified as Rosamond about this issue. But that was small comfort for Rosamond. She didn't like thinking her security men had gotten the better of her.

Perturbed, she deliberately changed the subject. "So… has anyone seen Lucinda?" Rosamond asked. "I know she was dealing with the arrival of Mr. Blackhouse earlier, but since then—"

"Oh no you don't." Bonita shook her head, wearing a knowing look. "You're not sneaking out of this one that easily. We'll talk about Lucinda and Mr. Blackhouse later." She plunked her chin in her hands, appearing enraptured. "Right now, let's hear more about these made-up signals of yours, boys."

Seth caught Rosamond's reproachful look. "Nah. Let's hear about your plan to waylay Callaway with that made-up questioning session, Miss Yates," he suggested breezily, deflecting the attention from himself. "You know darn well there hasn't ever been a full tribunal to pick members for the mutual society."

Bonita's cheeks colored a dull red. "About those signals…?"

"I'd like to know about the made-up tribunal," Miles

put in from beside Rosamond. "Especially the turning-around part."

Several of the women became abruptly interested in clearing the table. Katie and Libby jumped up with plates in hand.

But Judah had no compunction about sharing his secrets.

"One of the signals was a whistle. Like this." He demonstrated. Ear-piercingly. Everyone winced…except him. "Turns out Daniel McCabe, the blacksmith, saw Callaway inching his way through town earlier. He figured he might be coming over here."

"'Inching'?" Miles protested grumpily. "I was moving at a steady, manful pace. I have broken ribs and a wrecked knee."

"I'm sure you were magnificent." Comfortingly, Rosamond patted his uninjured knee. She nodded at Judah. "Then what?"

"Then everyone else relayed the signal, I guess." Judah shrugged. "All I know is, it passed from man to man, lickety-split. First McCabe, then Clayton Davis, then Cade. I heard even that medicine-show man who comes through town sometimes—"

"Will Gavigan," Seth supplied knowingly. "The one who sells Tillson & Healy's Patented Miracle Elixir from his wagon."

"Yeah. Even he helped," Judah finished in a satisfied tone. "That's how we knew we had to try to delay you, ma'am, from leaving. We didn't want you to miss Callaway's apology."

"His proposal, you mean?"

"Nah." Judah grinned. "We wanted to hear him grovel."

"Well, you didn't hear that," Miles said gruffly.

"No, we didn't." Maureen O'Malley smiled. "All we heard was one big, whopping holler from one very happy man."

Remembering that, Rosamond smiled lovingly at him.

"I was hollering, too," she said as she squeezed his hand, knowing she was blushing. "Only on the inside, that's all."

Miles shook his head, still seeming disgruntled by her friends' machinations. "It all ended well, but I can't believe you were all so devious. You manipulated us. And the men!" Shaking his head in pretend dismay, he sighed. "To think that they were the ones who gave away my grand plan with all that cooperative signal relaying. I can hardly fathom it."

"I can." Pertly, Rosamond buttered another biscuit. "Here in Morrow Creek, the men have a powerful desire to see love conquer all. I can't explain it. But I definitely believe it."

"Hmm." Beside her, Miles seemed intrigued. His gaze dropped to her lips, promising more than temporary agreement. "I guess that means I'm going to fit in here even better than I thought."

"I guess you are." She felt drawn to his mouth, too…

"Not me! I don't have a single ounce of interest in seeing love conquer all!" Hands in the air, Seth stood up. "I think I'd maybe better take up faro dealing in Landslide or someplace."

"Yeah." Dylan Coyle rose, too. "I've got to be going." He caught Rosamond's skeptical look and added, "Truly, this time."

Little Tobe Larkin stood up, also. "Me, too, men!" He put his hands on his waist in a tough pose. "Who needs love? Pah!"

It was peculiar to see a thirteen-year-old try to look

jaded, but Tobe did his utmost to pull it off. While all the women laughed, Judah only sat there wearing a faraway look.

"Judah?" Rosamond prompted. "Don't you want to assert your own distaste for love and romance and all that mushheartedness?"

Her erstwhile security man met her gaze. "Nah." He glanced out the darkened window, still seeming preoccupied. "Not after what I saw between Mrs. Larkin and that Blackhouse man today. After that, I might be on the side of love and romance."

His exaggerated way of saying it made the whole thing sound slightly absurd. But everyone gawked at Judah, all the same.

"You are?" Tobe burst out. "You're a traitor, man!"

Judah winked, then stood. "Just kiddin'. Haven't you ever heard of the Morrow Creek Men's Club? I'm the newest member and the proudest. This here marriage bureau isn't the only club in town." Pointedly, Judah went to join the other men. "I'm siding with the bachelors this time. Sorry, but I know when I'm beat."

His significant gaze took in Rosamond, Miles, their joined hands…and all the love that radiated between them.

They'd already conquered all with their love, Rosamond knew. Now all that remained was…

"Me, too." Rosamond yawned, pretending—for once—to lose an argument. "I surrender." She stood, then glanced at Miles.

"Do you want to surrender with me?" she asked.

He was upright in a heartbeat. A wobbly, determined, soon-to-be-healed heartbeat. "Yes, ma'am. Anyplace. Anytime."

"In my parlor. Right now." Rosamond cast her assembled friends a playful look. "I think I still have some membership requirements of my own that ought to be satisfied."

The women kept on clearing the table, all pretending to take her business interests at face value. The men scattered, too, overtly intent on not falling in love anytime soon.

And Rosamond? Well, now that she was truly safe and secure—in her own heart, which was the only place that mattered—Rosamond took Miles's hand and led him away with her, ready to start their future full of love, trust, adventure, several pounds of Mr. Hofer's mercantile crackers...

...and a whole lot of all-over kisses, too.

* * * * *

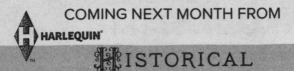

COMING NEXT MONTH FROM

HARLEQUIN®

HISTORICAL

Available March 17, 2015

PROMISED BY POST
Wild West Weddings • by Katy Madison
(Western)

When Anna O'Malley becomes a mail-order bride she hopes to find security by marrying a wealthy ranch owner. Instead she finds herself entranced by Daniel Werner—her fiancé's brother!

A RING FROM A MARQUESS
The de Bryun Sisters • by Christine Merrill
(Regency)

Stephen Standish, Marquess of Fanworth, sees Margot de Bryun as perfect marriage material—until a stolen family ruby is traced to her jewelry shop. Infuriated, Stephen demands she become his mistress...

BOUND BY DUTY
The Scandalous Summerfields • by Diane Gaston
(Regency)

When Tess Summerfield is discovered sheltering in Marc Glenville's arms, only marriage can silence the scandal. Marc's work tears him away, but reunited years later, can they rekindle their flame?

STOLEN BY THE HIGHLANDER
A Highland Feuding
by Terri Brisbin
(Medieval)

To end the feud between clans, Arabella Cameron is prepared for a loveless marriage. Until, on the morn of her wedding, outlaw Brodie Mackintosh steals her away to the mountains!

**YOU CAN FIND MORE INFORMATION
ON UPCOMING HARLEQUIN® TITLES,
FREE EXCERPTS AND MORE AT
WWW.HARLEQUIN.COM.**

HHCNM0315

REQUEST YOUR
FREE BOOKS!

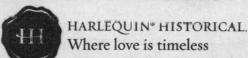

HARLEQUIN® HISTORICAL.
Where love is timeless

2 FREE NOVELS PLUS 2 **FREE GIFTS!**

YES! Please send me 2 FREE Harlequin® Historical novels and my 2 FREE gifts (gifts are worth about \$10). After receiving them, if I don't wish to receive any more books, I can return the shipping statement marked "cancel." If I don't cancel, I will receive 6 brand-new novels every month and be billed just \$5.44 per book in the U.S. or \$5.74 per book in Canada. That's a savings of at least 16% off the cover price! It's quite a bargain! Shipping and handling is just 50¢ per book in the U.S. and 75¢ per book in Canada.* I understand that accepting the 2 free books and gifts places me under no obligation to buy anything. I can always return a shipment and cancel at any time. Even if I never buy another book, the two free books and gifts are mine to keep forever.

246/349 HDN F4ZY

Name _____
(PLEASE PRINT)

Address _____ Apt. #

City _____ State/Prov. _____ Zip/Postal Code

Signature (if under 18, a parent or guardian must sign)

Mail to the **Harlequin® Reader Service:**
IN U.S.A.: P.O. Box 1867, Buffalo, NY 14240-1867
IN CANADA: P.O. Box 609, Fort Erie, Ontario L2A 5X3

Want to try two free books from another line?
Call 1-800-873-8635 or visit www.ReaderService.com.

* Terms and prices subject to change without notice. Prices do not include applicable taxes. Sales tax applicable in N.Y. Canadian residents will be charged applicable taxes. Offer not valid in Quebec. This offer is limited to one order per household. Not valid for current subscribers to Harlequin Historical books. All orders subject to credit approval. Credit or debit balances in a customer's account(s) may be offset by any other outstanding balance owed by or to the customer. Please allow 4 to 6 weeks for delivery. Offer available while quantities last.

Your Privacy—The Harlequin® Reader Service is committed to protecting your privacy. Our Privacy Policy is available online at www.ReaderService.com or upon request from the Harlequin Reader Service.

We make a portion of our mailing list available to reputable third parties that offer products we believe may interest you. If you prefer that we not exchange your name with third parties, or if you wish to clarify or modify your communication preferences, please visit us at www.ReaderService.com/consumerschoice or write to us at Harlequin Reader Service Preference Service, P.O. Box 9062, Buffalo, NY 14269. Include your complete name and address.

HHI3R

Brodie stood in their way, hands on hips and a dark
expression in his eyes. She was still far enough from him
that she could get the black horse into a running start that
would force Brodie to move or be trampled. Before she
could, he strode quickly at her, his long legs eating up the
space between them.

The horse reared up and whinnied loudly, blowing and
huffing his displeasure at being threatened so.

"Are you willing to take the risk, lady?" he asked in a
quiet voice and not in the loud, angry shout she expected.

"Risk? He is mine. He knows me. He can take me out
of here," she said.

"The dark of the moon is upon us. The fog rises quickly
in the mountains. And you would take that horse onto a
hillside path that you do not know and have never seen?
If you have not a care for your own life, I thought he was

more valued to you than that, Arabella." He crossed his arms over his massive chest and glared at her.

Accusation mixed with disappointment. That was what she heard in his voice. And, worse, it bothered her, though she did not wish to admit that. She wanted to run. She wanted to knock him out of their way and escape. But—damn the man—he was right.

He walked the final few paces and reached up to take the reins from her. The horse shuffled his hooves in the dirt and nuzzled him just as he had her. The traitor!

"Give me the reins," he ordered.

"I want to go home, Brodie. Just let me pass." She hated that her voice trembled and sounded, even to her, as though she begged this of him. .

"Give me the reins, Bella," he said.

So shocked to hear that name, she let the reins slip from her hands. No one called her that except…except… Malcolm. And this was the man who had taken his life. The same one who now held her life in his hands. She stared at his hands, remembering the sight of them and him covered in her brother's blood that terrible morning.

Arabella did not realize she'd launched herself at him until they tumbled to the ground.

Don't miss
STOLEN BY THE HIGHLANDER by Terri Brisbin,
available April 2015 wherever
Harlequin® Historical books and ebooks are sold.

www.Harlequin.com